Canuck and Other Stories

ISBN: 0-9668536-2-8
Library of Congress Control Number: 2005908558

To order additional copies, please contact us.
BookSurge, LLC
www.booksurge.com
1-866-308-6235
orders@booksurge.com

or

Rheta Press
641 So. Main. St.
Brewer, Maine 04412
or http://www.rhetapress.com/

Canuck and Other Stories

Edited by Rhea Cote Robbins

Rheta Press
2006

Canuck and Other Stories

TABLE OF CONTENTS

ACKNOWLEDGEMENTS

Many people, in addition to the translators, Sue Huseman, Sylvie Charron, Jeannine Bacon Roy, and Madeleine C. Paré Roy, aided in the proof reading, and fact checking as well as bringing to light the living history of the connection of the families of the authors. I wish to thank them all. If I leave anyone out of the listing, please forgive me. I would like to thank, first and foremost, the translators for their dedication and interests in preserving these works. I also would like to thank Bridget for her typesetting of the texts. Researchers who aided in the project in the community and on the internet as well as proof readers: Noel Mount, Corinne Prézélius, Claire Quintal, Paulette Terry, Ruth Maré, Mary Freeman, Jocelyne Schael, Gilbert Albert, Arthur Greenspan, Doris Provencher Faucher, Norman Faucher, Adrienne LePage, Adèle St. Pierre, Claude Poirier, Clifford Boram, many students at University of Maine at Farmington, Charles A Rocheleau, Madeleine Brodeur Westerback, Adèle Boufford Baker, Ann Rocheleau, Madeleine Brodeur, Robert L. Courturier, Julien Olivier, Margaret Langford, Janet Shideler, and others who offered encouragement and insight into the work over the long process of bringing the books to fruition. I would like to thank my husband, David, for his support of the work and also my family for their continued encouragement.

To Franco-American women everywhere

INTRODUCTION

Why translate the books contained in this volume? Why go beyond the ordinary to bring to the reader the texts that are printed in this book? What was the incentive and inspiration to put out a call for translations as I did? It is my dream and my wish to bring these texts, originally written in French, to those who cannot read the French in order for them to know the literary tradition in the Franco-American culture. As Franco-Americans, we have a rich and long literary tradition, and these three women are part of that tradition.

I had been reading and preparing to teach the Franco-American Women's Experiences course where I examined the Franco-American women's literary tradition for the start of the course a few years ago. Reading fiction, nonfiction, histories, and more of these women's lives who came to settle New France, and the later writings of those who came to work in les *États Unis,* I read deeper and deeper into the meaning of these women's lives and contributions. In doing these readings, my life was being transformed. Some of the books I read were written in French. I realized that these texts, as I was reading them, were the bridge to the knowledge of the French heritage woman on the North American continent: I wanted others to be able to read these books.

It is not easy to be calm in the face of such life-changing work. I can barely contain my excitement or my sense of being, a "displaced" person in my ordinary existence with this new knowledge: I am now becoming someone else as a result of these books. I have entered a higher plane of self-knowing—a self-knowledge to be found among a community of women; an explained self with reference and contextuality.

I know I am not the only one who sometimes feels like an island of Franco-Americanism. I realize now that I am at sea, afloat in a flotilla of other vessels long on this journey of knowing and learning the French woman self. Can such a thing happen in my life? I again realize the richness of my woman life—I find myself looking for the right words, and I would say it is very much like relief at recognition. Hearing and seeing those sounds and images reflected which makes sense of the self in print.

Something from "home," and a much deeper conscience, and consciousness of self. Mostly, I feel explained or known. Freed from the long, time-held silences surrounding the self. The woman self.

The translation of the knowledge gained and the testimony to these women's lives can be a possession and a goal of all Franco-American women. It is my dream and my wish that they can arrive at this kind of self-knowledge, and also to know the worth of each woman in the work of the culture.

As a result of the readings I was able to do in French, and because I wanted others to read these writers, I posted the following notice (see below) to many on the internet and four remarkable women responded to the call for translators: Sue Huseman, Sylvie Charron, Jeannine Bacon Roy, and Madeleine C. Paré Roy. They each agreed to the long and arduous task of translating these early women writers of the Franco-American women's literary tradition: Camille Lessard Bissonnette, nom de plume, Liane and her book, *Canuck*; Corinne Rocheleau Rouleau, *Française d'Amérique*; Alberte Gastonguay, *La Jeune Franco-Américaine*.

> **Notice: Translators, Faculty and Students**
> Translations are needed of several important and historical works of fiction by a body of Franco-American authors. These works were produced in the late 18th and early 19th century. They are seminal works of fiction forming a body of literature of the Franco-Americans who immigrated/emigrated to the United States. These works, written in French, are important to the tradition of literature of the Franco-Americans in the U.S. and Canada. What is so ideal about these works of fiction, is that they are already written in French and are available for course work that is conducted in French; what is needed are translations of these works to accommodate many Franco-Americans who do not have access to the language due to the ravages of assimilation to which they were subjected.
>
> These works contain the clue to tying the lost generations of our forbears in literature. The National Materials Development Center preserved these works in the 1980s, and now it is this generation's turn to do a service for the coming generations. We need to make these works of fiction available to all Franco-Americans in both French and English.

Anyone who has the ability, desire, fortitude, and possibly in need of a scholarly project, could contact me for further discussion about doing the work of the translations.

Sensitivity to North American French is a must.
Preservation of the original language's nuances and richness creates the criteria for success in transmitting the message of the author's intent. What follows is a partial list of the works that are available as well as others that I will be adding to the list as time goes on. Please pass this on if you know of someone who would be highly capable in translating these works. Thank you, merci!

The books were translated into the English and then that left the task of creating copy for the French language text to be read online and information about that aspect is located at **http://www.fawi.net/Transcriptions/Transcriptions.html**. Bridget Robbins Grant, a teacher of languages, and my daughter, offered to type up the entire three volumes of the French texts. Her contribution to this process enables the reader to read the texts, if they so wish, in comparison with the English. Without her work, this book would be one less step away from reality. Her contribution makes this a work that continues through the generations.

A few words from Bridget of her experience in relation to these books: The texts, *Canuck, Françaises d'Amérique, and La Jeune Franco-Américaine,* are a patchwork of sketches that adds to the amazing tapestry that is feminist history in the Americas. Reminiscent of the triumphs and trials of other women, these books reemphasize the imminent, natural quality of ambassadorship in women; particularly the heroines of the French-Canadian pioneers. As a quilter, and a typesetter, the piece-work of these texts fell together incredibly well; tales to be told and compiled, the final product are these colorful tales.

***Canuck*, by Camille Lessard Bissonnette, (1883-1970), translated by Sue Huseman and Sylvie Charron** is a book which reflects the immigration experience from a young woman's point of view. The protagonist, Vic, is a very modern young woman who sets out to accomplish many things in her new country, the U.S. The book, written as mixed genres, includes many elements of the culture in its compact and succinct storyline. The book is unique in that, it provides a word bridge for the generations back into the era of immigration, and it gives explanation to the conditions of the immigration with understanding and candidness. Other topics that the author explores with authenticity in regard to the culture are: mother/daughter relationships, religion, education, farming, medicines, folklore, intimate relationships and more. I cannot say enough about the importance of this book as a cultural literary map in examining the territory of immigration and resettlement. Translators of this work are: **Sue Huseman, Ph.D.**, is a member of the Project Maine France Exchange Committee responsible for student and faculty exchange opportunities as well as opportunities for collaborative research and other forms of academic cooperation between The University of Maine System campuses and partner universities in France. **Sylvie Charron, Ph.D.**, is professor of French at the University of Maine at Farmington. She also served on the Kennebec-Chaudière International Corridor Commission.

La Jeune Franco-Américaine, The Young Franco-American **by Alberte Gastonguay, (1906-1978), translated by Madeleine C. Paré Roy**, is a book that was first published by the Lewiston French language newspaper press, *Le Messager* in 1933. This book is situated in Lewiston, Maine, and it is a study of the life of a young woman who is seeking her way in the world. She meets many suitors and comes to the conclusion of a satisfactory ending in the ways of traditional culture. This book could be cited as a romance with a moral to the story—how to fall in love Franco-American style. It is an important book because of the many nuances of the culture that it examines. Like *Canuck*, this is a blueprint to the culture. **Madeleine Paré Roy** is the translator of this book. She was the Coordinator of the Franco-American Reading Room at University of Maine at Lewiston-Auburn. She is fluently bilingual and she worked on the translation for credit in a degree in the Arts and Humanities. This translation was a supervised piece of work with a University of Southern Maine French professor in an independent project.

Françaises d'Amérique, Frenchwomen of North America **by Corinne Rocheleau Rouleau, (1881-1963), translated by Jeannine Bacon Roy**, is a one-act play which features the heroines who helped settle New France. They are: Mrs. Louis Hébert and Guillemette, her daughter, first settlers of Québec; Mrs. Samuel de Champlain; Mrs. de la Peltrie; Mrs. de la Tour, baronne de St. Estienne; Lady in Waiting; Jeanne Mance; Mrs. Jacques de Lalande; Mrs. Louis Jolliet; Madeleine de Vercheres; Jeanne le Ber; Jeanne le Ber's cousin; and Mrs. de la Mothe-Cadillac. This play was commissioned by the *Cercle Jeanne Mance* of Worcester, MA. in 1915. This play is an important historical document and link to the lives of the women who immigrated to the New France. This play proves their presence on the North American continent and as written in the Preface of the play by its author:

"We have often discussed the major feats and accomplishments of the French colonists, but we have left their "better halves" in semidarkness. I believe that it is time to introduce these French women pioneers. As a young lady once asked me, "'Were there ever any?'"

Indeed there are French women pioneers, and to have this text written and now translated makes it an important book to add to this work for its perspectives. The translator of this work is **Jeannine Bacon Roy.** Jeannine was brought up bilingually in Rhode Island and remembers being taught about some of these women in her grade school years when Canada was a part of the curriculum for Franco-American communities in New England. Jeannine has done much cultural, linguistic, and genealogical independent research and has traveled in Franco-America, Québec, and France.

I am delighted to have had the opportunity to edit such a volume as this one. I hope that you will enjoy reading it and will be inspired by these women writers as I have been inspired.

Rhea Côté Robbins, Editor
Author of *Wednesday's Child*

CANUCK

A Novel by
Camille Lessard Bissonnette
Translation by Sue Huseman and Sylvie Charron

FOREWORD AND ACKNOWLEDGMENTS

My sincere thanks to Rhea Côté Robbins for originally suggesting this translation project and for her continued interest, commitment, and support. My thanks also to Sylvie Charron, my translation partner on several previous translation projects, who has worked with me over the past year and a half to complete this very special undertaking. What began as a project of personal and scholarly interest has become a labor of love. Finally, I offer a heartfelt tribute to Camille Lessard Bissonnette, who gave us this extraordinary account of the lives of French-Canadian immigrants to the United States based on her own life experience. I have included below a translation of the biographical sketch of the author that appears on the back cover of the French version of her novel which was republished in 1980 by the National Materials Development Center for French in Bedford, New Hampshire, through a grant from the U.S. Office of Education, Department of Health, Education, and Welfare. It is that published version of the novel that we have used in preparing our translation.

Sue Huseman

INTRODUCTION

According to the 1990 census, persons of French origin constitute the fifth largest ancestry group in the United States, numbering 13.15 million[1]. Most French Canadian immigrants arrived in New England between 1850 and 1920 to work in factories. Yet, novels written in French by Franco-Americans representing this vast New England immigrant group are exceedingly rare. *Canuck* is one brilliant exception[2]. It plays an essential historical and literary role considering the scarcity of immigrant writing in French within the American novel. It sheds light on the effects of immigration as well as on the specific fate of French-Canadian immigrants to the United States at the turn of the century. This text is almost all that exists for the recovery of Franco-American women's voices at the turn of the 20th century. It relates the life of millions of working women in New England factories and tenements.

Camille Lessard-Bissonnette emerged from a society and time firmly rooted in traditionalism and nationalism, having left Quebec for Lewiston, Maine, in 1904. Two years later, the schoolteacher-turned-millworker-turned-journalist would begin to boldly articulate her views on a variety of topics such as the suffrage movement, racism, and national allegiance. In 1936, Lessard-Bissonnette, the novelist, would do much to explode cherished myths about French-Canadian society.

Canuck was written in feuilleton form in 1936 for the French newspaper *Le Messager* located in Lewiston, Maine. Soon after, the novel was published as a single volume and was so successful that a Laurence, Massachusetts; newspaper also featured it as feuilleton a year later[3]. The novel has fundamental historical, sociological and literary value.

The author, Camille Lessard Bissonnette and her family emigrated to the U.S from Québec in 1904. Camille was born in 1883 in Sainte-Julie-de-Mégantic, Québec, near the Maine border. She was bright and ambitious, finished her schooling at age 16 and became a school teacher even though her parents were illiterate[4]. In 1904 her teaching career was interrupted when her entire family immigrated to Lewiston to improve their condition (A factory worker in the US would receive ten times the wage of a school teacher in Canada). Camille began work in the filature Continentale, a textile mill where she worked for four years. She also started working as a columnist for the local paper in 1906 and was hired as editor for its Pages féminines two years later. These pages were similar to pages commonly found in Quebecois newspapers but, because Camille Lessard was familiar with working women's woes, she used her columns to affirm the right to work for equal pay, speak against family violence, demand the right to vote, and addressed many other social issues affecting women, marriage and family. This journalistic writing helped sharpen her social views, until she published her only work of fiction, *Canuck*, for *Le Messager* almost thirty years later.

Canuck is a minutely descriptive and evocative novel, largely based on autobiographical material from Camille's life and the life of the larger community around her. It is written in precise, elegant French, sprinkled with a few vernacular expressions. It presents the perspective of an immigrant family struggling to establish a life in a less than welcoming host environment. For the student of French, this novel demonstrates that Franco-American literature in French can be easily understood and highly literate. It helps deconstruct the stereotype that New England French, somehow, is an obscure 'patois,' not meriting public attention.

Canuck (a derogatory term used to refer to French Canadian immigrants, recovered by the author to claim a positive identity) is divided into twelve chapters of similar length, as can be expected from a feuilleton. The first six chapters, constituting a vivid and tightly woven whole, describe the arrival of an immigrant family to Lowell, their struggle to adapt, and their life till the death of Besson, a sickly but angelic child who keeps the family blessed, in a manner predating Jack Kerouac's main character in *Visions of Gerard*[5]. *Canuck*'s realism echoes Balzac or Flaubert and recreates the environment of work and home so vividly that the modern reader can recover this past in its most minute and compelling details (cockroaches, food culture, noisy looms, crowded spaces, tenements, poverty and prejudice, countered by dignity, pride, joie de vivre and a desire to succeed). When the child dies, the family returns to the family homestead in Canada while Vic, the young and courageous heroin, stays behind to continue working in US factories and sending money to her family. One of her first priorities, consistent with tradition, is to pay for her younger brother's education towards the priesthood. At her father's death, she returns to the ancestral farm with the intention of running it, reversing expected gender roles. Camille Lessard sets the beginning of her novel in Lowell, Massachussetts, rather than Lewiston, Maine, to create some geographical distance, but retains the year of her own immigration to Maine, 1900.

Chapter 7 represents a major shift in tone and point of view since it is a first person narrative, an intimate journal written by Vic, which spans five years of her life. It addresses the issue of love relationships but demonstrates her inner strength. Vic's journal is the turning point of the book before Vic re-enters Québec after her sojourn in the U.S. The journal draws the female reader into the story by its intimacy. The preface of the first edition states: "Le chapitre 'Je T'aime, Jean!' nous bouleverse, tellement cela sonne vrai[6]." "The chapter moves us because it rings so true". The author shows how relationships develop in the culture and insists on Vic's chastity and morality. She stands up against the commonly held view that French women are 'loose'. She purposely undoes the suspicion that surrounds ethnic women and their sexuality.

The remaining four chapters return to a third person narrative and tell of a temporary repatriation into Québec: they represent a quilt of multiple themes, incorporating folklore, myth, recipes, folk medicine, pig slaughtering, while also paying tribute to traditional values in the culture. Life in the country is romanticized as was customary in the Quebecois novels of the period, contrasting the bleak view of the town and factory at the beginning of the novel. These chapters are sociologically relevant as a detailed and accurate depiction of rural life and Quebecois customs.

Chapters 9 and 10, entitled Père L'allumette and La vie d'un errant, introduce an old beggar from Louisiana, who depends on the charity of his hosts but also provides the family/reader with stories from the wider Francophone world. He is a wandering soul and healer, providing a long list of herbal medicines for the women of Lewiston. This list is a tribute to the Franco-American faith in folk medicine. The saga of his family and travels resemble a Greek tragedy, giving the tale mythical overtones.

Finally, the last two chapters of the novel serve as an epilogue with Vic's marriage to her benefactor, a benevolent, educated man substantially older than she. Vic also discovers that her farm is sitting on precious minerals, which enables her to sell the property at substantial profit, travel the world and live happily ever after. Life on the farm, then, is not shown as entirely desirable, as would be the case in most Quebecois novels of the period. Camille Lessard Bissonnette does not propose a return to the rural past, and certainly not to the traditional situation of women.

In short, the novel tells a story of immigration, resettlement, and the many cultural shocks the French-Canadians faced when newly arrived in the U.S. The literary establishment has largely ignored immigrant women's writings, especially in cases such as *Canuck,* because the text was not written in English and does not belong to either the American or French tradition. Current criticism is reevaluating the importance of immigrant writing, border crossing and writings by women like Bissonnette.

Canuck is a particularly bold piece because it criticizes the traditional dependence of women on their fathers or husbands, their constant fear and silencing. Camille Lessard-Bissonnette proposes a new kind of Franco-American heroine: young, smart, independent, ambitious and self-reliant while respectful of contemporary morality and religion. The author challenges the patriarchy inherent in a French culture largely ruled by the priesthood and the supremacy of the adult male. She also examines the discrimination faced by newcomers from prior immigrants. She describes the poverty of new immigrants and their desire for social promotion. She examines the stereotypes (typified by the title), the more prominent and recognizable elements of the culture, and goes beyond to add realistic dimension to the stereotypes by presenting a full-bodied view of the values and belief systems of the culture.

Canuck is also characteristic of immigrant writing and border crossing in the way it weaves life and text. Camille Lessard was herself a free spirit who moved often and traveled widely in the US and Canada. Her mobility, geographical distance, and time separation from her subject played a part in her formation as a writer. She wrote *Canuck* while working as Colonization Agent for the Louisville and Nashville Railroad whose head office was located in Louisville, Kentucky.

The writing in turn serves as repatriation into the culture for the reader, generations removed from the original voices. Ethnic writing is an act of taboo (telling family secrets) and breaking taboo at the same time. A difficulty of writing the oral tradition is that the nature of writing does not easily resemble the oral tradition of storytelling. Oral tradition, myth, and storytelling may explain why Camille wrote in mixed genres. The absence of books in the home, the inter-textuality of the oral tradition—folklore, songs, medicines, recipes, poems, complaints—lends itself to the mixed genres.

Camille Lessard's work is complex because she writes the cultural Other, in French, as a woman, and as an émigré. She "reversed the stereotype of submission... invalidates the external naming process that makes them outsiders"[7] through her act of writing, and particularly by writing in mixed genres. She opposes the traditional in literature and the patriarchy in the culture.

In the first half of *Canuck,* Vic challenges her father and the dominant ethos. She demonstrates her courage by leaving her family. She does it to keep her wages and help her mother and siblings, while still adhering to traditional values by supporting her brother's aspirations towards the priesthood. *Canuck* exemplifies border crossings and re-entry into the culture. Camille, through her writing, stands up against the oppression of women long before the Quiet Revolution in Québec gave women "a newly rediscovered female mythology"[8]. Camille Lessard also points out that Vic's freedom is linked to the financial independence gained from her comparatively high wages in US factories. These wages are the necessary basis for social promotion and respect: "nous permettre de vivre comme du monde!" (33). Without financial independence, Vic could not rebel against her father's stinginess and constant humiliation or physical harm, which keeps the family in poverty and fear. Through her heroine, the author enunciates a new mythology of the French-speaking woman on the North American continent and denounces the oppression of the women within the culture.

Finally, *Canuck* deserves reading for its colorful representation of culture. Camille Lessard-Bissonnette includes oral tradition, family life, seasonal rites, folk medicines, folk tales, history, death and burial rites, religion, and more. She pays tribute to the culture renewed. It is very much her patchwork and her quilt. Her signature as a writer grew organically out of her cultural past, lived and redefined. *Canuck* serves the double purpose of breaking the bonds that keep women in their place by its form and its message.

A quilt is cut from squares of the past which a seamstress sews in the present, using a traditional pattern or devising one of her own, for future use by herself or for others, and still the quilt goes on much longer than she does; a writer like Camille, takes pieces of women's lives, the culture's oral traditions, the language and its nuances, the men and their redemptions, healing medicines, gossip, the dark side of life, the fortunate, and pieces together a story, quilted by her design—pieces of the past, in her present/presence for our future use.

--Sylvie Charron and Rhea Côté Robbins

ENDNOTES

[1] For the 1990 census, see Armand Chartier, *The Franco-Americans of New England A History* (ACA Insurance, 2000) p. 417. Also see Gérard Brault, The French Heritage in New England (Univ. Press of New England, 1986), pp. 1-2 (1980 census).

[2] "Only a few Franco-American novels have been written in French , perhaps a dozen in all, and about half of them were published in the years from 1935 to 1960" Chartier, p. 318.

[3] Janet L. Shideler, *Camille Lessard-Bissonnette The Quiet Evolution of French-Canadian Immigrants in New England* (New York: Peter Lang, 1998), p.98.

[4] Shideler, p. 114.

[5] Jack Kerouac is considered one of the foremost Franco-American and American writers of the beat generation. *Visions of Gerard* (1968) describes his growing up in Lowell's Petit Canada in the 1950s.

[6] Camille Lessard-Bissonnette, *Canuck* (Lewiston, Maine: *Messager* 1936). Reprint. Bedford, N.H. : NMDC, 1980.

[7] Lippard, Lucy R., *Mixed Blessings: New Art in a Multicultural America* (New York : Pantheon Books, 1990), p. 202

[8] Gilbert Lewis, Paula, ed., *Traditionalism, Nationalism, and Feminism: Women Writers of Quebec* (Westport, Ct : Greenwood Press, 1985), p.8

CAMILLE LESSARD BISSONNETTE, (1883-1970)

Camille Lessard was born in Quebec Province on August 1, 1883. In 1904, she emigrated with her family to Lewiston, Maine, where she learned firsthand of the arduous work of the cotton mills.

Under the pen-name of "Liane," she became the editor of the women's page for the French language newspaper *Le Messager* in Lewiston.

She held, in turn, each of the following positions: librarian in Edmonton, Alberta; store manager in St. Louis, Missouri; "colonizing" agent for one of the largest railroad lines in the southern United States; editor of several women's pages for the newspaper *La Patrie* in Montreal.

Throughout these years, she continued contributing to *Le Messager* in Lewiston. And, on January 23, 1936, the newspaper announced that a novel entitled *Canuck* would be published in the newspaper in serialized form beginning February 14th of that same year. One month later, the novel was published as a single volume.

Camille Lessard Bissonnette eventually moved to Long Beach, California, where she died in 1970.

CHAPTER I

Life in the Mills

It was an early March morning in the year 1900. A train locomotive on the Boston and Maine Railroad line arrived in Lowell, Massachusetts pulling, in addition to its luggage cars, three passenger cars full of French-Canadian immigrants. With the sound of engines puffing and worn wheels screeching, the locomotive, its nose pointed towards Boston, gradually slowed down and finally came to a complete stop about a hundred feet from the train station.

Passengers poured out of the wagon's front and rear doors like swarms of bees, jostling each other, pushing their way forward with knees and elbows, anxious to vacate, as quickly as possible, the smoky, dusty, putrid atmosphere in which they'd been packed like sardines for hours. Perhaps their rush towards the exit was also due to the fact that they'd arrived, at last, in the States!

Old and young, men, women, and children, all looked weary and sleepy-eyed from an endless night spent on train benches.

The men carried huge sacks under their arms, packs on their backs, bulging suitcases in their hands, the girls pulled younger children along by the wrist, the women held babies in their arms, and the entire crowd, like a flock rushing towards the same destination, pressed towards the welcoming train station where lamps were still burning.

These French-Canadian immigrants that the Boston and Maine Railroad discharged in Lowell on that frigid morning of March 1900, were exceedingly poor. But the following day, the same 45th railroad line would deliver a wealthier class of passenger: merchants, business men and professionals who also came to finger the gold in Uncle Sam's coffers.

While the passengers exited the train cars, the luggage men carelessly unloaded enormous crates with holes drilled in the sides to insert rope handles: without these, the crates couldn't have been loaded onto a passenger train. Next, trunks, large and small, rusted and new, some tied together with laundry line, some with camel-hump lids, were unloaded as roughly as the crates. The male travelers kept an eye on the luggage being unloaded and, now and again, you would hear one of them call out: "There's mine!" or "Here's one of them; I hope the others all made it!" When all were accounted for, the owner would breathe a sigh of relief and set off to find his family inside the station while his fellow travelers went through the same routine.

The train station was filled with babies crying, toddlers whimpering, children squealing. The mothers handed out bottles of milk as fast as they could to stop the screams of the youngest; the older children unpacked bags filled with slices of buttered bread and devoured them gluttonously, smearing their faces with butter and jam; the girls, damp cloths in hand, couldn't keep up with the number of hands, noses and chins to wipe.

In one corner, a family of five was nervously huddled together. The father, Vital Labranche, a tall dark man with bright eyes and blade-thin lips that suggested you'd better not get in his way, appeared to be about forty.

The mother, a small, frail woman with large, soft, dreamy eyes and the fearful look of an animal that expects to be slaughtered at any moment, could easily have been the same age as her husband but looked fifty.

Victoria (whom they called Vic) was a girl of fifteen, tall and thin as a reed, with eyes as deep as night, long braids as black as the wings of a crow, and the slender fingers of an artist seeming out of place attached to the body of this unsophisticated young country lass. She would have been pretty if she had been dressed differently. Nevertheless, even in a dress that bespoke the misery and poor taste that result from poverty, her young, shapely figure stood erect in a stance of defiance against the world. A careful observer would have noted a certain bravado about her lips and a flash of rebellion in her eye that suggested that she, for one, would not be easily led to slaughter.

Maurice, age ten, a handsome blond child with dreamy eyes like his mother, fine features and an intelligent face, huddled against Vic as though he knew that the surest protection and understanding would come from her.

Besson, Maurice's twin, whose lungs and bones had been weakened by an untreated pleurisy that had left his body twisted and hunch-backed, was curled up on the bench, his pale, slight head resting on his mother's lap. His large eyes, opened so wide that they seemed ready to devour you, his tiny face like the face of an angel, pale as wax, showed that he wasn't asleep but had simply reached the end of his strength.

"It's comfortable here, you can wait for me," Labranche said, "while I go find us a place to stay. When I've found a place, I'll buy some beds, a stove, a table, chairs, some fire wood, and whatever we need for cooking. Don't be concerned if it takes me most of the morning. When everything's ready, I'll come back here with a cart to get you and to transport all our belongings."

He buttons his coat, pulls his hat down over his eyes, puts on his woolen mittens and sets off into the cold, dark morning while the rest of the family remains seated on the waiting room bench without a thought of food or conversation.

Vic, whose eyes explore everything about her, stands up and looks out the window. "If you'd like, mother, I could take a look around. I'll watch out for carriages and I won't go far. Besides, father won't be back for a while and ... he won't even have to know."

"I'll go too" says Maurice who, without waiting for permission, sets off beside her.

"You can go out for a while" their mother calls after them, "to stretch your legs, but I'll stay here to take care of Besson who seems pretty exhausted out from the night on the train. Don't be gone too long, though, or I'll be worried."

Vic walks around the platform with Maurice at her side, stops on the sidewalk in front of the station, looks at the dirty street just coming to life, the grey, dilapidated houses, the dull windows behind which shades are just being raised, and a frown creases her forehead. There is a hill beside the station. The girl climbs it with Maurice and, from the top, she briefly contemplates the tenement houses which all look alike, the dust-covered shops, the smoky factories, and these words escape her lips: "So, this is the United States! And this is where I'm going to live!" Maurice, who is younger and less observant, is too excited about this enormous change in his life to bother to take stock of things.

That same evening in March 1900, the Labranche family found themselves settled into a four room apartment on the fourth floor of a tenement, at $3.00 a month rent. The front of the apartment looked out over the dirty street. At the back ran the canal from the mill, with muddy water and banks where no grass or trees could grow since the canal had been lined in cement. All traces of paint had disappeared from the neighborhood buildings, inside and out, long ago. The wooden frames of the doors and windows were eaten away along the edges, probably from having been open and closed too often and too violently. The window panes, completely free of putty, were loose with pieces of glass missing in places. The plaster on the ceilings and walls had fallen off in spots leaving cavities resembling rat holes through which you could see the wooden lathe underneath. The softwood floors were knotty and rough all over guaranteeing that on every uncarpeted threshold barefoot children and kneeling washerwomen would gather splinters at the slightest contact.

The cupboard door hinges were loose and the locks no longer worked. The corners of the cupboard shelves, as well as the top and bottom of the iron sink were crawling with cockroaches of all sizes and colors. The faucets in the bathroom were covered with mildew and there was not a trace of enamel left on the sink.

The area immediately surrounding each of two nails driven in the wall just above the sink, designed for hanging a cup and a mirror, was completely devoid of plaster right down to the wooden lathe into which the nails were driven. These two dirty holes had become a haven for cockroaches. Next to a kitchen window there was a shelf on which a lamp was stored during the day. In the evening, at dusk, it was lighted and placed in the center of the table.

The stairway remained unlit in order to conserve oil. You had to grope your way up and down, feeling your way along with your feet and with a firm grip on the banister. The steps were sunken and thin in the middle from use. The wooden edges had broken off in places and posed a threat to working men in their big heavy boots.

The banister was worn and wobbly from the army of boisterous children who slid down it's railing more often than they used the stairs. The newel posts had served to hone the skills of every child who owned a knife just as the plastered walls had served as a canvas for every would-be artist with a pencil.

There was no porch or stoop of any kind. One step down and you were walking on the beaten earth since there was no sidewalk along the street.

When she first entered their new quarters, Vic wandered curiously from room to room, which only took a minute, and, for the second time that day, she whispered: "So, this is the United States! And this is where I'm going to live!" Anyone who had observed the girl at that moment would have seen a fine wrinkle crease her forehead and a spark of rebellion flash in her eyes.

The afternoon and evening were spent unloading things, unpacking, getting the beds ready, setting up the stove and adjusting the stove pipe (a task accompanied by a great deal of swearing on Labranche's part), doing the most essential washing, cleaning the cupboards, and scrubbing the sink, in order to get to bed as quickly as they could so they could show up at the mill at 6 a.m. the next morning: there was no time to lose before starting to earn some money.

Labranche had already been to the States in his youth, and, since he'd been trained as a weaver then, he was sure to find work easily. His wife was going to learn the same trade, as would Victoria because that was what paid the best. Maurice was big and tall for his age, so they would say he was fifteen and, instead of sending him to school, find work for him either in the carding department or the spinning department where they always needed young lads. As for Besson, who was too weak for either school or factory work, he would take care of the house. He would peel potatoes, wash dishes and do other light housework. In the evening and on Sundays, Vic and her mother would tend to the meals, laundry, ironing and so forth. With life organized this way, they should be able to save enough money, in four or five years, to pay off the mortgages on their farm in Canada and go back there to live.

And hence their new life, that is, LIFE IN THE MILLS, began for the Labranche family.

Labranche and his wife each worked a set of looms in the same section. Hence, Vital was able to urge his wife on so that her work would be more perfect and their pay envelopes fatter! She didn't rebel because her life was the life of all peasant women where she came from. She moved forward like a beast of burden, feeling the blows of her master's whip, but making no effort to shield herself from them.

They tried to teach Vic weaving but, on the second day, the child fainted, falling onto the loom and crushing her shoulder under the shuttle before they could stop the motion of the heavy machinery. The injury healed and they were able to get the girl hired in the loom threading department. Loom threading is always done by women for the logical reason that you need patience, delicate fingers and soft skin to handle the thousands of fine threads of cotton, day after day, without breaking them.

Iron frames are set up facing the windows. Male workers (strong arms are needed) use wheelbarrows to carry in huge iron spools covered with yarn and then install the spools on the frames. Next, the female workers, using a special hook, must thread each strand of yarn (and there are hundreds and hundreds, perhaps thousands, of them) from these spools through the eyes of a set of metal or linen heddles . The set may consist of as many as fifteen heddles, all fastened tightly together. When a special pattern is to be woven, the heddles must be carefully threaded with strands of yarn following special instructions written on a piece of paper by the overseer. But most of the time, the pattern is simple and no written directions are needed for an experienced hand.

After the heddles are threaded, the same strands of yarn must be threaded through the teeth of the "reed" with a special hook for that purpose. If a single strand is threaded incorrectly or if a single tooth of the "reed" is missed, or if a strand of yarn is threaded through the tenth heddle when the instructions specified the 5th heddle, the spool, after having been tried out on a loom in the weaving room, is returned to the loom threader who made the mistake. And the entire process has to be completely redone, without pay. Hence, it's absolutely essential to give one's full, sustained attention to one's work, and to learn to work quickly if one hopes to have a fat pay envelope on Saturday.

The department where Vic went to thread looms was on the fourth floor and you could see part of the city through the large windows of the room. Sitting quietly at her workstation, no longer within immediate earshot of the infernal noise of the working looms, Vic felt that, in this new position, she'd taken a step forward since her arrival in the States.

At the end of her workday, at 6 p.m., the girl would put her heddle and "reed" hooks in her pocket so they wouldn't be stolen (the hooks were expensive) and then she'd walk at a slow pace back to the dark, ugly apartment.

At home, it was the same routine every day. In the morning, they'd set out about 5:30 a.m. carrying a sack lunch for their noon break. Since the family hadn't been able to find work in the mill near their home, they had to go to work in another, more distant mill, one too far from their apartment to permit them to eat lunch at home.

When they got home from the factory, at about six-twenty, they'd rush up the stairs despite the darkness. Maurice and Vic, with the energy of youth, would often climb the stairs four at a time, sometimes missing a step, losing their balance, righting themselves and continuing on at the same pace. On these occasions, their father would never fail to say: "Can't you walk up the stairs like normal people; you sound like stampeding cattle when you clatter up that way!" No one responded to this well-placed remark and a scene was thus avoided.

After climbing the three long, steep flights of stairs, they'd rush into the kitchen which served as dining room, living room, and parlor —in short as everything but bedroom. The table, which normally stood against the wall between two windows, had been pulled out by Besson before the family arrived, for the two younger brothers sat on the wall side of the table at mealtime. Vic sat across from them. Her father sat at one end of the table, his back to the door, and his wife at the other end facing her husband.

When six o'clock came, Besson placed five straight-back chairs around the table. On the oilcloth, he set five large earthenware plates with the same number of bowls and saucers, a large spoon beside each plate when there was soup, otherwise just a knife and fork. There was only one teaspoon and it was placed in the sugar bowl in the center of the table. Everyone used it to sweeten their tea (no one ever talked of coffee in the Labranche family), very sparingly under the watchful eye of the family patriarch. A jug of syrup was placed on a saucer so that it wouldn't stick to the oilcloth that covered the table and ruin its thin protective coating. A bottle of vinegar accompanied the sugar bowl whenever beans and lard were served.

When the table was set, Besson would go to the window and gaze out at the street for a long while. Days were incredibly long and boring all alone at home, and he couldn't wait for his family to return.

After a few minutes of reflection, his nose pressed against the window, the crippled boy would climb on a chair to take the lamp off the shelf. With the utmost care, as if it were a treasure (and woe to this poor child if ever the lamp slipped from his fingers and broke), he would descend from his perch and set the lamp on the chair. Then he'd remove the lamp globe, check to see if it was clear, and if not he'd clean it with a large wad of crumpled paper that he pushed down into the globe. He'd turn it so that, rubbing against the inside of the glass, the wad of paper would remove the black streaks of smoke inside the globe. This operation complete, he'd check to see that there was enough oil in the lamp for the evening and add some if necessary. He'd turn up the wick and trim it off with a pair of scissors, taking special care not to leave any loose strands that might smoke. Then, taking a piece of kindling from the woodpile and touching it to the glowing coals of the stove, he'd light the lamp and place it carefully in the center of the table.

Besson always had the potatoes ready on time, cooked to perfection. When the fork prongs entered the potato with just the right amount of pressure to assure the invalid that no one would criticize his cooking, he'd pour the water in which they'd been boiled into the sink—taking great care not to scald himself. Then he'd place the pot on the back of the stove so that it would get cool and he'd crack the lid ever so slightly so that the steam could escape, preventing the potatoes from becoming mushy.

Once this was done, the child would verify that everything was in order, that nothing was missing, and then he'd curl up in the only rocking chair in the house. This chair was a great luxury for the family, but Mrs. Labranche had been so insistent, to the point of tears, that her husband had decided to spend a few dollars to purchase the chair, intended to provide a bit of comfort to the poor little soul, whose days on earth were numbered.

So Besson would settle down in the rocking chair and wait for his family. He'd pose his thin arms on the armrests, lean his head back in the chair, and close his eyes, his big beautiful eyes, so gentle and deep they seemed to reflect the earth and the sky.

He barely had time to fall asleep before the banging doors and the clattering of footsteps on the staircase alerted him that the factory folk were returning home. His mother, as she entered, would devour him with her eyes as if she were surprised to find him alive each time she returned from the mill. His father would cast a worried, protective look at him. Vic never failed to pat his head as she went by. Maurice was the only one to greet him playfully with: "Hello, Besson, is our supper ready? Are our potatoes cooked?"

While Labranche and Maurice took turns washing their hands and faces in a basin placed in the sink, Vic and her mother brought out the pots of meat, stew, fricassee, or soup they had cooked the evening before. They placed them on the stove after removing the burner covers so that the food would warm up more quickly and supper wouldn't be delayed.

A loaf of bread was cut into thick slices, the reheated food was put into stoneware dishes which were placed on hot pads in the center of the table. Then everyone was ready to dip their spoon into the dishes, to fill their plates and devour their supper after a long day's work.

There were never any pies or cakes or pastries, not only because they would have taken too long to prepare, but also because they would have cost too much. On the other hand, there was always a jug of diluted "cassonade", a brown-sugar syrup. A small amount of this syrup would be poured into a saucer and then a slice of bread was dipped in , on one side only and very lightly in order not to waste any. When they tired of syrup for dessert, they'd eat a kind of mixed fruit jelly (made from jelly that had passed the fruit too quickly to make contact). It was purchased in tub-sized buckets that would last a year or more.

When supper was over, while Vic and her mother cleared away the dishes, Labranche would take off his boots to rest his feet and, donning thick country wool slippers that smelled of sweat, he'd fill his tobacco pouch and go across the hall for his evening card game at the neighbor's. As soon as he was gone, the mother and daughter, without looking at each other, would breathe a sigh of relief: they were guaranteed a few hours' peace. Labranche was moody, hot-tempered, and violent. You never knew what to expect when he was around. He was a man who'd invent powder, if he had to, for the pleasure of lighting it.

After supper, Maurice would bury his nose in his books—the school texts his mother had once used when she taught in a small country school—and he'd put them away only when it was time to go to bed. Either his mother or Vic would have him recite his lessons and solve his math problems. The only thing the boy ever talked about was becoming a priest and no one discouraged him, even though they wondered how his father could ever be persuaded to loosen his purse strings to permit him to go to college.

As for Besson, since playing and studying wore him out, he'd usually follow his father to the neighbor's and spend his evenings curled up in a chair, watching the men play cards and smoke. Sometimes the smoke got so thick that his weakened lungs would explode into coughing. Then, doubled over with pain, with a racking cough that brought up blood, he'd return home and, without the least complaint, put himself to bed.

CHAPTER 2

Canuck

As is often the case for newcomers to the States, Vic, at the beginning of her stay in Lowell, was the butt of jokes and derision on the part of the other factory girls. They found it comical that her enormous braid of black hair, looped in half, was tied with a piece of shoe lace instead of a ribbon; that the tips of her worn leather boots were protected with a piece of yellow metal that sparkled like gold in the sun; that the style of her old hat had disappeared from fashion long ago; that her dress was tight to bursting on her—the girl had to wear out her clothes because she didn't have a younger sister to hand them down to. She couldn't show her face without hearing someone shout "CANUCK!" at her. And this derogatory label was accompanied by jeers, insults and often blows. She wasn't alone in her torment, for Canadians who leave the shores of the Saint Laurence to earn their living in New England factories are often derided with the term "CANUCK!" And not by Americans, but by fellow countrymen who have arrived under the star spangled banner before them.

So Vic, with her air of a princess in rags, became, from the first day she appeared on the streets of Little Canada in Lowell, the scapegoat for young Canadians like her who'd lived in the States a few years longer than she. Three girls of eighteen or twenty, in particular, pursued her relentlessly, shoving her, pinching her, snatching her hat, stomping on the yellow toes of her boots.

At first, Vic tried to run from her persecutors, but they quickly caught up with her and then the three of them would hold the girl prisoner to torment her. All that Vic could do was to try to walk next to an adult, but even so, she was sure to get a fist or a knee in the back at an opportune moment.

Did she complain? No, this child of the Canadian countryside was too proud for that. Did she defend herself? How could she, alone against three much older girls? So the harassment continued and intensified as time went on.

Anyone who has ever worked in the New England mills has probably witnessed this kind of treatment; perhaps they've even been victims of it themselves. Perhaps this compulsion to persecute newcomers, those who look even more cowed than their comrades, finds its origins in our American colleges where new students are initiated so fiercely that some of them die from it!

Whatever the cause, Vic was, week-after-week, the scapegoat of three misguided minds. One evening, having retraced her steps to get something she'd forgotten, the girl was the last one to leave the factory gate. She held her head high: at least this time she'd be able to walk home without being attacked. She hadn't counted on her tormentors waiting for her, hiding in a dark corner of the street. It was past six o'clock and since it was late March and the sky was overcast, it was dark. What's more, there wasn't a single soul in the street: everyone had hurried home as quickly as possible for the evening meal. It was the perfect opportunity for mischief.

The three thoughtless attackers came running out from their hiding place and, without slowing their pace, charged straight into Vic, knocking her to the pavement. Then they came back at her, pretending at first to help her up, only to knock her down again each time she tried to get to her feet. They snatched off her hat and then shoved it down over her ears; they pretended to trip over her so they could fall on top of her with their full weight; and they shrieked like madwomen: "Hey, Canuck, we'll fix you up!" "Here, we'll make your cursed hat fashionable for you! And those bits of gold on the toes of your boots, we'll shine them up for you!"

Her face smeared with blood, her hands and knees torn and bruised, Vic lay still on the pavement. What was the use of trying to get up again to fight these three big girls, each stronger than she was? One cried: "Let's give her a bath in the canal! Yeah, that'll clean her up; you can tell she doesn't take a bath very often!" With the three demons bending over her, all Vic could do was to grab hold of a board lying within her reach. At the least attempt on the part of her three tormentors to throw her into the water, Vic was determined to scream for help at the top of her lungs.

But the scene had had a silent witness for the past few moments. And a bomb wouldn't have had a more powerful effect on the three furies than the deep voice that suddenly bellowed: "Help that girl to her feet right now or I'll call the police!" Releasing Vic and bounding upright, the three savages tried to take flight. "Oh no, you don't; you're not going to escape like that. Help that child to her feet just as I said or beware the consequences!" Fear-stricken, they obeyed, for if the stranger didn't know their names, Vic certainly did and would be sure to tell him.

"You can't have much honor or courage to do what you've just done! But... I'm not too surprised since I recognize one of your faces under the gas light. Yes, you're the one who committed infanticide a few years ago and whose picture made the front page. Because of your young age, you were spared a long jail sentence, but, given what you've just done this evening, it's clear that the judge should have sent you away for life. You'd better get out of here as fast as you can, you band of vipers! I'm going to report your brutal act to the police immediately, and, from now on, they'll be keeping an eye on you!"

Like hyenas, three shadows fled into the night.

The stranger came towards Vic who was trying to stop her face from bleeding. He picked up her poor old-fashioned hat, shook the dust off of it, and held it out to her without a word. This simple gesture seemed to open a floodgate inside her and uncontrollable sobs gushed forth, as her whole body shook convulsively. Through her tears, she kept repeating: "Why do they keep on hurting me, when I wouldn't hurt a soul?"

In a comforting gesture, the stranger put his hand on the girl's shoulder and, without thinking she pressed herself against him like a young bird nestling under a protective wing...

"Come on now, you mustn't cry like that. Those girls attacked you because they're ignorant misfits. If they had any intelligence they wouldn't act that way. They're going to behave themselves now because I'm going to alert the police this very evening. In view of the fact that they have a bad reputation to start with, they'll be under close surveillance from now on. So don't be afraid, they won't hurt you again. Here, take my handkerchief and wipe your face. Can you walk? Yes? O.K., I'm going to walk with you part of the way so you have a chance to put yourself back together before you get home. And when you get there, don't tell your parents about what happened tonight, for that would worry them needlessly."

As they walked, the stranger deftly questioned Vic, gleaning her name, her address, her family, her life, and so forth...and seemed astonished at the refined manners and elegant language of this child. He didn't know that her mother had carefully instilled in the child all the knowledge that she herself possessed. Nevertheless, he was beginning to understand why the factory misfits resented her: in spite of her misery and her ragged clothing, the girl had the bearing of a princess.

"Now that you've recovered a bit, I'm going to leave you. Here's my card. If you ever need a friend, don't be afraid to come and knock on my door. I'd like you to go, at your convenience and with your mother's permission (once she's been told of this evening's events) pay a visit to my mother and make her acquaintance. Here, I'll write her address on my card. She's almost always alone because my work often keeps me away. You'll like my mother; she's a wonderful woman. I'll tell her about you tonight and I'm sure that, once she gets to know you, she'll like you, too. Now, give me your little hand and don't forget to call on me if you need me. Good night, child, and keep your chin up."

Vic took time to read the words on the vellum paper, "Raymond Fénélon, Mining Engineer." Then she slipped the card into the top of one of her stockings and went up the stairs to explain to her family how she'd tripped and fallen and put her face in its current condition. They all accepted her explanation, but that night the girl dreamed of a purple and gold throne, floating in the clouds, on which sat, a halo circling his head, a mining engineer who answered to the name of Raymond Fénélon.

CHAPTER 3

A Friend for Besson

The next day, Vic's life resumed its monotonous course. Three years passed this way, in work and deprivation of all kinds in order to amass the necessary sum to permit them to return across the border, to the farm encumbered with mortgages that they'd been forced to abandon.

Maurice continued to spend his evenings and his days off with his nose in his books. And in all this time, Labranche never once missed his card game at the neighbor's, nearly always accompanied by Besson.

One evening, instead of following his father, the little invalid went and sat with his back toward his mother and Vic, next to Maurice at the table from which the supper plates had just been cleared. After an awful fit of coughing, he reached out and timidly touched Maurice on the arm:

"I'm not going to go outside in the street anymore!" He said in a low voice so that no one except his brother could hear him.

"No? Why not?" Maurice asked distractedly.

"Because the other children all call me 'frog,' and walk all twisted up to make fun of me and stuff balls of paper in the back of their sweaters to pretend to have a hump like mine. It's not my fault if I got sick and ended up this way...I'm never going out again, I tell you!" And huge tears rolled, unchecked, down the sick little boy's emaciated cheeks. Maurice suddenly shifted his attention from his books and clenched his fists. He answered in the same tone Besson had used:

"Just wait until Saturday afternoon or one of my days off. I'll go out in the street with you and you'll see what I'm going to do to the ones who hurt your feelings."

"Oh, no! I'd rather not go out any more, because, if you try to defend me, ten of them will jump on you and you wouldn't stand a chance. I saw them do that one day to a little boy who told them to stop making fun of me. It's better to run away from a gang like that. They're like the wolves at home: they only attack when it's ten against one."

From that day on, Besson, without complaining to anyone but Maurice, no longer went to sit outside in the sun whose rays were obscured by the dust of the street. He spent his free time at the window on the fourth floor, looking down at the street but more often gazing up at the blue canopy of sky above him...Sometimes he would fall asleep in his chair and, around his head, the sun would trace a golden crown...In the healing warmth, the little boy dreamed of the trees, green fields, and flowers on their Canadian farm. He also dreamed of the gurgling streams, the wild blackberries and strawberries, and the blue sky...

One day at noontime, Besson was busy at the sink, washing the plate and utensils he had used for his meager lunch, when he heard a timid knocking at the door. His hands still in the dishwater, he called out, as he had heard his parents do on similar occasions: "Come in!"

The door creaked on its hinges but didn't open wide enough for the sick boy to see anything from where he was, for the cupboard hid the door from view. Quickly drying his hands on his pants, he walked over and saw, framed in the opening of the door, a head that opened its mouth wide to say, softly, as if fearing it might be heard:

-Hello, Besson!

-Hello, Cadet Roussel[I], come in and close the door.

The lad that Besson had called Cadet Roussel appeared to be about ten years old. He had an intelligent face, eyes that sparkled with life, a body plump with health, but a head nearly devoid of hair. Some accident of birth had left him with a denuded scalp on which the hairs were so sparse and so pale in color that pitiless scamps had—from the first time he appeared in the street as barely more than a baby,—baptized him "Little Three Hairs". Later on, whenever they wanted to infuriate him, they would chant, "Cadet Roussel has just three hairs" ...and a whole litany of related couplets would follow. This nickname stuck. The boy got used to it over time and even his family, without intending any harm, adopted it. Aside from his parents, no one on the street seemed to know what his real name was.

His bald pate had exposed the youngster to many a blow and a jeer, particularly whenever a new family teeming with children moved into the neighborhood.

In contrast to Besson whose frail, twisted body had difficulty standing, Cadet was stronger and sturdier than most children his age. He knew how to respond blow for blow, an eye for an eye, a tooth for a tooth, unless his attackers were full-grown good-for-nothings, twice his size and twice his age.

But if Cadet had hardened his fists by returning blow for blow, his heart, on the other hand, had remained pure as gold. He was the one who had dared, one day, to come to the defense of Besson when he was being cruelly mocked. Cadet was rewarded for his efforts with a bloody nose and broken teeth. He had silently promised himself to take revenge by bloodying noses and breaking teeth in return as soon as he was big enough, but, for the moment, he was simply Cadet Roussel, a child of the Little Canada section of Lowell.

Today, from the landing outside the small Labranche apartment, Cadet, at Besson's invitation, had stepped inside, closing the door softly behind him. Leaning back against that same door, he had stood, smiling, looking at the hunchback boy without saying a word. Then he glanced down at the pocket of his sweater into which one of his grimy hands was tucked.

Besson noticed this movement and understood that something was afoot.

"What are you hiding in your pocket?"

As if he had been waiting for just that question, Cadet triumphantly pulled his hand from his pocket, and held tight in its fingers, was a ball of immaculate white fur with a pink nose. It was a white rat!

Cadet presented the animal to Besson and the two boys spent the rest of the afternoon laughing and making plans for the rat and his future descendants. Cadet kept a dozen rats in the basement of his house, but in the tenement where Besson lived, they couldn't think about using the basement for this purpose since it belonged to all the tenants in common.

With a stealthy step and a smiling face, Cadet left, only to return a few minutes later with a round hatbox. The boys pierced the lid with a multitude of small holes: this box was to be the rat's palace. Cadet suggested hiding the box under Besson's bed from six at night until six in the morning. But what would happen when Saturday came and all the floors were scrubbed? This dilemma was too difficult for the two boys to resolve: they decided to wait and see what would happen.

Besson was so happy with Cadet's gift that, that very evening, when he climbed into bed after saying his prayers, he, who had neither cat nor dog to pet here in the United States, reached down, lifted the lid off the rat's palace, and thrust in his hand. And a small ball of snow-white fur with a red nose took its place in the boy's bed, snuggled against the chest of the invalid.

Everything would have been fine if the little boy's fingers hadn't relaxed as he slept and if the rat, feeling suddenly unfettered, hadn't begun to explore the space in which he found himself. A moment later he was climbing down Maurice's neck, and Maurice, awake with a bound, began to scream that the devil was under the covers and that he'd felt his claws!

Besson, suddenly awakened, didn't realize at first that his rat was the cause of Maurice's terror. Only when his father, his mother, and Vic arrived, in response to Maurice's cries, and when, by the light of a lamp, they found a little white ball paralyzed with fear hidden in the folds of the sheets, only then did the boy understand. His frail body began to tremble, his lips pressed together, and tears welled up in his eyes. In a broken voice, he explained the presence of the rat in the house and under the covers, and he promised his father that if he would let him keep the animal, he would see to it that it stayed in its box. Labranche, who never lost his temper with his sick son, went back to bed without a yes or a no, which, as everyone understood, was the same as giving permission.

After the rat incident, Cadet saved a poor sparrow from the jaws of a cat before the bird was completely mutilated. Unfortunately, the bird's wing had been broken by the feline's claws. Cadet brought the bird to Besson, in the pocket of his sweater as always, and the two boys spent hours together making the bird a cage out of bits of wood so that it wouldn't run about the house making a mess. Besson would have loved to have a singing canary so that the bird's song could keep him company when he was alone, but a sparrow with a broken wing was better than nothing.

Ever since Cadet had first found the courage to come and knock at Besson's door, he had developed the habit of coming by frequently after school. When there were religious holidays for which the mill didn't close, he would spend the entire day there, slipping away only when dinner time came.

Besson, who had a prodigious memory and a fertile imagination, recounted to an enthralled Cadet the most marvelous tales, and, in return, Cadet described in detail, and often with amplification, all the adventures that happened at school and on the street. His stories often made the sick boy shout with laughter, and, when they did, Cadet was happy as a prince.

The boy knew himself to be healthy and strong and, with a good heart that embraced all of life, he felt proud when he could serve as a champion for those less strong than he. His had a heart of gold, a TRUE Franco-American child's heart.

Cadet was to play a very short but truly sublime role in the life of this poor little exile from the French Canadian woods. Once his role had ended, after the "grand departure" of his protégé, he slipped away—like a ship setting out to sea—toward a destiny that is not part of this story. In time, he became one of the most brilliant writers in North America. God smiled on the magnanimous acts of this small outcast's heart and, in turn, gave him the talent and good fortune to realize his dreams.

In the modest apartment of the Labranche family, the two little boys almost always sat at the only table on the premises—the kitchen table—and when they weren't spinning tales and adventures, they played at marbles, dominoes, Parcheesi, and other simple games.

But when the old family clock, which hung above the table, chimed five o'clock, all games ceased. Cadet would quickly pull out the cap he had stuck down inside his shirt in order not to lose it or forget it, and, with a "Good-bye, Besson" he would dash off down the stairs so that the little hunchback could begin the preparations for his family's supper.

[1]The name "Cadet Roussel" (Cadet is pronounced kah-day with primary stress on the second syllable) makes reference to a French nursery rhyme about a child who has three of everything but is nonetheless a good child:

Cadet Roussel a trois maisons
qui n'ont ni poutre ni chevron...
Ah, mais vraiment,
Cadet Roussel est bon enfant

In taunting Besson's friend about having little hair, the children sang the Cadet Roussel nursery rhyme adding/inventing a stanza about Cadet Roussel having only three hairs. As a result, the name of the nursery rhyme character, Cadet Roussel, stuck as a nickname for the nearly bald boy.

CHAPTER 4

Vic's Rebellion

One day a cloud burst that set off a chain of events that would eventually completely transform the lives of every member of the Labranche family.

Labranche and his wife were always the first ones home, unless they stopped at the store for groceries. Their work stations were on the first floor next to the exit doors near the factory gates. As soon as the looms slowed their movements—a sure sign that it was quitting time—the couple was almost instantly outside and headed toward home in haste.

Vic would arrive a few minutes later, since she not only had to go down three flights of stairs but, in addition, walk the entire length of the mill before reaching the gates. Next home was Maurice who invariably arrived at least fifteen minutes behind the rest of the family because he worked in a more distant factory.

One evening, as she opened the door, the girl heard her father raging and her mother and Besson crying.

"What's the matter now?" Vic demanded. "Our lives are difficult enough as it is; we don't need these angry scenes every day on top of everything else. What's going on?"

"It's our fancy Mr. Maurice," answered Labranche, "who's changed jobs without asking my permission and, in doing so, is going to lose half a day's salary!"

"Did he change to a better paying job?"

"Yes, but he still should have talked to me first," insisted Labranche. "I had to hear it from the others. If I had known, I could have arranged for him to change jobs without losing the half day of pay."

"He surely didn't do it to cause trouble." Vic pleaded. "Besides, if he hadn't acted when he did, I'm sure somebody else would have seized the opportunity to take the better job. Before you get angry and upset everyone, why don't you wait and see what Maurice has to say about all this?"

"Sure, that's it, take his side again," raged Labranche. "What do you care if your father is losing his soul to the factory as long as Maurice can do as he pleases?! Maurice comes before me, I suppose? I'm going to show all of you, once and for all, who's the master here, Maurice or me! When he gets home he's going to get the worst beating of his life!"

These last words set Vic off like a charge of dynamite. Eyes afire, nostrils flaring, lips pale as death, she strode toward her father:

"If you so much as touch Maurice tonight, my room will be empty tomorrow."

"Your room will never be empty, shouted Labranche, because if you leave, the police will bring you back here, to your own shame! I still have rights over you, even if you are eighteen!"

"Yes, you still have rights over me," Vic replied, losing all reserve and all respect, "But I dare you to claim those rights! If you have me brought back by the police, I'll see to it that you take my place in the police wagon while it's still warm! Don't forget, you committed a crime in forcing Maurice to work in the factory when you should have been sending him to school! You made him pass as a fifteen year old so you could sacrifice his blood, sweat, and health for your own profit. What do you think the police will say if I tell them that? Whatever happens as far as I'm concerned, you'd better leave the police out of it! You can go on sacrificing Maurice's health and his future...you can drive Besson into an earlier grave by forcing us to live in this hole and depriving him of fresh air and sunshine, so you can fatten your bank account!...you can keep on making my mother a martyr... in short, you can keep on killing us all little by little, but, take my word for it, you'd better leave the United States police out of it!...If you had worked the land half as hard as you work here in the factory, we would never have had to leave the farm!...As for the field work and the stable work, it was Mama and I, as soon as I was big enough and I wasn't very old even then, who did all the work!...While you were busy riding around in carts and buggies, playing cards, drinking and womanizing!...And when you finally did come home, if we hadn't managed to finish all the heavy work, there was hell to pay!...You even dared, one of those times, to hit Mama because a gate hadn't been mended and the animals had roamed into a neighbor's field!...You hit Mama who has more worth in her little finger than you have in your whole being!...Mama and I are willing to continue helping you so you go back to acting like a king in the village we came from as soon as possible, but, take my word for it, you'd better not lay a hand on Maurice tonight!"

Labranche, his eyes bulging out of his head as if he were having an attack of apoplexy, fell back in a chair, overwhelmed by the unexpected violence of this attack. As for Vic, without another word, she turned on her heel, and walked through the boys' room to shut herself in her room.

A door opens and closes...It must be Maurice...Some cursing...A small voice trying in vain to make itself heard...Then hinges creak and a slip of a boy throws himself on his bed weeping...Yes, it's Maurice followed by Besson who talks to him softly, between sobs...Vic would like to go comfort the boys, but she's afraid of another scene if her father opens the door to their room. She waits. A chair pushes back, shoes thud, a door slams. Her father must have left for his evening card game at the neighbor's. Vic gets up and, on tiptoe, crosses to the boys' room, and, just to be safe, peers through the keyhole into the outer room. Her father is, in fact, gone and she hears her mother sigh. She peeks her head out the door:

"Come here, Mama."

Her mother, slump-shouldered, eye reddened, lips trembling, comes toward her murmuring: "Dear God, your Calvary is too steep for me!"

Vic leans over the two sobbing children and, her head resting on theirs, breathes:

"Don't cry any more; we're going to talk."

Madame Labranche collapses at the foot of the bed and Besson, shaking with a horrible fit of coughing, throws himself in her arms. Vic puts her arm around Maurice and pulls him to her. For a few minutes, the girl rests her eyes on the embroidered bedspread, giving them all some time to collect themselves. Then, in a serious tone, she addresses the three unhappy souls:

"I've been thinking about all this for an hour and I've decided that the only way to help all of you is for me to leave!...Think about it! I'm earning twenty dollars a week right now, and that, even with all the other money that comes into the house, isn't enough to permit us to live decently. We dress like beggars and live like social outcasts in the saddest, poorest section of Lowell! When Sunday comes, we have to beg Papa to get the ten cents we need to go to mass! We have to cry to get a two-cent stamp to mail a letter! We can't go out walking, because that would wear out the soles of our shoes! There are no curtains on the windows and no rugs on the floor and Besson can't even have any cough syrup to ease his coughing fits!...The only way I have of helping you is by leaving. I work next to a Miss Vaillancourt who lives just five minutes from here. Her mother is a widow and, as a result, there are no men in the house to...make life miserable!... They had a female boarder who paid them three dollars a week, but she just got married. Madame Vaillancourt would probably let me stay there for the same price. I could sleep in the same room as her daughter. If I could manage my own money, I could buy medicine for Besson and books for Maurice. Little by little, I could find a way to dress you decently, Mama, and the boys too. From whatever I have left, I would spend a little to clothe myself and I'd put the rest in the bank for Maurice's education. This child has to go to college and I'm the only one who can help him. Don't worry that Father might send the police to look for me; he'd be much too afraid that I'd report him for keeping Maurice out of school. He's always beaten down anything and anyone that didn't bend to his tyrannical will; it's time he learned that he can be escaped! If I stay here, I won't be able to do anything for any of you. To be able to help you, I have to leave."

"But, my poor child, what if you get sick?" wails Madame Labranche.

"Why would I get sick? And even if I did, you wouldn't be far away. Besides, I'll be with good people; they wouldn't let me die without taking care of me. I could see Maurice every evening when I come home from work, and if Father goes out on Saturday or Sunday, you could all come to see me—it's not far. I don't want you to cry. What I propose will be difficult but it has to be this way if we're going to be saved. Look at me, I'm brave...don't take away my courage...Tonight I'm going to put my few rags in a sack and tomorrow I'll have someone come for them once I've reached an agreement with Madame Vaillancourt. Tomorrow evening, the scene Father's going to make, once he's realized I'm gone, isn't going to be pleasant...but you'll see, it won't last long. Things will get better little by little as he comes to realize that he can't drive us with a whip and a spur anymore as if we were animals."

End of Part One

PART TWO

CHAPTER 5

Besson's Death

Vic is now installed at Madame Vaillancourt's. If she often has a heavy heart when she thinks about her mother and her little brothers, she tries to console herself by remembering that it's for them that she's working now, so that a few rays of sunshine and some moments of happiness can brighten their lives. The first pay check she receives to do with as she pleases makes her a bit dizzy. Just imagine, after she pays her rent, she still has seventeen dollars, a huge fortune for a young woman of eighteen who, until this very moment, has never felt the thrill of holding a bank note between her fingers.

The first Saturday following her emancipation, or rather her liberation, Vic set out alone on foot in the direction of rue Merrimack (la GRANDE rue)—without the fear of being told that it would wear out her shoes—to window shop at her leisure and to decide what she might buy to ease the lives of those at home. Shoes? Hats? Shirts? No, her father, in a fit of rage, would be capable of throwing the whole lot into the fire. He would probably never forgive her, not so much for having fled, but for having, by that act, taken from him a large weekly sum he would have added to his own bank account. He would surely also always begrudge her for having hung over his head a sword that would inevitably fall on his neck if he ever made the mistake of having his daughter brought home by the police. No, Vic wouldn't buy anything just yet that might be noticed by her father. Later on, she'd see. She'd surely find a way to buy a nice black dress for her mother who, like all rural Canadian women of the time, wore only black. It was the custom that once married, young women stopped wearing bright, cheery colors. Perhaps her father wouldn't notice a new dress if it were a black one. Soothing syrups for Besson and books for Maurice, those she could have Maurice smuggle home in his pockets at night. She would also give fifty cents a week to each of her little brothers without her father knowing and then the children could buy themselves a few treats.

After many longing looks and much hesitation, Vic decided to buy herself a pair of ankle boots and a hat. She would buy other necessities another week. But every week without fail, she would put ten dollars in the bank for Maurice for college. Always this obsession: college for Maurice. If only her father wanted to, it would be so easy to make everyone happy...but no point in thinking about that: the task fell on her shoulders alone. She didn't complain, quite the contrary, but she was saddened by the suffering of her loved ones and by the happiness in their lives that was lost through the tyranny of her father.

One of the first things that Vic also did was to enroll herself in a night course to learn English.

One evening, Maurice informed his older sister that Besson wasn't doing well at all, that he was confined to bed and that their mother had had to quit working in order to care for him. That very evening, since there was no English class, Vic went to the rectory to see the parish priest and tell him about her family's situation.

"They'll no doubt call for you soon to administer last rites to my little brother. Perhaps you could work your way into my father's good graces and get him to consent to let Maurice go to college. I'll be responsible for the cost of instruction. However, I have to warn you that, short of a miracle, it's not likely that my father will ever agree to stop exploiting that poor child. You see, as our father he has the power of life and death over us...Couldn't you help me, Monsieur le Curé, to bend my father's will regarding Maurice?"

"I'll do what I can, young rebel, but God Himself will take care of things without my intervention. The designs of divine Providence are difficult for us to apprehend, my child."

A few days later, at the advice of the doctor, Labranche went to see the priest to ask him to give last rites to one of his sons who was dying.

In the bare room, only the face of the dying boy was calm. He wasn't suffering; he was simply growing weaker and weaker. He had asked his father's permission to send for Vic who had rushed to his side. Kneeling beside Besson's bed, she held one of the child's small, transparent hands against her lips to keep from crying aloud and covered it with kisses. On the other side of the bed, Madame Labranche was crying softly, her head leaning on one hand that hid her eyes. Labranche was standing, his hands clutching the footboard of the bed, his eyes never leaving the face of the dying boy, and, without his realizing it, or being able to stop them, the FIRST tears of his life streamed from his eyes, unabated. Death, with his grand scythe, had cut down a tree to make a coffin that would open the doors of a heart that had never before known anything but egotism.

As for Maurice, at times he devoured his little brother with his eyes and at others he buried his head in his arms which were flung across the back of the chair. Then his shoulders would shake violently with his sobs.

The attention of all those present was focused on the bed where a small form, frighteningly thin, could barely be distinguished beneath the covers. Every gaze was riveted on the small, emaciated face, dominated by two large eyes that looked like feverish stars. No one heard the knock at the front door.

However, Besson, with the great understanding and clairvoyance of the dying, heard it, and he immediately divined who was knocking at this final hour. In a weak voice, he interrupted the grieving of those who surrounded him and asked Maurice to go open the door for Cadet.

The little boy had heard on the street that his friend was very ill and, without stopping to think that he might be intruding, he had come running to see him. He approached, bare-headed, on tiptoe, with an anxious face. Without fully understanding, he sensed that something grave was happening. Timidly, as if fascinated by the small, pale face, he came right up to the edge of the bed on the side where Madame Labranche was sitting.

Besson, whose eyes still had the strength to hold themselves open, knew his friend well and asked Cadet:

"What did you bring for me today in the pocket of your sweater?"

As if caught in some mischief, Cadet stammered:

"I took some pennies from my bank and bought you a gold fish. I put it in a little bottle half filled with water to bring it to show you. Since there's no cat here to pounce on it, you can put it in a dish and watch it swim. Look how tiny and pretty it is." And as he finished, the boy took out the bottle and held it gently swaying above the bed.

A smile—his last in this world—lit the features of the dying boy's face. Death paused. The heavens opened and the angels, delighted, looked down on two of their small earthbound brothers.

Besson reached out with one of his small, thin arms. Cadet, with two strong, vigorous hands that trembled with emotion, placed the bottle in

Besson's hands and then guided it to his lips. His lips, through which not a single drop of blood seemed to circulate, opened to pose themselves radiantly on the clear glass, inside which a tiny gold fish wriggled. It was the trout from the streams of his native land that the dying child rediscovered there!

Cadet took possession of the bottle again, for Besson's arm had fallen back onto the bedspread. The boy, his throat constricted, his eyes burning, said in a low voice:

"Good-bye, Besson, I'll come back tomorrow to see if you're better."

Without waiting for an answer, which surely would not have come, he vanished like a shadow, pulling his cap down over his eyes. Later, he would remember this moment when, for the first time in his young life, he came in contact with death without realizing it.

Besson watched his friend depart with the heart-broken look of one who is left behind to watch the sails of a ship disappear over the horizon never to be seen again..., then he seemed to pull himself together and gather his forces one last time as he turned to the priest and asked:

"Monsieur le Curé, do angels ever have hunchbacks?"

"No, my child, death takes away all deformities. Only perfect bodies and flawless beauty exist in heaven."

"Then I'll be happy to die so I can be like everyone else. I was afraid that, even in heaven, they would still call me 'frog' and laugh at me because of my hump. It's not my fault, Father, if I have an ugly hump on my back."

The good priest could only shake his head. He couldn't say a word, he was so overcome by emotion.

As for Vic, sensing that this moment belonged to the GOOD LORD in Heaven, she released the hand of the child who was poised on the threshold of eternity and went to kneel beside her mother whose silent suffering was heart-rending.

"Papa," said Besson, "I have something to ask of you. This is the last and only thing I will ever ask. Once I'm gone, you'll have one less mouth to feed, fewer feet to buy shoes for, and one less body to clothe. Vic is earning a living. It won't cost you and Mama much to live. I saw you calculating your savings. You're several thousand dollars ahead now. Why won't you let Maurice go to college? Vic would pay for him to go, so it wouldn't cost you anything. Wouldn't you be proud if he became a priest like Monsieur le Curé? Then one day when it's your turn to come join me in heaven, maybe he could be the one to administer last rites and bless you the way M. le Curé did for me. Tell me, Papa, couldn't you give permission for Maurice to go to college? Don't you see, I could go away really happy if you'd just say yes."

Labranche, in an impulsive movement, suddenly knelt down beside his son:

"Forgive me, Besson...Forgive me, all of you...I have been truly wicked and I didn't even realize it...I understand now how unhappy I've made all of you...I swear to you, Besson, Maurice will go to college if he wants to and I will do my part to help with expenses...But don't leave us, Besson, your father needs you...With Maurice in college and Vic off on her own, your mother and I are going to be very lonely without you..."

"I'm not going far away, Papa, and where I'm going, I'll be much more handsome because I won't have a hump any more. You'll see when you come to see me...Papa?"

"Yes, Besson?"

"When I'm dead, I'd like you to put my grave where there are lots of trees and flowers and birds...I'd like you to bury me in our village, because here in the United States it's dirty and dusty and ugly...and, even when I'm dead, if you buried me here, I wouldn't be happy...Will you take my coffin to Canada, Papa?"

Labranche, his voice strangled by sobs, could only nod his head in assent. Besson, in a final, supreme effort, lifted his arm and, unable to do more, let his icy fingers fall on his father's hand. The latter, his head leaning over the small heart that had almost ceased beating, divined rather than heard these words:

"Thank you, papa...you're very kind..."

The uneven pulse in the child's tiny neck showed that his heart couldn't keep him alive much longer. Two large eyes opened wide, turned heavenward, glazed over...A puff of air, like a small ball bursting, passed through his white lips...It was over...An angel flew away.

In the doorway to the room, the priest, his hand raised in a sign of final benediction toward the angelic soul that was separating itself from its earthly shell, spoke softly: "How unfathomable your plan is, Lord!"

FAITHFUL to his promise, Labranche—an unrecognizable Labranche—took the train with Besson's coffin and went to bury his son in the country woods where he was born.

In the meantime, Vic helped her mother dispose of their meager furnishings, then Madame Labranche, in tears, accompanied by a sobbing Maurice, bid farewell to her grown-up daughter and followed the route of the tiny coffin that had preceded them back to Canadian territory.

Shortly thereafter, Maurice entered the college in Victoriaville, thanks to the combined assistance of Vic and their father. The years that followed saw him become an ecclesiastic at the Seminary of Montreal and then a priest.

CHAPTER 6

Vic's Story

Besson's death and the departure of her family were such a shock to Vic that she took to her bed overwhelmed by a feeling of despair that refused to leave her. But, at last, youth triumphed in spite of it all. Once back on her feet, she plunged into her work and her studies with more vigor than ever. She gave up her position as "loom threader" to work in a shoe factory where, thanks to her ability, she soon doubled her salary. This permitted her to dress a bit more fashionably, to live in a better neighborhood, and to take better care of her mother, all the while continuing to put something in the bank for Maurice each week.

One day, while rummaging through a trunk, the young woman accidentally came across the business card that, one evening, five years ago, had been slipped into her hand by the engineer who snatched her from the clutches of the young hyenas from the mill. She was only a child then, yet she had been aware that she was too miserably dressed to dare go knocking at the door of the well-to-do. Older now, more sure of herself, better dressed, she could risk paying a visit to Madame Fénélon as her son had asked her to do that day long ago.

Once an idea entered Vic's head, it was a deed accomplished; for it was no sooner thought than executed.

Hence, on a Sunday afternoon, with a hand that trembled slightly, she rang the doorbell of a luxurious house in a nice residential neighborhood in Lowell. A woman of about sixty, with white hair and an aristocratic air, opened the door with a smile.

"Are you Madame Fenelon? I'm Victoria Labranche. My name won't mean anything to you, but let me add that, five years ago, your son saved my life by preventing three girls from throwing me into the canal near the mill. He told me to come and see you, but I haven't been able to until today."

"Ah, yes, I remember now. I had, in fact, forgotten your name but not the incident. Come in, child. I'm glad you came."

Intimidated at first, Vic quickly regained her composure thanks to the genuine warmth with which she was welcomed into this milieu so different from her own. How beautiful everything was here, how peaceful and good! Vic's eyes were drawn to the enormous rows of books that covered one entire wall. Her hostess noticed at once.

"Do you like to read?"

"Oh, yes! You see, my mother was a country school teacher and gave us her love of books. If I had the means, I would spend all of my free time studying. That's the one thing that interests me. I never go out, since I don't know how to dance. And after my day at work, I'd much rather read than spend my energy learning to waltz."

"In that case, the door to my library is open to you. You are welcome there any time."

"How kind you are—thank you." And, in the sweetness of the moment, Vic shared some details about her life with no particular order or emphasis.

"Would you like to stay and have supper with me, my child? I'm alone here since my son won't be coming until later this evening. I'm sure he'd be pleasantly surprised to find you here, but I doubt that he'll recognize you."

Vic laughed.

"Yes, I've changed a lot in five years. I was a child then, and here I am already twenty. On the other hand, I wouldn't recognize your son either, for the evening that I met him I was blinded by my childish despair. I may even have seen him on the street since without recognizing him as my rescuer."

"In addition to my son, who should be here before nine o'clock, I'm expecting a friend, Madame Guay, who is coming to play chess with me. My husband was bedridden for several years, and during that time I learned to play chess to help him pass the time. It so happens that my friend Madame Guay learned the game in similar circumstances. So when we both found ourselves widowed and alone, we continued to play chess with one another on the rare occasions when we see each other. Madame Guay has a large family and hardly ever goes out. As for me, my broken foot—you've noticed that I limp—keeps me from visiting others. But I don't really mind, since I love my home. Perhaps you know how to play chess?"

"I have to admit," said Vic blushing, "that I've never even seen a chess piece."

Madame Fenelon smiled.

"You'd learn quickly, I'm sure, for I can see that you're a bright student. I'll teach you the game and, in return, I'll ask that you come and play it with me from time to time. Can you spend the evening?"

"I don't know if I should accept. You see, I'm afraid to be out alone at night."

"Don't worry about that. Jean, Madame Guay's son, always comes to get his mother when she visits me. He will no doubt be pleased to escort you to your door. And if Jean doesn't come, my son will accompany you home."

Vic accepted the invitation because she felt her heart warm in the presence of this old woman whom she already loved.

When Raymond, her son, arrived, sooner than expected, Vic saw, without recognizing him, a tall, serious young man in his mid-thirties, with manners as aristocratic as those of his mother. After a warm hand-shake, she sensed that she was going to like the son as much as the mother.

"I insisted, Raymond, that Mademoiselle Labranche spend the evening with us with the understanding that Jean would accompany her home, or that you would."

At the mention of Jean's name, Vic, a careful observer, saw a frown appear on the engineer's brow. She was to remember that frown later and understand its significance.

Madame Guay, Madame Fenelon's friend, displayed a refinement and elegance of manner further distinguished by a frank openness. Her son was a handsome young blond, probably nearing thirty, but who appeared a bit too sure of himself. As pre-arranged, Jean accompanied Vic home and the young woman felt a rush of emotion at the touch of his hand on hers. The warm, velvety eyes that held hers for a moment moved her strangely.

After this first evening, which was to play, at first, such a devastating role and then, later, such a providential role in her life, Vic saw Jean again frequently, either at his mother's house, where she was warmly welcomed, or at the Fénélon's house. She, whose childhood and adolescence had lacked the slightest demonstration of love or affectionate physical contact of any kind, fell completely in love, irrationally, impetuously, with all the force of her ardent young being, with a man whose only glory seemed to be stealing young hearts to display like trophies.

The FIRST GREAT LOVE that occurs in every life came knocking at Vic's door and she welcomed it in only to find herself stabbed to the quick.

Had she been less innocent, less naive, less kind, perhaps she could have fought back and triumphed, but, poor, half-opened blossom that she was, she lost the struggle before it began.

Since meeting Jean, it was no longer blood but molten lava that coursed through her veins. The pent-up love in her heart had broken the gates of the dike through which devastating torrents now flowed.

A noble heart, a worthy soul, would have given his fortune and his life's blood to be loved the way Vic loved Jean.

Even he, who had a mistress in every port, couldn't help being touched by it. On one of the rare evenings when he accompanied her home, she had twined her fingers through his and, like a child, had plunged their two joined hands into the pocket of his overcoat. She felt so close to him this way, it made her feel as if Jean belonged to her more. Touched by her gesture for a moment or two, he had squeezed the long fingers that clung to his own and murmured:

"Vic, will you wait two years for me? I'm not ready to get married right now, because my business isn't established solidly enough yet to permit me to think about supporting a household without risk. Tell me, will you wait two years for me?"

Pressed up against him, her eyes half-closed to hide the joy that glowed there, Vic replied, her voice choked with happiness:

"Jean, I'll wait for you forever—for years and years if I must—you're my whole life."

The young woman shouldn't have let Jean see that she loved him so much, but she was carried away by a flood of emotion she couldn't control.

Her charmer, sincere for the moment, untangled his fingers to capture her face which was tilted up amorously. He saw her lips tremble, and, not yet content with his victory, Jean whispered against her neck:

"Let me show you what a soul's kiss is."

And she, foolishly, offered her lips to the man who had just asked her to be his wife.

From the instant that Vic first experienced the sensual delight of that devil's drink they call a soul's kiss, not even fire could have kept her from Jean. And through fire she would pass, for life, in it's unfathomable plan, had deemed that she would, in fact, be separated from Jean.

However, we must add in fairness, while Jean broke her heart, he preserved the honor of this girl who loved him to distraction.

From the day that she found Jean in her path, Vic's small boat carried her straight towards the rapids that would break her into a thousand pieces. Knowing nothing of life or its vagaries, she set off on the waves with a smile, her eyes on the stars, while at her feet the demons raged and foamed.

Jean shared only bits and pieces of his life with Vic. He was, he told her, too wrapped up in his business dealings to court her openly or to go strolling with her in public. She, in her naiveté, trusted what he told her, for she didn't yet suspect that he had so many lady "friends" that he had to be careful in courting each not to be found out by the others. He was intent upon keeping them all in order to create a realm of love and delight for his own selfish pleasure.

Questionable conduct always ends up being exposed, and Vic began to see things clearly through a fog of tears. Had she been more experienced, she could have responded in kind, but in her state of naiveté, even if someone had advised her to, she wouldn't have been capable of it. Aside from Jean, no one else in the world existed for her. If she had loved him less, perhaps she could have closed her eyes and kept silent, relying on his PROMISE, but she was so hurt by his deviousness that she had to let him know that she didn't deserve to be treated this way.

Many a scene followed, but Jean always found some excuse for his strange behavior. These explanations, and the kisses with which he devoured her after each confrontation, disarmed her. For when one is in love, one grasps at the slightest straw.

One evening, Jean had told Vic to go to the ballroom alone, because he was going to be detained at the office too late to accompany her, but he promised to meet her there later in the evening. Vic was happy because Jean, HER Jean, was going to meet her at the ball. She wouldn't be able to dance with him, of course, because she didn't know how to dance, but, after each waltz, he would come and sit beside her.

Suddenly, the young woman's eyes, which had been watching the door, flashed and her whole body stiffened. HER Jean has just come in, arm-in-arm, with a young woman, beautiful as a dream, with the figure of a goddess, dressed like a princess. The couple walked straight over to the chair where she is sitting and Vic heard, as if in a fog:

"Allow me to introduce you to my friend, Mademoiselle Colombine Girardin." Vic's mouth didn't open to respond to this introduction, for her blood seemed frozen in her veins. Noting this cool reception, Jean and his new companion set off swirling to the orchestra's stirring rendition of a waltz.

It's time to escape, Vic, why don't you? But no, faint-hearted as those truly in love, the young woman remained glued to her chair, and, if it weren't for her trembling, one would have thought her a statue, a statue of despair.

Soon it was time to go and Jean seemed to realize that perhaps this time he had gone too far. Whether out of pity or because he wasn't quite prepared to give up the unhappy girl who loved him so dearly, he abandoned his dance partner and came to accompany Vic home.

"Mademoiselle Girardin came looking for me at the office," he said, "and asked me to accompany her to the ball, so I did so without hesitation, never thinking of the pain it might cause you." The same carefully phrased excuses as always, and because she loved him SO MUCH, Vic felt her pain melt away and, with a kiss, forgave him once more.

There were other occasions when Vic went to the ball alone because HER Jean didn't have time to accompany her, and how many times did she glimpse him blending into the crowd to avoid being seen...He was always alone, it's true, not willing to compromise himself by being seen with one or another of his flames.

These deceptions and the scenes that followed them went on for years, and the two years that Jean had proposed multiplied and threatened to become an eternity.

However, since everything in this world must eventually come to an end, an evening finally came when Jean brutally announced to Vic:

"I saw Mademoiselle Girardin today and she's so unhappy that she's threatened to enter a convent if I don't marry her!"

"And so?" Vic questioned, holding her breath.

"So, I've decided not to marry either of you, since there would be too much suffering on either side if I did."

The coward! The cad! This was too much. Vic pulled away from Jean, who made no effort to detain her, and ran off into the night. She ran on and on, headed instinctively toward the home of her old friend, Madame Fenelon, whom she loved like a mother and who always found a way to rekindle a spark of hope in her soul. She arrived and knocked at the door. Since it was only ten o'clock, the door opened immediately. Without a word, Vic rushed into the open arms of the old woman who read the signs of another crisis in the young woman's distraught face and in the wild gleam of her eyes. Without noticing Raymond who was sitting near the fireplace reading and smoking, the young woman allowed herself to be led into one of the bedrooms. Madame Fenelon removed her hat and her coat, pushed her into an arm chair, and bathed her face with cold water, all the while murmuring: "You poor child! He's made you suffer again! That miserable man! He'll pay for all this one day!" She made the young woman drink a calming potion and then undressed her and put her to bed.

"No, don't try to talk this evening, you're in too much pain. Try to rest. Tomorrow you can tell me everything."

Then the white-haired angel turned out the lamp and exited quietly leaving the door open a crack in order to be able to hear the slightest summons.

Vic felt the effects of the sedative spread through her body. The pain in her heart was numbed but she didn't fall asleep. She could hear the voices in the next room:

"What can she possibly see in him to make her love him this way? As for him, the cad, the day of reckoning will come and he'll pay in blood for all the evil he's done today. Why did a child like Vic have to fall in love with THAT SORT of man?" The voices continued, but the young woman felt sleep overtake her under the effect of the sedative...She fell asleep thinking that it was wonderful to be loved by kind-hearted souls like Madame Fenelon and her son.

Now we see Vic back in her own bedroom, kneeling at the side of her bed. In her folded hands, with her lips pressed against it, is the crucifix that Besson held next to his heart before he died.

"Dear Lord," she moans, "what's the use of being good when I'm rewarded this way? I never did anything bad in my entire life and in return what have I gotten? Nothing but tears and torment! Dear God, give me a miracle now or tomorrow I'll stop being virtuous and I'll start down the slippery slope where they say the roses have no thorns. If you don't offer me a helping hand today, tomorrow will be too late. Dear Lord, don't I have the right to a little happiness here on this earth?"

Vic, you don't know what you're saying. Your despair has blinded you and led you to blasphemy. God doesn't create the kind of miracles you wish for deep in your heart, but in his own time he creates even more spectacular ones. He's leading you over this thorny, rock-strewn path today so that he can offer you something better tomorrow. You don't understand, but He does, and He is not leading you blindly. If you had the wisdom of the ages, my child, you would understand that everything that happens to us happens for the best, even in this world.

The next day, Vic, but a Vic with fierce eyes and scornful lips, set off for the office of Raymond Fenelon. After waiting an hour for his meeting with a client to be over, the girl was ushered in. She sat down across from the engineer who looked at her mystified. They exchanged pleasantries, but Vic cut them short and leaned forward toward her companion and said:

"Do you remember the March evening eleven years ago when you saved my life on Canal Street? Do you remember that you told me that night that if I ever needed you I could come and knock at your door without fear?"

"Yes, I remember very well."

"Well, the day has come when I need you! Your mother has doubtless told you about my unhappy love affair with Jean Guay? I've been virtuous until now and look how I've been rewarded! Well, I'm done being virtuous since it appears that loose women have all the good fortune!...Only hussies manage to make good matches and find good husbands!...You know yourself that the most happily and richly married women are often the ones who threw virtue to the wind when they were young!...No doubt because he was afraid of the obligations that might ensue, Jean respected my reserve...but maybe if I'd been one of those girls who give themselves freely, he would have married me!...I'm through being good, I tell you!...I want reckless abandon, I want happiness, and you're the one who's going to give them to me!...Take me and make me forget!...I don't want alcohol or drugs to dull my senses, I want two arms around me and a heart that loves me!"

Raymond leaped up as if launched by a spring. He put his arms around Vic and pressed his lips to hers...but it's was the icy mouth of a statue that touched his...Slowly, even reverently, he lifted the girl's face to his.

"Look at me, child, look deep into my eyes...Giving you the oblivion that you seek would be a crime that I'd never forgive myself for! You don't love me today, and you would despise me tomorrow if I gave in to your foolish desire! But I want you to know that, even if your lips had responded to my kiss, I wouldn't have helped you find the oblivion you seek in your despair...My gesture was intended to wake you out of your delirium and make you realize what a foolish act you were about to commit...Oh, if I were younger—I'm fifteen years older than you, child, and young blood responds to young blood—if I had thought I could compete successfully with the man who brought despair into your life, I would have given my mother a daughter-in-law long ago. You would have a home today and... maybe even children to love...our children, Vic...but even though I loved the quality of your mind and the tenderness of your heart, even though I admired the shape of your body, no one knew, not even my mother, because I'm the sort of man who knows how to step aside in order not to obstruct the path of those in pursuit of happiness...Right now, Vic, if you married anyone, it would be in spite of the presence of another in your heart and that would be the curse of your marriage. Think of your personal happiness, but don't forget the happiness of the man who becomes your husband. In spite of everything, the good Lord loves you, since He led you to me during the greatest trial of your young life. This storm will pass and you'll end up understanding that everything that happens happens for the best. God will take care of things for you without my help. The designs of divine Providence are difficult for us to understand, Vic.

The girl, pupils dilated, took a step back and then another. "Those words, those words! Those are the same words our parish priest said when Besson died! A prophesy that came to pass all too quickly! Is yet another tomb going to open up before me to change the course of my life?"

Vic rubbed her eyes as if she'd just awoken from some hypnotic trance. She slowly approached the engineer, took his hand, wrapped it around her waist and leaned against him.

"No, don't misjudge me. It's not forgetfulness I seek, I just want to be close to you to talk, my heart next to yours...Why didn't I fall in love with you instead of Jean? But from the first moment I saw him, everyone else ceased to exist for me. Perhaps I could find forgetfulness, but to do so, I'd have to have a change of scene. And since the necessities of life hold me here, I'll just continue on, with my head held high, thanks to you, Raymond. Twice you've been placed in my path to save me! If I could see into the future, perhaps I'd see you appear in my life again, in a moment of crisis, to save me a third time!"

"If that moment comes, teased the engineer, I'll expect to receive the same reward they give to all those who save others' lives."

"And what reward would that be?"

"Your unconditional love, Vic!"

"Who can say," murmured the young woman as if to herself, then, stirring, she said:

"I won't come to your office again, Raymond, but, before I go, would you kiss me the way you would kiss a younger sister? I want to be able to remember a kiss from the purest heart that ever existed."

The next day, when she returned home from work, Vic found a telegram with the following message waiting for her:

YOUR FATHER PARALYZED. NEED YOU HERE. COME. MAMA.

The girl, holding the telegram in her hand, unconsciously repeated the words of the old priest and Raymond: "How difficult it is to understand your divine plan, Lord!" and she burst into tears, forgetting her own heartache and thinking only of those who needed her, in the northern territory

Vic telephoned Madame Fenelon with the news, then she called the train station to get the departure schedule, and finally she set about packing her trunks to leave on the next train. When she opened the last drawer, she found the diary in which, for the past several years, she had poured out her heart, in burning prose, as it overflowed with her love for John. Her first thought in seeing it was to destroy this silent confidante without rereading it, but then, realizing that she couldn't take the train until the following morning, she sat down in an armchair and, for the next hour, immersed herself in re-reading these pages, written with her heart's purest blood.

CHAPTER 7

I Love You, Jean! Vic's Diary

November 1, 1906.—There are times in your life when you have to pour out your heart to keep it from exploding under the pressure that's building. Ever since LOVE came into my life with the suddenness and fury of a hurricane, I've felt as if I'm suffocating from not being able to tell anyone about the emotions that tear at me. So, in order to have an outlet for my thoughts and feelings, I've decided to keep a diary, not on a daily basis, but from time to time, depending on my heart's need to express itself. So, I'm beginning tonight, on Halloween night.

Jean, my dearly beloved Jean, I'm going to talk to you in my diary tonight since I won't be able to see you. Tell me again what you whispered in my ear before we went into Madame Fénélon's house last Sunday night? Tell me again: I LOVE YOU, VIC! If you only knew what incredible ecstasy those words brought me, my love! If one day life leads me to climb a Calvary of my own, I'll find the necessary courage, in the midst of my blood and tears, by remembering the night of October 30, 1906, when, with a kiss, you said "I love you, Vic!" And then you said: "At first, I wanted to make you love me without loving you in return, but I got caught in the very trap I'd prepared for you! And now I love you, Vic, and we'll get married in two years, but let's keep it a secret, our secret, so no one suspects a thing!" As you spoke, your voice was thick with emotion and my happiness knew no bounds. "I love you, Vic!" When I close my eyes now, my whole being trembles with the magic of those few little words, words that fill my entire universe!

I don't know if I'll see you again before Sunday night, Jean. If I do, I'd like to ask you something: You're supposed to arrive at Madame Fénélon's with your mother at 8 p.m. If you wanted to—(you could give your mother some excuse for not getting there at the same time she did)—we could meet fifteen minutes earlier at the post office and go for a walk together, just the two of us, arm in arm, my hand clasped in yours inside the pocket of your overcoat. You see, I long to hear you tell me again: "I love you, Vic!" When we get to the house, you could ring the front door bell while I go in through the back door to take off my coat. That way, no one would know we've been together, since you don't want it known. What do you think, Jean? Look, I'm putting my lips to your ear to ask you this. Can you feel my breath on your neck?

8 Nov., 9 p.m.—Jean, bend down, take me in your arms like you did last Sunday night when you walked me home and tell me softly: I LOVE YOU, VIC! I want to hear you say those words to me every day of my life. Do you have any idea how much I love you?... You may never really know how much! I love you even when you hurt me... Did you know that I nearly choked the other day when you asked me to go to the party Thursday evening with your favorite cousin? People associate her name with yours so often, people say so many things about the two of you together, that I just couldn't agree to your request. I simply sent her the tickets you'd given me and offered some sort of excuse. Thursday after work I'll wait for you like I do every night, so I can walk with you, and those few moments of happiness will be a million times more precious than going to the party. And don't think for a moment that you've deprived me of a chance to amuse myself by making the request you did. I promise you, I have no desire to go to parties now that I have a love in my heart that fills my entire existence. Why would I care about parties, anyway, Jean, if you're not there?

How wonderful it would be to lean my head against your chest as I write this and to stay there, close to you, and forget the rest of the world... I want to hold on to the beautiful dream that made me tremble constantly and that vanished when you asked me to go to the party with your lady friend. Let me pick up my dream again where I left it...Good night, my dear Jean, I lift my face to yours and my entire soul is in my kiss.

23 Nov.—You said you loved me, Jean, and then you repeated it again and again. I believe what you say, I have faith in your love, but why do you insist on hiding that love in the shadows as if loving each other were some horrible crime? I want to shout our love from the rooftops so the whole city knows how happy I am... But since you're so insistent, I've contented myself with very little: talking together for an hour every now and then, trembling as I take your arm when you come to walk me home after work, feeling your presence at parties that I go to only because you're there...And

that's it! And even though it's so little, now you tell me that your acquaintances have seen us walking with our heads close together, as if dreaming, and that tongues are already wagging about Jean and Vic being in love...So, in order to wrap yourself in the cloak of mystery you insist upon, you want me to give up the little you've given me? All right, you'll see how reasonable I can be: I won't wait for you at the edge of the park any more. I'll go back to my room alone; since that's your wish, so be it... And if I'm sad, if I need to cry, only my diary will know. I'll tell you, in these pages that overflow with my writing, what I do each day, what I think about, who I dream about, I'll tell you that I love you and I'll ask you to tell me again: I LOVE YOU, VIC! I don't believe those words could be uttered insincerely, since, when I say them to you, it transfixes me and my throat tightens as if they were holy words drawn from the depths of my heart.

Jean, since you made that strange request that we not see each other, even for a few minutes every night, my heart has ached, but, clearly, you must have your reasons, and I need, I want, to respect them because only you can know what you want and why. And yet, under the circumstances, I wonder whether it wouldn't be better if I went away while we wait for the two years you've insisted on to pass...At least then, if I were far away, I'd have to resist, whether I wanted to or not, the overwhelming desire to see you, to talk to you, to feel my hand in yours, my shoulder pressed against yours...But here, the temptation is too much for me: to know you're so close and yet so far!... My forehead is burning tonight, let me press it against yours, Jean.

27 Nov. 1907.—My soul was filled with joy all day today at the thought of seeing you tonight. That single thought made me as happy as a child. But when the time came and went and I realized you weren't coming after all, I was so unhappy that I burst out sobbing and couldn't stop... You called to tell me that you'd been detained at a friend's house (was it a male or female friend, I wonder?) and that it was impossible for you to meet me. And yet you managed to steal a whole day away from your business and spend it with your friends when I would have been happy to have just ten minutes... Ten minutes!... It seems like so little to ask, just the time to slip my arm through yours, to squeeze your fingers, to feel the caress of your eyes on mine, then I would have raced up to my room with a song in my heart... I sense the wings of a huge vulture circling over my life and I'm afraid, Jean. I love you so much, and you cause my soul so much anguish...

Now that I've learned to love you, do I have to learn to forget you? It was so much easier to give myself up to you than it will be to tear myself away... When you told me that you loved me and that I should wait two years for you, I was in ecstasy; will I have to pay for that enormous happiness now?... Will I have to search for forgetfulness, Jean, in an abyss of tears, bitterness and despair?

What price will I have to pay to forget you, Jean? Since I met you, everything but you has disappeared. I've loved you too much...me, the same girl, who, at twenty, thought that her heart would never quiver...Our paths had to cross, Jean, before the fire sleeping inside me could be kindled...but that divine flame has leaped out of control, devouring everything in its path, and now I have to put it out with my bare hands...Put it out before more ruins accumulate on this pile of charred debris... Will I be able to do it?

Jean, it takes more than a day or a month or a year to eradicate from one's soul a feeling as deep and as pure as the one I hold in my heart for you... And yet, if you don't love me any more, I have to rid myself of my love for you, this love that was my whole life... I have to have the strength to uproot it and toss it so far away from me that it can never take root again... And after that Herculean task, only a tiny spark of life will be left in my weary limbs, heavy heart and broken soul...and never again will those tendrils of love which cause so much pain push their way down into my soul... Instead, another plant, one called indifference, will take root in my heart. Its shoots will be brittle, its leaves withered, its flowers faded, but at least this plant of sorrow won't make me suffer, Jean, like the burning bush of flame that was my love for you.

I'm only dreaming, aren't I, Jean? ... And perhaps tomorrow I'll see you again and you'll offer some excuse for your behavior and I'll forget everything, everything, in order to love you.

December 4, 1908.—I spent the afternoon writing to my family and then I went to mail the letters at the post office. When I got back to my room, I lay down on my bed to read a book by Pierre Loti, the great dreamer who spent his whole life pursuing an impossible dream... I tried to read but I had to close the book because my eyes rebelled against my mind's will. I folded my arms behind my head and, staring off into space, I went back over my life since we first met. Jean, I'm just now beginning to understand some of the puzzling things you used to say. Before now I didn't really give much thought to anything except my love for you. Maybe you had a purpose in mind, but I was just stumbling along in the dark with only your love to guide me!

The other night you told me: "I love you Vic, but not as much as you love me. I never imagined that anyone could love the way you love me." I know perfectly well, Jean, that you can't love me as much as I love you, but I'm content with the little piece of your heart that you've given me...There have been other loves in your life,—as you've told me,—that have diminished the intensity of feeling in you that corresponds to this feeling that is consuming me... If you can't love me as much as I love you, just love me as much as you can and I'll be happy.

I didn't fall in love with you instantly, Jean, you had to mount a full assault to conquer my heart, a heart that had been deprived of any display of tenderness or affection, and that had withdrawn into itself saying, "I want EVERYTHING or NOTHING!" When you forced open the doors of that heart, you must have been amazed at the violence of the feelings you awakened there.

Jean, if only I could snuggle up against you, my hand clasped in yours, my heart beating next to yours, and tell you tonight and every minute of my life: I LOVE YOU, JEAN!

Why do I love you, Jean?... Just because you're you! I love to talk to you, I love the way you look, I love the way you are, I love everything about you. Just hearing someone say your name makes my eyes glow and I have to turn my face so no one sees...so no one knows that I love you.

Jean, do you remember that unexpected business trip you had to take to Paris? Do you remember the long letter I slipped into the pocket of your vest before you left and your promise not to read it until you had set sail across the Atlantic? Do you remember that in it I told you that whenever I try to get control of myself, to escape from your love, I feel your thoughts hovering over me like a huge wing holding me captive?

Isn't that at least partly true?

You said you regretted having insinuated yourself into my life and having asked me to wait two years for you. You also added: "If I hadn't said anything, you wouldn't have hoped for anything or suffered from anything." In the balance of human emotions, will the happiness you brought into my soul be outweighed by the suffering that has come with it? If you hadn't said anything, Jean, I wouldn't have experienced the ecstasy of loving you, and that's why, in spite of everything, I don't complain too loudly about the suffering you cause me.

December 13, 1909.—It's as if I'm paralyzed, sitting here in front of my diary... It seems as if my life stopped yesterday and I don't know how to set it in motion again. The storm that racked me hasn't abated yet...and with each blast, my head bows further, because I no longer have the pride or the courage I used to have. Jean, love must have put strong roots deep down into my soul to withstand the violent blows you deliver... When you seem unaware of my existence, my whole being rebels but, like a coward,—like all those who love,—instead of fighting back, I can only scream my pain at you.

Jean, I love you so much and that love is killing me... My whole nervous system is out of whack and I don't even understand myself any more. And yet, I have to pull myself together, because I'll need all my strength to continue on...alone...Bend down to me, Jean, see how my head is burning, hear how my heart is beating... Let me rest my head on your shoulder for just a moment; maybe that will soothe my fever.

Jean, how I regret the day I met you, how I wish I could remove this love from my soul and your face from my sight, but I can't, I can't!

I had a dream so beautiful, so grand, so pure, that God himself must have been jealous of it, for today he cut off its wings and let it fall, lifeless, back to earth. It never should have tried to fly so high.

Jean, I put you up on a pedestal in my soul and brought you all the offerings of my heart, without reservation. I couldn't see, with my eyes gazing into yours, that the base of the pedestal was set on shifting sand and that one day it would collapse, burying me in the ruins of my grand and beautiful dream.

December 14.—Jean, you punish my soul one minute and you sing me words of love the next...And in the face of your love, I grow fainthearted and forget the pain you've caused me.

Jean, I'm happy again tonight after my brief walk with you, leaning against you, my fingers laced through yours. You asked me what my idea of perfect bliss was and, with my head resting against yours, oblivious to the street noises, I said: "My dream is for you to love me as much as you can; and for me to be able to shout my love for you from the roof tops, standing arm in arm with you, in broad daylight. My dream is to spend my life giving you moments of pure happiness; to have little angels to cradle in my arms and smother with kisses, our children, Jean... My dream would be to grow old beside you with my shoulder always there ready for you to rest your head on in times of sadness. My dream would be for our home to always be a haven of tenderness and understanding; for my hand to always be ready to lift your face and dry your tears when dark moments came; for my tenderness for you to be so deep that you would never be ashamed to come and cry on my shoulder in times of trial and have me understand you and love you... That's my whole dream. And what about you, Jean, what's your dream?" Our time together had sped by as I described the dream that sings in my soul, so, instead of answering, you looked at your watch and told me you were already late and that we would continue our conversation another night. Will we really?

December 15.—Joy yesterday, tears today, this is my life since you stole my heart, Jean. This evening when you came to walk me home I was happy knowing that it was your turn to tell me your dream just as I had told you mine yesterday. But instead, as if obsessed by a thought you had to express, you said to me: "Vic, I can't love you the way you love me because your love is so overwhelming that it frightens me at times!" Choking back a sob, I replied: "Love me as much as you can, Jean, and I won't ask for anything more. It's not your fault, is it, if I have to love you the only way I know how?" You answered me with: "Vic, I know I asked you to wait a couple years for me, but my business affairs are in such a state that I'm still not ready to get married yet. What's more, I've been thinking about all this for quite a while now, and I don't think I'll ever get married. You should find yourself a boyfriend, Vic, and make a life with someone else." Then, after a moment of anguished silence, you continued as if talking to yourself: "What a pity for both of us, oh, if only you knew, Vic!" After those words, I couldn't see clearly anymore, Jean. It was as if I'd received a violent blow to the head. So, without a word, I fled. I wept, I wailed in despair in my room, and yet, despite all the pain you've caused me, I still love you, Jean! But if all you can feel for me is pity, it would be better if you finished wringing the last drop of blood from my heart right now, without relenting.

I can't help thinking that we won't be taking any more walks together, leaning against each other, that you won't hold my hand in yours any more, that you won't tell me that you love me anymore or that I should have faith in you. Is it really over, Jean, forever? With a sob that echoes the sobs of all those souls who have loved and suffered like me, I call out to you: I LOVE YOU, JEAN! But if you no longer love me, Jean, create a crevasse, with a single blow, between us. In crucifying pain, I'll close my eyes and my mouth in silence for a long time so no one can hear me... I'll lean against the wall so no one can see or feel the shudder that runs through me, killing me...And then it will all be over...Jean! Oh, Jean!

And so, with an unclear mind and a heart surely engaged elsewhere, you want to tear yourself from me and me from you, Jean? But what if tomorrow, without reason, without squeezing your hand, without a kiss, I were to say to you: "I'm going to disappear from your life forever, since that's your wish, but if one day your heart aches with a pain that no one can heal—since no one will know it's there—and you think of me, it will be too late! If one day you remember the years we spent together when I embraced you with a love so strong that it frightened you at times, and if, your head in your hands, you murmur: "Vic would have given me a better home than the one I have now, but I banished her from my life after breaking her heart!" it will be too late for regrets, Jean.

If I were to disappear from your life tomorrow, Jean, your heart would ache a little, for you've loved me as much as you could, in your own way! If you were playing a role when you first entered my life, the role didn't last long. If you were acting, then I was acting, too, but in the great human comedy, where hearts are captured only to be tormented later! You loved me, Jean, you may still love me without realizing it, but now you're attracted by a passing fancy, you're intrigued by intoxicating perfumes offered by hands other than mine...You struggle against your heart and at times you don't even know where your head is leading you.. You cried out to me: "If only you knew, Vic!" Knew what? What do those words mean? There seems to be a mystery in your life that I can't decipher, a riddle that I can't solve. Sometimes you let a word escape and it seems as if there's an iron collar around your neck...And every time you try to reach out to me, it's as if some invisible chain pulls you back. I asked you about it. You looked at me for a long time, your lips pressed together, then you shook your head and changed the subject.

January 9, 1910.—Jean, you're playing at cat and mouse with me. After the brutal words you'd said to me, you came to me, took my hands and held them to your burning forehead, and, with your eyes closed, you cried: "Vic, I'm a coward! I'm struggling in a web I can't escape. Forgive me for the pain I cause you at times, I'm not to blame!" Then I hugged you close, shaking with sobs of joy, I was so happy to have you back, if only you knew, Jean, my Jean!

I don't know if this perfectly pure feeling I have for you is love or if it's the wind of madness blowing through my mind. Put your arms around me, Jean, Close my eyes with the touch of your fingers—these eyes that cry now and then because they desperately need for you to love them.

January 20.—We said goodnight to one another two hours ago and for two hours I've been dreaming about you, Jean! If there are times when I curse the love you brought into my life, there are also times when I bless it.

Tonight, when you were talking again about the sudden trip you had to take to Paris, I had a glimpse of a vision so beautiful it staggered me. What a dream, to go away with you over the ocean, following the seasons around the world and loving one another under every sky...This vision was so beautiful that I was dazzled by it for a few moments before I was brought quickly back to earth by the realization that it could only be a mirage. Wherever we are, I will love you just the same, Jean. I will love you on the banks of a river, or a lake or an ocean. It doesn't matter where, as long as I can nestle in your arms like a child, with my head against your heart, and feel you there, close to me. It doesn't matter where, as long as I can share with you, openly and without fear, the love song that bubbles up constantly from my heart to my lips and that now I always have to suppress!

It's ten o'clock now. The silence in my room is interrupted only by the tick-tock of my alarm clock. My eyes close and my thoughts all fly away to you. Good night, Jean!

May 4, 1911.—After the dance. Yet another night when I had eyes only for you, Jean, and when you had eyes only for all the other girls, except me! It's cold in my room but my head is burning and I hurt, here, in my heart, oh, how it hurts! What good does it do to talk so much, to write so much, when it doesn't amount to anything? Wouldn't it be better to suppress these thoughts, these words, these feelings, and to stop the mad pounding of my heart? Wouldn't it be better to disappear into the distance, casting my dying soul into the vastness of the sky and then tracing myself a new path, empty of joy perhaps, but free of tears as well? The high hopes and idealism that have played such a huge role in my life so far have to help me now to hold up my head and to walk courageously into the fray—they just have to! I'm still young. Who knows what the future has in store for me?

November 14.—Jean, do you know what two names I was given when I was christened? For months I've been wanting to tell you, but for some reason every time I open my mouth, nothing comes out. Since everyone is given one or more names at birth, I hadn't attached any importance to my given names until that night at the dance when you introduced me to the young woman—by the same name as one of my own—who was leaning so happily on your arm while my heart stopped beating! I inherited the name Victoria from my grandmother, while my godmother dubbed me with the same name as hers: Colombine. Now do you understand why the OTHER Colombine, the one who isn't me, broke my heart when she captured yours? Victoria, the Vic that I am, loves you with her nature of fire, with her ardent, impetuous, insatiable temperament...while Colombine, who I am too, loves you timidly in the shadows, always ready to forgive and forget in return for a smile, a touch, a kiss.

Colombine suffers the torments of hell, but Vic comes to the rescue, eyes flashing, ready to destroy the other Colombine, my shadow, because a mere shadow can't love you like the real Colombine. And when Colombine, at night in her tiny room, huddles at the window, her head pressed against the glass in the hope of seeing you pass, and says feverishly: "He will walk over my grave on his way to the other Colombine!...oh how can I love this man so much when he breaks my heart without pity?" Vic replies: "You're a coward...You, the independent one, here you are licking the boot that kicks you! You who've spent your whole life displaying an energy and courage beyond the ordinary, you're reduced to letting yourself be battered, beaten, and destroyed by a man? Come on, how is it possible? If he prefers other women to you, let him pursue his other loves; they'll pay him back in kind one day. Do you really believe there's a man worth destroying your life for? If you allow yourself to be carried away like this, then you're a coward to those who love you, a coward to yourself, and a coward in life!"

November 17.—The sadness that has dampened my spirits these past months has once again invaded my heart. I try to free myself from its awful, suffocating embrace, but it's as if I no longer have the strength to struggle. Jean, I can't bear to hear you tell me again that you love her, this Colombine. The blow your brutal declaration dealt my heart wounded me so deeply that I can't heal, and my blood is seeping slowly from the wound.

Love her if you must, if you can't help yourself, but for God's sake, don't tell me about it!

November 29.—How happy I was to hear you tell me, whispering softly in my ear, that it's all over with the other Colombine, that I'm the one you love the best. Since the night you told me you were in love with her and that she, in return, adored you, my heart has bled so, that some strange malady seems to be sapping my energy, my strength, my life. I did nothing to fight off this disease, for I was content to feel my flesh gripped in claws that had the power to carry me away. Constantly, when my eyes weren't closed in sleep and even in sleep, I saw before me the image of the one to whom life had given one of my names. It was no use shaking my once proud head, her image had penetrated the depths of my soul and was carrying me away.

You told me last night that it was over between the two of you, that you had parted after a terrible quarrel...Lovers' quarrels are quickly forgotten, Jean! You've come back to me today, but if tomorrow she holds out her arms to you again, you probably won't have the strength to resist her. I'd like to smile in the face of tomorrow, to laugh at life, but since knowing you, Jean, I've forgotten how to laugh...In a moment of bravado one day I said: "I want to know all about life and everything it offers!" My wish was granted and now I've known life and all it holds!

December 10—When I die I would like to be buried wearing, as my final ornament, the chain and cross that you gave me, Jean. I'd like to carry that lugubrious piece of jewelry with me into the next world so that no other young woman can wear a chain and cross from you, Jean!

A cross on a chain? What were you thinking when you gave me that gift, Jean? Nevertheless, when I feel them around my neck, touching my skin, it makes me smile to think that they came from you, Jean!

I didn't say anything about the incident at the last dance. I don't think I have the strength left to say anything. The only signs of my distress you saw were the tremors that shook me. A tornado was sweeping through my mind. What was your purpose, your plan, after breaking up with her, in bringing her back to Lowell to display her proudly on your arm? Whatever your goal was, I guess you've achieved it, Jean...I asked too much of life, the last small bits of my beautiful dream have been destroyed...Oh, if only I could hurt you as much in return...But no, I'm a coward like all those who truly love.

I'm afraid of tomorrow, Jean, for tomorrow you'll no doubt talk to me about "her". Maybe you'll tell me that you still love her...I'm afraid, so afraid of tomorrow, for tomorrow it's YOU, and HER, and ME!

When the last sentence danced before her tear-clouded eyes, Vic got up and went to get some logs and some kindling from a box hidden behind a piece of furniture, and then set about making a fire in the fireplace: an enormous FIRE that resembled a FUNERAL PYRE on which she sacrificed her LIFE'S DREAM! Her fire prepared, Vic struck a match and held it next to the dry twigs. There was a crackling and soon long tongues of flame lapped at the stones of the fireplace.

The young woman crouched before the fire, her face, illumined by the light of the burning logs and flushed from the heat of the flames, resembled that of a vestal virgin watching over a sacred fire in some pagan temple. But in place of incense, Vic offered up the pages of her diary, ripping them out one by one, with a sound like ties or fetters breaking. Vic tenderly offered the corner of each page to the fire, holding on to each twisting sheet of paper until the flames licked her fingers. And Vic saw, rising up from each page that she fed to the flaming holocaust, these words written in huge red letters: I LOVE YOU, JEAN! When the last page had been destroyed by the fire, Vic didn't weep, for there seemed to be a vast empty space in the depths of her soul. In one corner of it a sick man struggled and in another a heart was dying. There were no tears in Vic's eyes as she looked into herself, horrified. She was certain of one thing: her dream would never rise up again from the cinders of the fire that had consumed it; as for the sick man, early tomorrow morning, she would set off to find him and, with the help of her family, she'd pit herself against the threat of death that circled around him.

End of Part Two

PART THREE

CHAPTER 8

Life in the Country

Having received the telegram alerting her to the serious illness of her father too late to leave that same evening, Vic took the first train the following morning. Since she didn't have enough money on hand for this unexpected trip and since the banks weren't open in the early morning hours, the Fenelons lent the young woman the necessary funds.

It's December 22nd. It's not terribly cold but it's starting to snow. The stations along the route —Nashua, Manchester, Concord, Laconia, St. Johnsbury —are bursting with people taking the train, since there are large numbers of Canadians returning to their homeland for the holidays. Vic, seated on a train bench with her nose pressed against the window, pays no attention to the clamor and movement about her. This is the first time she's taken this route since she traveled it with her family by night eleven years ago. Since Besson's death and the departure of her family, Vic hasn't taken a day of vacation, spending all her days at work in order to support Maurice and to put something aside for herself in case of emergency.

This is the route, so desolate in winter, that leads from Lowell, Massachusetts, to the asbestos mines in Quebec Province, but Vic sees neither the bare trees, nor the white ground, nor the waterways covered with ice. The same image drifts constantly before her eyes: her father struck down by illness, her father who —according to what her mother wrote —hasn't been himself since Besson's death.

Will she get there in time? How slowly the train wheels turn! And the huge flakes of snow are falling faster and faster. What if the storm gets bad enough to disrupt rail service all together?...And that's exactly what happens. The locomotive is blocked by banks of snow and can no longer move. A veritable tempest is unleashed. It grows cold in the compartments. Children are crying and everyone is nervous and worried. Finally, after a two hour delay, the track is cleared and they set off again slowly.

Late that night, Vic gets off the train at the village station where she must find lodging for the night. The next day she will try to find a carriage to take her to her destination.

"The roads are covered in snow," the local cart drivers tell her the next morning. "We can't do any traveling today; we'd risk getting the horses bogged down in the snow." Since, in the end, money always speaks more loudly than any objections, Vic finally manages to convince one of them to take her. She leaves her baggage claim checks at the hotel with instructions to send her trunks along as soon as the roads are passable, and prepares herself for the trip.

Bricks are heated to place at the travelers' feet, a bearskin carriage blanket is spread out over the seat to keep out the cold, another bear skin is spread over their laps, two pairs of snowshoes and a snow shovel are stored in back, and they're ready to undertake the six miles of roadway along which all the fences have disappeared under mounds of drifting snow.

The horse advances with short steps, testing the moving ground beneath his hooves. A wool blanket on his back is held in place by the harness, but the sweat freezing on his head and chest show how exhausting his task is. Nevertheless, the courageous beast, seeming to understand what is expected of him, continues to pull steadily ahead.

Several times, the cart nearly turns over, but rights itself thanks to the courage and skill of the driver. He has thrown off the blanket that was spread over his lap at the beginning of the journey and is now standing up leaning first to one side and then to the other in order to help balance the cart.

Now he places the nearly useless reins in Vic's hands, and jumps out to walk behind the cart holding firmly onto the back of it to keep it from tipping over. The young woman tries to guide the horse as best she can along what she thinks is the middle of the road but it's hard to tell which direction is which since the road signs have been blown over by the wind and buried under the snow drifts.

Suddenly there's a snow bank that appearsf higher than the others: perhaps they're at the edge of the road. The horse, who appears unafraid and determined not to be defeated, puts forth an extraordinary effort to pull out of the drift but, labor lost, he remains buried in the white shroud.

They can see the buildings of a farm a short distance ahead. The cart driver, up to his waist in snow, cups his mitten-covered hands around his mouth and calls out as loudly as he can. His voice carries a considerable distance in the white stillness. Some men come out of the farmhouse and wave their arms. There are travelers lost in the snow —they'll come to the rescue.

Up to their hips in snow, the rescuers succeed in tracing a path to those adrift in the snow. They set about casting aside great shovelfuls of snow, clearing away the moving desert of snow in which the poor beast is buried up to his back. They unfasten the harness, pull the animal by the bridle , and the gallant charger is freed at last from the frozen ruts.

Several minutes later, Vic is standing before the open flames of an enormous cook stove in the kitchen of the welcoming farmhouse thawing her frozen extremities. The cart horse is exhausted and can't take them any further until the roads are cleared. Soft-hearted, like all Canadian country-dwellers, Poleon Auger, the farm owner, immediately offers to take Vic by sleigh to her parents' home which is just a mile further on. Auger knows the difficult spots in the road and will be able to avoid them. Two boards are placed length-wise on a bob-sleigh and, with a "Don't worry —if the roads are too bad, I'll stay at the Labranche's tonight!", they're off.

There are lights at the Labranche's —it's time for the train. At the sound of approaching bells, a man comes out of the barn carrying a smoking lantern. It's Maurice who has preceded Vic by a day and who's come out to take care of the animals. Maurice, a tall, handsome lad whom Vic hardly recognizes, for the last time she saw him he was just fifteen and here he is already twenty-one.

Bone-crushing handshakes, as when fingers are squeezed in great pain and Vic's only words are: "How is Father?"

"Still in the same condition," Maurice replies sadly. "He hasn't regained consciousness since they found him paralyzed two days ago."

Maurice climbs up to stand on the back of the sled saying: "I'm going to go as far as the house with you so I can bring Mr. Auger's horse back to the barn. The roads are too dangerous for him to return home tonight in the dark."

Vic, bracing herself against the emotions that threaten to suffocate her, enters the old house. She sees several figures gathered in the large kitchen, but she doesn't recognize anyone or notice anything familiar because of the mist clouding her eyes.

She walks straight ahead to the large bedroom, her parents' bedroom. Distractedly, she hugs her mother who has come to meet her. Her eyes are fixed on the bed where her father is lying, eyes closed, his left arm limp at his side, his right arm folded across his chest.

Vic walks slowly, automatically, forward toward the shape on the bed which appears lifeless. She slips off her glove and places her hand on the sick man's forehead.

"It's me —Vic. I've come to help Mama take care of you, Father, so you'll get better sooner."

Somewhere in the fog of his sluggish mind, the voice of the child he hasn't seen for several years, —the child who dared to defy him one day but whom he never stopped loving all the same, in his own way, —seems to strike a resonating chord. For the first time in two days, the sick man opens his eyes and looks steadily at the young woman leaning over him. He opens his mouth, makes an effort, then brings his left hand slowly to his lips to indicate that he can't speak. Huge tears well up in the dying man's eyes.

"It's all right, Father," Vic says, stifling a sob, "Don't strain yourself; it will all come back. With both Mama and me to take care of you, you'll see, you won't have to stay in bed long...Now then," Vic offers this excuse, for she knows that if she stays there at her father's side one moment longer, she's going to burst into sobs, "I'm going to go take off my coat, and then I'll come back and sit beside you." A gleam of light shines in the eyes of the paralyzed man as he watches Vic go off in the direction of the kitchen.

The priest is there. A neighbor went to get him during the night to minister to Labranche. The priest insisted on staying, as much to console the family as in the hope that Labranche would regain consciousness and be able to say confession. The tempest struck and now the priest can't leave until the roads are open. So he's spending a second night in the Labranche home where the closest neighbors are already gathering for the wake. One never knows what might happen and it wouldn't do to leave the family of the dying man all alone. Such is the lovely and touching custom of Canadian country folk.

The struggle with death begins. It is a battle lost in advance, for without having regained his ability to speak, Labranche is slowly dying, fully conscious but without being able to say a word!

Five days after Vic's arrival, between Christmas and the New Year, they carry the farmer's coffin to the Charnel House of the village cemetery. In the Spring, when the ground thaws, they will place his grave next to Besson's.

With the neighbors gone and the large bedroom where the body had been on view closed up, Madame Labranche and her two children now find themselves alone together in front of the huge two-decker, cast iron stove[1] that heats the whole house. The silence is interrupted by Maurice who is poking about in the stove moving the brightly burning logs aside to give space and air to those less well lit. After completing this task, he hangs the poker from a nail, brushes his hands together to remove any clinging ash, and, without raising his head, says:

"Mama, I've decided not to go back to seminary."

"Not go back to seminary, Maurice, but why?" asks Madame Labranche in alarm.

"Because with Father gone, you're going to need a man here. This farm has become too important in the last six years to risk losing all the money and work you and Father have put into it by neglecting it or abandoning it. Perhaps, in time, we could rent it or sell it, but we'd doubtless have to wait a long while to get the desired price. Don't you see, unless we have some income from the farm, it's not fair to leave the responsibility of supporting me at seminary entirely on Vic's shoulders. You must leave the money you have in the bank right where it is in case of hard times to come; I'll take Father's place and continue to pay off the land."

Vic listens to Maurice without interrupting him. When he's finished, it's her turn to speak:

"Maurice, you're going to go back to seminary and I'm going to try to take Father's place here. I'm strong, I still remember something about farm work, and, with Mama's help and advice, we'll get along fine. And what's more," she adds, as if talking to herself, "it will help me forget! During the peak seasons when there's lots of work to be done —sowing, haying, harvesting, threshing —we'll take on extra help. I'll go to the orphanage right away and get a lad of about fourteen or fifteen. If we offer to clothe him, give him a place to live and a few dollars a month to spend, he'll be happy and so will we. Your classes begin again in just a few days, Maurice, and you're going to be there. While you're at seminary, I'll help pay off the farm so that we can all make a living."

Maurice, with the same gesture he used to make as a child when his heart was breaking, knelt at Vic's feet and rested his head in her lap, weeping. The young woman, impulsively, as if in a gesture of unconscious benediction, placed her hand on the blond head bent before her, then, overcoming her emotion, she lifted the young man's face and said teasingly:

"You're setting a bad example! One day, I'll be the one kneeling at your feet, Monsieur l'Abbé! Say, what will we call you when you're the minister of God? Can we still call you by your first name?"

"Come on, you ninny! To you and Mama I'll always be just Maurice!"

And, when Maurice set off to return to the seminary, Vic took the path to the stable.

At Madame Labranche's request, the director of the orphanage had promised to send one of the most capable orphans to help them as soon as the necessary formalities had been completed, but, in the meantime, Vic undertook the heavy work alone. Nevertheless, she set her shoulder to the task with the same valiant spirit she had shown during all the difficult times in her life. For the moment, her sorrow over Jean was frozen, her grief at seeing another coffin carried off to the cemetery was dulled, and her boredom at finding herself isolated in the desolate countryside after having known the comforts of the city was cast aside. Her soul seemed to soar overhead in another realm while her body mechanically moved ahead.

Winter passed amid work of all sorts shared among Madame Labranche, Vic and Alfred, the boy from the orphanage.

Sugaring time came and it was an amusing diversion for Vic to go up to the sap house. Light-footed and singing, she went from maple to maple inserting the taps and hanging up the metal buckets into which the sap would drip.

That task accomplished, the young woman readied the hut where the sap would be boiled. She cleaned the kettles, the large pots, and the cloth strainers and set out the long wooden molds into which the syrup would be poured to become solid blocks of maple sugar. She washed syrup bottles, jugs, and barrels as well as funnels. She also sorted through specialty molds in the form of hearts, crosses, anchors, triangles, tiny houses, all made by her father in his free time while he watched over the boiling sugar. As for the birch bark molds that would be used to make sugar cones, she left that to Alfred.

When the sap of the maple trees started to flow, it was Vic who went from tree to tree to gather the sugary sap and pouring it into barrels arranged on a light sleigh drawn by a calm, steady horse. When it was time to boil the sap, she stayed at the sap house all night and slept there. Sometimes Alfred or her mother would come to join her.

For the orphan boy, these excursions into the woods became a real sugar orgy: licking the stirring sticks, dipping biscuits or bread, pulling sugar, an egg cooked in sugar, etc. He usually ended up with a stomach ache, but he was always ready to start all over again the next time.

While her mother and Alfred rested, Vic watched over the remaining cauldrons without feeling her sleepiness and fatigue. She tended the fire watching the sparks fly up into the night, stirring the thickening liquid with an enormous ladle, listening to the sounds that rose from the giant cauldrons and the wounds in her heart healed little by little.

Easter came and the Spring had been so mild that the snow had already disappeared and in places the soil was ready to be tilled.

Maurice came home for Easter vacation and decided to take two young horses from the stable and use them for a little field work. He harnessed the animals, full of energy after an entire winter of resting in the stable, to one of those new disc ploughs that his father had bought, shortly before his death, from a foundry salesman who had sung the praises of these new perfected machines.

The young man set off for a plot of virgin soil, proud to be able to lend a hand. Everything was going fine on the first pass through the field when, suddenly, one of the horses caught his foot on a tree root and, taking the bit in his teeth, charged off causing the second horse to bolt in fear as well. Maurice, seated on the plow, the reins wrapped around his wrists, thought himself strong enough to regain control over the two terrified beasts. But in the uproar, he lost his balance and fell head first beneath the rear hooves of the horses. The slicing discs of the plough ran over his face, but fortunately his head was buried in one of the fresh furrows that had just been ploughed.

Alfred was in the stable, Madame Labranche was weaving in the attic, and Vic was preparing the meal when a figure appeared in the kitchen doorway, his face covered in reddish mud, his cap dangling from his hand. In a semi-conscious state, Maurice's first thought, as he got to his feet, had been to pick up his cap!

"My God," exclaimed Vic, "What happened to you?"

"Oh, the horses got spooked and, in trying to reign them in, I tumbled under their feet and the disc ploughed my face. That's all."

"That's all!" echoed Vic. "Sit down while I heat some water to wash your face. Mama," cried the young woman, "Maurice has had an accident. Run tell Alfred to go to the Payeurs and ask them to bring the doctor as quickly as possible."

Madame Labranche came down the stairs as fast as she could; she saw Maurice's face, as red as.... and started to wail: "Oh, my God! My God!"

"It looks worse than it is," said Vic to stem her mother's panic, but she was afraid that it was worse than it seemed, for it looked as if one eye had been injured.

"Go quickly," she said, "while I'm washing Maurice's face, and tell Alfred to go to the Payeurs!"

With water and boric acid, Vic washed the torn flesh of Maurice's face, opening the wounds from which blood now flowed more abundantly, working to remove the dirt lodged in the cuts. She worked without a tremble, having once again found her nerves of steel to face this tragedy.

"Can you help me to bed," said the faint voice of the wounded lad, "because I can't see clearly anymore and I'm afraid I'm going to lose consciousness."

Vic half dragged Maurice over to the bed, made him drink a little cold water, and then continued, gently and tenderly, to disinfect the wounds. Alone, for her mother in her terror could only sit and cry, the young woman kept at her difficult task until mid-evening when the doctor from the neighboring parish arrived in the Payeur's carriage. Then she gave up her place and went to reassure her mother with words of hope that she herself didn't believe.

Alfred came to tell her that he had found the two horses, exhausted from their wild escape, and that he had led them back to the barn. Neighbors came by to offer their sympathy, but Vic didn't hear them, for her soul was in the room where the doctor was tending to Maurice's lacerated face.

An hour later, the doctor announced that, aside from a scar near Maurice's eye, where he had had to apply several stitches, there would be no lasting signs of the young seminarian's accident. If they would be kind enough to come to his office in two weeks, he would remove Maurice's bandages and the young man could return to seminary.

Her nerves giving way at last, to joy rather than sorrow, Vic rushed off to shut herself in her room where, kneeling, with her head in her hands, she sobbed: "Thank you, dear God! You must truly want this child in your sanctuary since, three times now, you have removed the obstacles that would have kept him from pursuing his calling. The first time, my father refused to let him get an education; the second time, he was determined to end his career in order to work the farm; and this time, you've saved him again in a miraculous way! Thank you, oh, thank you!"

As the doctor predicted, two weeks after his accident, Maurice resumed his studies and life continued peacefully on the Labranche farm with Vic in charge.

Each year, a herd of pigs was fattened for market on the Labranche farm. Most of these pigs were killed, disemboweled, and skinned before being sent to market. Normally it was in December, after the first real freeze, that the butchering was done.

Richard Payeur, the Labranche's neighbor, was the "professional" butcher of the parish, not because he was involved with selling the meat in any way, but because he was the one who was summoned when it was butchering time. He possessed an assortment of knives that would have been the envy of any professional butcher in the city, and, what's more, he was gifted with incomparable speed and skill.

The morning of butchering day, in the middle of the field near the pigsty, two solid long tree branches—two small trees were often used—with a fork on the end were planted firmly in the ground. A pole was placed with one end in each fork, connecting the two branches like a bridge. Next, with the aide of a strong hook, a huge iron pot like those used to boil syrup was suspended from the middle of the pole. The pot was filled with water and a fire was lit beneath it. If it was raining or snowing, a similar arrangement was set up in the shed, with the risk you might suffocate from the smoke that accumulated inside.

As soon as the pig was slaughtered, Alfred would run to the house with half a kettle of warm blood so that they could immediately begin preparations for making boudin (black or blood pudding). In the meantime, the men would pour huge pots of boiling water over the pig, so that they could more easily scrape off the bristles, with the aide of special knives, until they were completely gone. Next they disemboweled the beast, removing the entrails, the pluck, and the heart. These were also taken to the house, while the carcass of the pig was hung up by its back feet from a ladder mounted in the shed for that purpose.

The fat from the innards was carefully extracted to conserve as much of it as possible. Cretons, a type of pate, was made from this fatty residue. The intestines were then placed on a smooth board to be emptied, scraped clean, and rinsed. The small intestines were used to make sausages, and the larger ones to make boudin or blood sausage. When it was a small pig that was being slaughtered for the family's use, they would debone it and butcher it with the use of knives, saws, and hatchets. The legs and feet were set aside to make stew once the hooves had been seared. The head was reserved for making head cheese. They put aside the roasts, the cutlets, and the meat for tourtière or meat pies to be kept in the cooler. The rest, after deboning, was carefully arranged in large wooden salting tubs and covered with brine. This constituted the salt pork with which they made beans and lard, pea soup, and vegetable stew. Pieces of fatty lard, salted or not, were cooked and set to cool. These were served on the days when the family ate baked potatoes accompanied by pickled beets or salted cucumbers. This sort of meal was finished off with a large platter of "grand-pères". "Grand-pères" are prepared a bit like beignets or fried dough, except that the dough is cooked in boiling water instead of being fried in hot lard. Once cooked, they're taken out of the water and served with maple syrup.

And life flowed along...In the Spring they were busy with sugaring and sowing; in summer with haying and fruit gathering; in autumn with harvesting and threshing; in winter with butchering and the holidays. Time passed without exciting events, it's true, but without nerve-wracking shocks as well.

The years flew rapidly by. Alfred was a man now and Madame Labranche paid him a salary commensurate with the work he did. Economical, like many who start life in the school of hard knocks, the young man watched his savings accumulate in the bank and he nurtured the hope that, in a number of years, he, too, might be able to own a farm where he wouldn't always be worrying about tomorrow.

Apart from going to church on Sundays and holidays, comings and goings were few on the Labranche farm. The neighbors often came by to gossip, to smoke, and to play cards, but they always left early since everyone goes to bed early in the country in order to get up at dawn or even earlier.

The days of real happiness on the farm were those when Maurice came home on vacation. In two years, he would be ordained as a priest, and what wonderful dreams everyone had about that!

However, yet another loss occurred to sadden Vic's life: the death of Madame Fenelon. The young woman grieved as if she had been her own flesh and blood. Raymond kept in touch through cards that he never failed to send two or three times a year, and that was all. He never made the slightest allusion to anything in the past, and Vic hadn't seen him since she'd left Lowell.

[1]Two-decker, cast iron stove known in French as poêles à deux ponts.

Les premiers poêles à deux ponts furent fabriqués aux Forges du Saint-Maurice (Trois-Rivières) ou importés de Grande-Bretagne comme en témoigne la documentation du TLFQ pour le dernier quart du XVIIIes.

Bibliographie : Marcel Moussette, *Le chauffage domestique au Canada,* 1983 (présente plusieurs illustrations et photos des nombreux types de poêles ayant été utilisés au Canada depuis les débuts de la colonie); R.-L. Séguin, «Le poêle en Nouvelle-France», dans Cahier des dix, no 33, 1968, p. 157-170; G. Gauthier-Larouche, *Évolution de la maison rurale traditionnelle dans la région de Québec,* 1974, p. 142-152.

La locution poêle à deux ponts est attestée depuis 1808 au Québec, poêle à trois ponts depuis 1867. Ces appellations sont à mettre en relation avec l'anglais decker «applied to a kind of oven», notamment dans ces passages datant de 1884: «Mason's Patent Hot-Air Continuous Baking Two Decker Oven» et «Patent continuous-baking "decker" ovens – i.e., ovens piled over upon each other, which are heated by one furnace» (voir : Oxford English Dictionary); cp. en outre l'adjectif two-decker «having two decks, levels, layers, or classifications» (dans Webster 1986; Funk 1909, s.v. two) et le three-decker «a structure as a piece of furniture, having three levels (used also attributively)» (v. Funk 1909, s.v. three).

Also, These combination kitchen-parlor cast-iron stoves came into use in Quebec in the 1800's. They were of two or three chambers stacked atop each other. The bottom chamber was the largest and wood was fed into it through a side door. The oven was above it. If there was a third chamber on top, it served as a warming oven. These stoves were only used during the long winter season and were dismantled during spring cleaning. They efficiently heated both ground floor rooms and were a major improvement over the single fireplace used during colonial times.

CHAPTER 9

Le Père l'Allumette

It was July. The last wagonload of hay for the season had just reached the threshing barn where from the top of a haystack, Maurice (home on vacation) and Alfred stood alert for the forkfuls of millet that the hired hands tossed them so that they could be distributed uniformly here and there.

The smell of human sweat mixed with that of freshly cut hay for they had been working solidly since daybreak in order to finish the haying and, in the barn, the heat was suffocating.

Seated on the porch, in the shade, Madame Labranche and Vic looked at the trail of hay left by the overfilled carts as they passed.

The two women didn't speak, perhaps because they had nothing to say, but perhaps also in order not to break the peaceful silence or to better contemplate the beauty of nature that surrounded them.

From behind them,—from the shed that had been partially converted to a summer kitchen in order to keep the main house cooler during the summer season,—came the wonderful smell of Canadian cooking, for dinner hour was approaching and pots, pans, and skillets hummed on the red-hot stove.

In the summer heat, the long, windy road bordering the farm looked, from a distance, like a huge gray ribbon rippling in the breeze.

In an hour the sun would set and then the majestic silence of the fields and woods would settle over the countryside where Vic had come back to work on the farm in order to help her family.

"Well!" exclaimed Madame Labranche, "I think we're going to have a visitor."

Neither age, nor fatigue, nor the weight of the sacks that hung from the stick he carried balanced across his shoulders seemed to have the power to bend the back of the old man with the long white beard who, on this late afternoon, was approaching the Labranche farm. Probably so as not to stir up needlessly the dust of the road, the old man took care to walk on the tufts of grass along the roadside. One of his hands clasped one ends of the stick that balanced his sacks across his back while the other gripped a thick cane made from the branch of a walnut tree. The cane must have served to ward off vicious dogs for he didn't seem to need it for any other purpose.

"I thought at first that it was an alms collector coming to visit," said Vic, "but it looks like Père l'Allumette (Father Matchstick). It's about time for his annual visit."

Vic had guessed correctly regarding the identity of the figure on foot approaching the farm. The person in question was not a beggar but rather a seller of matches (hence his nickname). He was also a healer, a bonesetter, a man who possessed all sorts of knowledge and who was even called a sorcerer. The truth was that, far from being a sorcerer, he was simply a trickster who enjoyed fooling people without causing anyone any harm.

Every summer at haying time for the past twenty years—with the exception of the years the family had spent in Lowell—this very Father Matchstick arrived at the Labranche home and where he came from, no one knew. They anticipated his visit in advance by gathering chairs with seats that needed to be mended with straw, horse collars that needed repair, and copper pots and cauldrons that needed to be re-tinned.

In their large shed the Labranches had set up a workbench for him, with tool chests, and a wooden "bed" that served for sleeping at night and as a bench during the day. This corner was the domain of the wanderer throughout his stay.

In the evening, the shed filled with neighbors of all ages, for Father Matchstick, who had apparently traveled throughout Africa and the Americas, had an inexhaustible repertoire of captivating legends, adventures, and stories to recount.

Where did the old man come from? No one knew. When they tried to question him on this account, he would reply vaguely:

"My home is in every land where French is spoken!"

His age? He never told that either and his long white beard may have made him appear older than he actually was.

He was six feet tall, straight as an oak, with the long fingers of an artist or a musician (or a gambler?!) or an aristocrat. His shoulders were thrown back and he had the high, handsome forehead of a deep thinker.

If, in his conversations, he sometimes used the local dialect in order not to discomfit his listeners, at other times he used expressions so subtle, so perfect, so refined, that Madame Labranche and her children had often asked themselves whether the old man had been born in a palace.

Married? No one knew anything. Like all old men, he liked to tease the women, young and old alike, but that was all. For him, his fellow beings seemed not to be distinguished by their gender.

He had once let slip that when the really cold weather came, he crossed the border to follow the birds south. Where? He didn't say.

Had he suffered? That had to be the case, for he always had a word of sympathy, or encouragement, or compassion for every trial, every unhappiness, every sorrow.

In addition to selling the matches he made himself to stores in every village, suburb, and district, he not only knew all the trades, but had remedies for all ailments. For all of his various services, he was generously remunerated.

When people learned that Père l'Allumette was in the area, they came from all over to consult him about livestock whose horns were sensitive; about cows whose milk appeared cursed, given that the cream, instead of thickening to make butter, turned into a muddy goo; about horses that had lung or hoof disease or colic. In addition to ointments, herb teas and poultices, the old man prescribed PRAYERS, for more rapid healing, he assured them...From whence came his title of sorcerer.

One year, he had succeeded in killing a canker sore that was devouring the nose of Malvina Fortier, one of the prettiest girls in the parish, by having her continually apply cotton swabs soaked in expensive gin, and, because of this cure, people had unlimited confidence in his medicinal knowledge.

If a farmer came to him crippled with rheumatism, the old man would give him the following prescription:

Rub on the ailing member:
I cup white vinegar
I cup linseed oil
I cup turpentine
I cup ammonia
10 c camphor

Mix and shake well before rubbing. With that, he also recommended the following tonic:

I ounce Smilax (for the blood)
I ounce Buchu leaves (for the bladder)
I ounce Mandrake root (for the liver)
I ounce Queen Meadow herbs (for the kidneys)

Boil slowly to make a pint of liquid. Strain through a thin cloth. Add a half pint of good Dutch gin. Drink one small wine goblet of this brew each night at bedtime until cured.

For DIABETES, he recommended a strict diet to prevent the formation of new sugar in the blood, then the following remedy to eliminate existing sugars: Boil a sliver of white cedar in a pint and a half of water. Reduce to one pint of liquid. Drink this brew instead of any other liquids. If bowels are too thin, simply blanch the cedar rather than boiling it.

For JAUNDICE, he prescribed the following: The first night, drink four large glasses of linseed tea adding one tablespoon of gin and a squeeze of lemon juice to each glass. The second night, drink three large glasses of the same recipe. The third evening, two glasses. The fourth and final evening, one glass only.

For the HARDENING OF THE ARTERIES: One clove of garlic to two parts pure alcohol. Place in a hermetically sealed bottle and expose to the sun for three weeks. Take 25 drops of this mixture three times a day before meals for one month. Stop this treatment for two months, then resume for another month. Abstain from meat, alcohol, coffee, and tobacco throughout the treatment period.

For WEAK LUNGS: Place 6 eggs in the bottom of a bowl without putting them on top of one another. With a knitting needle, make a multitude of tiny holes in the shells without breaking the eggs. Cover the eggs with the juice from a dozen large lemons. Cover with a napkin. Store in a dry, cool, dark place. Leave for 48 hours. Crush the mixture to make a paste. Pass through a thick press. Add one cup of brandy, one cup of cod liver oil, one cup of (pure) honey. Beat well with light strokes. Bottle the mixture and wrap the bottles in dark blue paper. Take 3 or 4 tablespoons of this tonic daily. In addition, drink milk, eat eggs and other fortifying foods. Get plenty of rest and as much fresh air as possible, day and night.

For KIDNEY DISEASE: Add four heaping tablespoons of linseed oil and one large unpeeled, sliced apple to two and a half pints of warm water. Boil until the liquid thickens. Add sugar to taste. Remove from stove. Add the juice from one large lemon. Strain if desired. Drink two large glasses.

For DROPSY: Make an infusion with Geneva berries. Use a cup of water for each ounce of berries. Drink three wine goblets full of this tea each day. You can also make a tea from thorny ash.

For BLOCKED INTESTINES: Pick walnuts from a tree, tender and young enough to be pierced with a pin. Use maple syrup to make a jam from the nuts with their shells. Store in a well-sealed container. Take one tablespoon as needed.

For PLEURISY: Make a weak potion from patience/dock (sang-dragon) root soaked in one cup of gin. Take a quarter teaspoon of this potion two to three times per day.

For DIARRHEA: Drink a concoction made from well-toasted bread dipped in boiling water.

For NEURALGIA and MUSCLE PAINS: Rub the aching spot with an ointment made from poplar buds dipped in alcohol.

For STOMACH ULCERS: Drink tea made from red clover.

For ABSCESSES: Employ the following poultice. Fill half a cup with yeast made from yeast cake, 7 cloves of finely chopped garlic, a quarter teaspoon of powdered tobacco, a pinch of pepper, a fistful of lard taken from the rind, minced very fine.

In addition to his many prescriptions for aches and diseases, Père l'Allumette seemed to enjoy mystifying his friends by hypnotizing hens, pigeons, toads, rabbits, and ducks; but he would never consider hypnotizing a human being, claiming that it would be too dangerous to play with the terrible, unknown forces of nature.

One night, appearing less guarded than usual, the old man pulled from his bag a superb ebony box with a lid encrusted with precious stones. After caressing the little box with his long, thin fingers, the old wanderer raised the lid and showed the neighbors gathered around him the carefully stuffed form of a tiny bird with feathers so beautiful and bright that everyone was dazzled. In a corner of the box in which the bird lay, there was a tiny glass compartment where they saw, immersed in a strange liquid, a heart the size of a small hazelnut, the ruby heart of a bird.

Where had this wondrous creature of the skies come from? In answer to this question, Père l'Allumette raised his arm and pointed towards the south and a ray of sun seemed to sparkle in his blue eyes only to be followed by a gray mist. Judging from the old man's behavior, those present understood that the stuffed bird must have belonged to loved ones from the past and must have come from a place where the wanderer had been happy long ago.

This little ruby heart, perfectly preserved, was reminder of his past that followed him everywhere, in every climate, under every sky.

But, they had dared to ask, how could the heart have been preserved to look so real when it was the size of a small hazelnut? He quickly explained that he had filled the small glass casing with pure honey, which possesses the property of preserving animal life.

After a three-week stay at the Labranche Farm—his usual stay—Père l'Allumette's visit was drawing to an end. One evening, the air was so muggy and hot that the old man asked whether he might spend the night on top of a haystack where it might be cooler to sleep than in his 'bed'.

Madame Labranche had no objection but she asked that Alfred join the old man on the haystack to ensure that Père l'Allumette would be safe during the night.

Alfred, a light sleeper, was sleeping when a movement in the hay woke him. In the darkness, he saw a shadow climbing down the ladder they had placed against the stack in order to climb up. A few minutes passed and the old man didn't return. Alfred, fearing that he might be hurt, climbed down from his perch.

A flash of heat lightning lit the horizon and allowed him to see the old man lying flat on his back in the grass. He ran towards him, called out to him, touched him and shook him but received no response and could see no movement. Overcome with fear, he was about to run to the house for help when he saw what appeared to be a firefly hovering over the white head that stood out against the dark grass. A few seconds passed and the old man sighed, rubbed his hand across his brow, and sat up.

When he opened his eyes, he seemed puzzled to find Alfred at his side. Still trembling, the lad explained to the old man what he had seen and the old man responded:

—I'm sorry to have unwittingly caused you such a fright. I understand now that the electricity in the air must have provoked a magnetic trance in me, and that,unknowingly, you witnessed an extraordinary phenomenon. However, if you should ever see me in this sort of state again—which is unlikely—you mustn't touch me or call me, and, above all, you mustn't tell anyone about this. What your human gaze mistook for a firefly was actually my spirit, which had left my body for a few seconds, returning home because my final hour hasn't yet come.

—Your spirit left your body and you're still alive? How can this be?

—Sometimes, my son, there are beings who belong less to this earth than to the hereafter. For that reason, they sometimes have enough strength to escape their earthly shell and rise to the stars. Down here on earth, there's probably no more than one spirit in a hundred million that has the power to free itself briefly from its captivity and then return. Knowing this, charlatans, take advantage of people's gullibility and present to the world hordes of impostors solely for their own financial gain.

—But, insisted Alfred who didn't understand any of it, if it's true that your spirit leaves your body, where does it go and what does it see?

—I can't explain that to you, my child, for you wouldn't understand—in fact, no one would understand—and you'd probably think me mad. I only want you to know that my spirit, during these rare moments of perfect bliss, is very close to God!

Alfred thought that the old man must be sleep walking or in some sort of hypnotic state and, as he followed him up the ladder to the top of the hay stack, he promised himself that he wouldn't spend another night on the hay stack for anything in the world, for he could sense death lurking near Père l'Allumette. He reluctantly lay down again and managed to fall asleep but he kept waking again with a start and seeing fireflies all over the haystack.

A few days later—two days before the planned departure of the old man—Madame Labranche and Vic readied the carriage to pick up Maurice and Alfred who'd gone off that morning to lend a hand to a farmer in need at the other end of the parish. When the two women invited Père l'Allumette to join them, he refused under the pretext that he had some work to finish. Madame Labranche didn't insist, but she advised the old man not to wait for them for supper and to simply help himself to the pantry if he got hungry.

Since the volunteers had decided to work as long as they had daylight, Madame Labranche with her children and Alfred couldn't begin their journey home until after dark.

They had almost reached the foot of the cliff when Alfred exclaimed:

—Look at those stars falling down the rocks!

The cliff in question was a bare rock wall several miles long and 300 feet high at its highest point. It served as the natural boundary between the Labranche property and that of the Payeurs. The entire Labranche farm was located on a plateau parallel to the top of the cliff, while the Payeur farm was located several hundred feet below in the valley. With a light pressure on the reins, Maurice stopped the horses at the side of the road. In the dark night, it seemed—as Alfred had noticed—as if stars, like a shower of molten gold, were flowing down the side of the cliff to extinguish themselves in the stream below.

Intrigued, the occupants of the carriage moved back about a hundred feet to get a better view of the cliff. That was how they happened to see, on the summit, an enormous log fire, from which a bareheaded old man with a long white beard was pushing burning coals so they would roll down the cliff.

After several minutes of this activity, the guardian of the fire stood up to his full height, which seemed majestic on the crest of the cliff. He threw his head back and from his mouth poured, in a rich, supple, and beautiful voice, the verses of a deeply touching ballad that golden throats had come to sing on our shores from ancient France long ago.

I have no roof to shelter me,
I have no friends or family,
All that I own, I wear upon me,
MY OLD RAGS!

When the hunchback from Landivisiau
Cut and tailored your collar to toe,
And bedecked you with trinkets all aglow
MY OLD RAGS!

And, thanks to you, on holy days
I set the maidens hearts ablaze
You have fewer holes than I have praise,
MY OLD RAGS!

At the farm and the factory,
They lock the door when they see me,
Because I wear you, they won't hire me,
MY OLD RAGS!

Now youth and happiness have flown
Spent before their value was known,
And this suit of sorrow is all that I own,
MY OLD RAGS!

As I drag myself along my way,
Like an inchworm inching from day to day,
You make children laugh and stop their play,
MY OLD RAGS!

In summer, you are my finery,
For as the sun beats down on me,
You glow like gold for all to see,
MY OLD RAGS!

But when harsh winter comes and the sun's rays wane,
I can no longer hobble along with my cane,
For you give free passage to the snow, wind, and rain,
MY OLD RAGS!

Doubtless with a bit of trickery and theft,
I could have found myself less bereft,
But you and my honor are all I have left,
MY OLD RAGS!

And when at last I go to meet
My Maker on His judgment seat,
I'll be wearing you as my winding sheet,
MY OLD RAGS!

The final notes of this touching melody that, in the echoing night, sounded almost like a sob, were extinguished in the mounting flames of the bonfire.

Without a word, Madame Labranche and her family slowly resumed their interrupted journey. They were haunted by the plaintive tune rising in the calm evening air from the rocky crest, from an unhappy old man who truly possessed nothing but the rags he wore.

Once the occupants of the carriage had arrived home, Alfred went to the shed to get a lantern so he could lead the horses to the barn. He declined Maurice's offer to help him unhitch the horses. That task accomplished, instead of returning to the house where supper was surely waiting, the young man returned to the cliff.

Lost deep in reverie, Père l'Allumette was sitting on a rock, his face faintly lit by the glowing log that had nearly burned itself out. He was unaware of Alfred's beside him until he felt the slight pressure of the young man's hand on his shoulder.

—Supper is ready, Père l'Allumette, and I came to get you, said Alfred.

—That's good. I forgot I was hungry, the old man whispered.

—We saw the light from your bonfire and heard your song, Alfred continued, sitting down next to the old man. Can you tell me why you were throwing burning coals down the cliff?

That, the old man replied, is just an old Indian custom. When the Native Americans were the masters of this Continent, they communicated by signals made with bonfires and burning coals. I must be returning to my childhood, because tonight, since I was alone, it occurred to me to revive that ancient custom. In order to do so, I used a sizeable portion of a cord of wood you'd cut.

I hope you won't be too upset with me. I got carried away with my memories and forgot everything else. As for the song you heard, I learned it in a theater, in Québec City, where I went to amuse myself years ago. I was struck at the time by the plaintive refrain of the song... and tonight the words came effortlessly to my lips, for it's only too true that all I possess are MY OLD RAGS!

—Père l'Allumette, Alfred said in a muffled voice, if I had a farm or any place at all that was mine, I'd ask you tonight to come live with me. I never had a home, never knew what it was to call someone 'father'. I would ask you to replace the father I never knew and with you to guide me, console me, love me, we would surely have many happy days together.

Père l'Allumette didn't answer for a moment, as if to give himself time to choke back the sob that rose in his throat. Then he laid his hand on Alfred's head in a gesture of benediction.

-May God bless you, my son, and give you success and happiness for the kindness of your heart and the goodness of your soul, but, believe me, it's better that things are the way they are. If you had a farm of your own, I probably wouldn't have the strength to resist the offer you just made, and perhaps you would learn to love me; but I am so old that your heart would break a little, one day soon when my coffin was nailed shut beside you ... Believe me, my child, everything God plans is well planned... Let's go eat now, my child, and rest for tomorrow, which may bring us who knows what???

The following day, after lunch, the old man announced that he was going to the forest to 'peel' an elm tree because he needed a little more to finish caning a chair. He left in the morning before the sun was too hot, taking along a hatchet and a knife, and asking that they not wait lunch for him as he wanted to take his time and didn't plan to return until late that afternoon.

The afternoon passed. The clock struck seven, then eight, then nine, and Père l'Allumette still hadn't returned. A very worried Madame

Labranche sent Alfred to the next door neighbors to ask them to come and help search for the old man.

Alfred, trembling with fear as he remembered the scene he had witnessed a few nights earlier, told himself that this time the old man's spirit could have left his body for good. He hadn't dared to tell the Labranches about the old man's somnambulistic trance during the night for fear that they would think him a liar, a madman, or a visionary: but deep inside he was convinced that after that night the old man no longer fully belonged to this earth.

Three quarters of an hour later, several neighbors, alerted by Alfred, arrived with lanterns and, with Maurice as their leader, they headed on horseback towards the woods, riding through pastures where cattle chewing mouthfuls of grass jumped to their feet, bellowing with fright, and galloped off into the darkness.

When they reached the woods, they all stopped as agreed while Maurice blew a bullhorn. The sound of the horn broke the stillness of the night and echoed throughout the woods, waking birds and animals from their slumber. There was rustling, yapping and grunting underbrush, but not the slightest echo of a human voice reached the attentive ears of the worried group. They voiced the fear that a famished mother bear might have come upon the defenseless old man and attacked him.

Maurice gave the horn to Alfred instructing him to stay behind and to blow the horn every fifteen minutes so that they could find their way back in safety: they all got off their horses, looping the animals' reins over branches so they wouldn't stray off to graze; and the group disappeared into the trees like ghosts.

The lower branches snapped and roots rising too far above the ground cracked as the men walked along, but when they stopped to listen, there was only the silence and shadow of the north woods.

Before leaving the house they had had Pataud, the old Newfoundland on the farm, sniff an old pair of slippers that belonged to the old man, in the hope that this scent would lead the animal to the right place. The dog ran faster than the men, his nose buried in the dead leaves of past years, following without hesitation a trail invisible to the human eye. His nose could smell what no human eye could perceive; he was following the smell of death through the woods, certain of his path.

They'd been walking for an hour, searching everywhere, when suddenly in the night everyone stopped at once: a prolonged, lugubrious wail had just pierced the night from some distance ahead. Unconsciously, the men removed their caps and the older men in the group crossed themselves: they knew that death was near.

Guided by Pataud's howling, they soon reached the edge of a clearing. The light from the lanterns enabled them to make out Père l'Allumette sitting on a fallen tree trunk, leaning back against a branch. His arms folded, bare headed, the old man looked as if he were asleep. They touched him: his body already had the stiffness of a corpse; he must have been dead for a several hours.

They cut some branches to make a stretcher on which they placed their lugubrious burden. The sound of the horn in the night enabled the group to return without difficulty to the place where they had left the horses in Alfred's care. After a great deal of resistance and rebellion from the horses who could smell death, they managed to tie the corpse on one horse's back and they began their somber journey home.

In the old man's bag they found a purse with enough money for a modest funeral. They also found a notebook whose pages had been written on in a strong, beautiful hand using a lead pencil. Madame Labranche, sitting on the 'bed' in the shed, began deciphering the freshly written pages, surrounded by Vic, Alfred and a few neighbors.

CHAPTER 10

The Life of a Wanderer

"It's past midnight," the old man had written, "And since I couldn't sleep, I got up. I feel an invisible presence beside me and I sense that the end of my earthly pilgrimage is approaching. Before closing my eyes forever, I'm going to try to give a brief account of my miserable life."

When I'm dead, perhaps people will say: "Poor old Allumettte was a good man." It wouldn't be honest on my part to allow my friends to have such a good opinion of me; that's why I'm writing these lines so that all of you will know that Père l'Allumette was a murderer who spent twenty years of his life in prison!

I was born, seventy-five years ago, on a large plantation in Louisiana, on the shores of the Gulf of Mexico. My parents were originally from France and lived in considerable comfort. I was their only child. As a young child I showed a disturbing tendency toward anger and jealousy. I broke anything that resisted me and I beat those who stood up to me. If someone or something vexed me, I would create a terrible scene. One day, over nothing at all, I whipped one of our young black servants so brutally that he lost his sight as a result. My quick-tempered, violent, despotic nature drove my parents to despair and finally became the curse of their life and mine.

At twenty, I married a young woman as beautiful as a dream and as sweet as an angel. I was divinely happy for several months until I gradually became jealous of the adoration showered upon her by friends, family, and servants.

One afternoon, my gun on my shoulder, I was coming back from hunting alligators. The soft grass muffled the sound of my steps and I saw, without their having heard me approach, my wife, seated on a bench shaded by a bed of azaleas, with her arms around the neck of a handsome man in an officer's uniform. The violence of my character and my jealous nature caused me to immediately shoulder my weapon and fire. I killed, with a single bullet, the couple as they embraced each other. In her agonized last breaths, my wife was able to tell me: "The man you just killed is my older brother who was on leave and came for a surprise visit after being away for ten years. If you doubt my word, look in his pockets and you'll find his identification papers."

The murder, the arrest, the trial, the life sentence triggered an attack of apoplexy that took my father's life within a few hours. As for my mother, after I was sentenced, she languished in the hospital for months in the grips of a delirium that wouldn't pass. When she finally left the hospital, the fever had completely destroyed all memory of the past. She had to start all over getting to know her own house, her possessions, and her servants. They spared her by not telling her of my crime or my sentence. For her, her husband and her son, whose portraits hung on the wall of her room, were dead: her husband's body lay at rest in the cemetery while her son had been buried at sea.

Having no close relatives, my mother made out a will leaving, upon her death, her immense property to charitable organizations to be made into an orphanage, but not without having first assured a generous annual stipend for all her servants.

My mother had always loved birds. After the illness that sealed off her memories of the past, her passion for the winged species grew to the point that she established on her plantation one of the richest, most complete aviaries in all of North America. She paid enormous sums of money to acquire birds unknown to the civilized world. Half her time was spent at the aviaries where she admired the richness of the birds' brilliant plumage while listening with delight to their enchanting songs.

As for me, within the confines of the four walls of my prison, I avidly acquired knowledge of every science and every profession. I became a model prisoner, striving, by leading a calm, productive, exemplary life, to atone for the crime I had committed in a fit of uncontrolled rage and unprovoked jealousy.

After twenty years in prison, I was pardoned. I set out for the plantation on foot, unafraid of inquisitive looks, for the proud young man I once was had become a poor old man with white hair. Gone were my proud demeanor, my haughty self-assurance, and my ambitious dreams. Nevertheless, to be completely safe, I didn't set foot on my home territory until a long beard as white as my hair had completed my transformation.

One afternoon, trembling with emotion, a mixture of happiness and remorse, I knocked at the door of the colonial residence where I had reigned as master twenty years earlier. When I asked to meet the owner of the plantation, I was led before an elderly woman whom I recognized as my mother, although twenty years had ravaged her looks as well. My entire being urged me to kneel at her feet, but, fearful of the effect that revealing my identity might have on her paralyzed memory, I lowered my eyes, dug my fingernails into my palms, and, in a muffled voice, asked for work. After a half hour's conversation, she engaged my services to help care for the lovely winged beings in the aviaries.

For ten years, I had the joy of seeing my mother every day, of walking in her footsteps, of kissing the wings of her favorite little birds. For ten years I lived in Heaven...and Hell.

In addition to the aviaries where birds from all corners of the world sang, my mother had succeeded in transforming our plantation—thanks to the cooperation of honest, capable stewards and an army of faithful and devoted servants—a paradise of flowers, bushes, and trees perhaps unique in the world.

She focused all the energy of her mind which could no longer look backward—toward the past that had been her life until the day I brought disaster into it—on the present and the future. In addition to the financial means my mother and father possessed, themselves during the golden period of our family life, significant inheritances from relatives who died in France had significantly augmented their fortune. Believing herself alone in the world, after the terrible tragedy that sealed off her memory and took my father's life, my mother spent her life and her wealth making her property on the shore of the Gulf of Mexico the purest, most beautiful jewel on the American continent.

With the help of botanists and explorers from every corner of the world, ten thousand different varieties of the most magnificent plants found on earth had been successfully transplanted onto the grounds of our property. More than a thousand azalea bushes of every hue bloomed in February—the month when these flowers open their petals—creating a veritable fairyland several miles long, lining the pathways where they grew. Bordering the wider alleyways were three thousand assorted camellias brought from China and Japan. And more than a thousand varieties of irises and thousands of other flowers of all kinds grew in fragrant hedges.

Immense flowerbeds overflowed with hibiscus, frangipanis and wild orchids. The purple of bougainvilleas mingled with the lavender hues of the swamp hyacinth, while the vivid yellow and red of the "canna" stood out against the azure blooms of the Texan blue-bonnet.

On one side of the grounds—in the right season—the flaming colors of the royal poinsettia gleamed. A little further on, one could see the fragrant yellow ball-like flowers of the acacia. Here appeared the intoxicating "asoka," the sacred flower used by certain Chinese and Hindu sects to decorate their pagan temples. There grew "Indian mahwas," whose petals are eaten as a delicacy by certain tribes in the tropical jungles.

Thousands of palm trees of all sizes and species bordered the alleys. The pathways were shaded by centenary oaks graciously draped with fine, mysterious Spanish moss.

Fifty varieties of bamboo, transplanted from Chinese, Japanese and Asian forests, rose up to heights of eighty feet above the ground.

Superb magnolia blossoms—so similar to water lilies—hid themselves under the dense foliage of the trees to protect their immaculate white petals from an irreverent caress. Magnolia flowers are so fragile and sensitive that the slightest touch, even from a breeze, wilts them, causing the petals to drop instantly, desecrated by being touched.

Inside the groves, banyan trees—a wild fig tree whose roots grow out from the branches to bury themselves in the ground and join the existing roots—and banana trees with heavy clusters of fruit and large, fiery, crimson and gold flowers, delighted the eye.

One could also find Brazil-nut trees, those forest giants with cup-like fruit that Americans call "monkey pots." Indian tulip trees with their magnificent yellow flowers. Camphor trees whose crushed leaves emit a strong camphor smell. Brazilian rosewoods which give off a rose-like scent. Cottonwoods, those Javanese forest giants from which the natives collect stuffing materials for mattresses. Ilang-ilang trees from the Philippines whose flowers, shaped like acorns, preserve their scent when dried and are sold by peddlers in the South Seas for sachet bags. Cow-trees which, when cut, give out a rich milk-like sap. Cork trees from India whose wood is the lightest in the world. Kola trees with red and white nuts that some African tribes use for currency. Umbrella pines. Giant tropical cedars. Candle trees, spear trees, shrimp trees. Australian Eucalyptus trees with nearly bare trunks trailing long strips of bark as if torn by claws. Kauri trees, also from Australia, the highest trees in the world. Tavachin trees whose flowers resemble coral. Naked-Indian trees whose branches and golden brown trunks are warm to the touch, like human flesh. Bread trees. Red geranium trees. Under some of these trees grow those sensitive tropical plants that close their leaves like tiny hands when touched, recoiling and then wilting instantly.

Bolivian bottle-trees whose live trunks are hollowed out by an Indian tribe in South America to use as shelters. The tree trunks are fat-bellied and naked like a bottle, and topped by a tuft of short branches about 20 feet off the ground.

In a dry, sandy plot of land, my mother had planted several hundred feet of a species of cactus called cereus. Like the well-known desert cactus, the cereus is covered with thorns and is greenish-grey in color. For six months of the year, the cereus has the same cold, prickly appearance as its father, the cactus. Then the protrusions—not to call them branches—start to cover themselves with tiny spikes one might call buds. As these buds grow and develop, they look like the candles on a candelabra. There are about ten of them on every 'branch'.

Since we knew in advance of the amazing phenomenon that would occur with the cereus buds, on that particular day, all our servants, neighbors and friends, were alerted that the cereuses were going to bloom. Late that afternoon, all work stopped, everything was put aside, so we could reach the enclosure, bordering a main road, where the desert plants grew.

The sun was low on the horizon. And then we felt something like an electric current inside us that seemed to connect us to the thorny plants. At that very moment it was as if some signal, a secret command, a general order was given to each plant. For at the very same moment, thousands of buds shook with a great trembling, and then slowly opened like the doors of some sacred tabernacle, forming a calyx (flower cup) the size of two adult hands. The petals were a delicate, fragile white, bordered by a fringe of stamen like golden threads, and, at the center of the flower, a frail pistil supported a kind of star.

In the moonlight,—so bright in the south—or, in its absence, in the gleam of the pine turpentine torches we had lit, the enchanting cups seemed filled with molten gold. Every passer-by, on foot or by car, would stop that evening and stay with us for hours to observe this miracle of nature.

Throughout the night, the cereuses would display their beauty in all their splendor and would spread their intoxicating perfume, but at the first rays of the morning sun, the cups would droop and begin to wilt. Their lives were over!

Incomparable flowers of the night, from year to year, era to era, season to season, I witnessed your birth, your reign and your death... and each time, my face inclined toward your open cup, I thought that your fleeting career was comparable in length to our poor human happiness.

Sometimes, when there was a breeze, I would spend the evening sitting under a Nubian caragana tree often called, for good reason, a 'singing tree.' Certain insects attack the bark of these trees and cause them to crack open. Then, when the wind blows, harmonious sounds are emitted from these cracks, one after the other, as if magical fingers were touching the keys of an invisible keyboard

The melodies that flowed from the cracked bark of these trees varied with the force and the direction of the wind.

A strong wind from the north caused harsh, staccato, irritating notes to ring in my ears, notes like the groans of snow under footsteps, of ice cracking on a lake, of sleet beating against the wall. If the north wind wasn't too strong, the melody it called forth made me think of powdery snow landing on the road, of the swishing of skis down snowy white slopes, of the flapping wings of a partridge seeking shelter under a pine.

A strong easterly breeze brought forth from the bark tunes of pleasure, activity, and jazz. Listening to them, we felt the blood run warmer in our veins, greater ambitions enter our lives, and sweeter hopes soar above our heads. We would listen, tremble, and feel alive. If the wind was gentle, it made sounds like oars slapping the waves, like huge winged sails beating the flanks of schooners, like waves rising and roaring, then breaking and dying on shore.

A western gale called forth notes that seemed to leap from the crevices of rocks, slide down from the mountain tops, and rise up from the desert's moving sands. A light breeze brought the sound of supple shapes sliding on rocks, of fine powder crackling on sand dunes, of wild flowers opening their buds to the torrid sun of a naked vastness. It was beautiful, it was grand, it was engaging like the very heart of untamed nature, wild and unconquered.

A gale from the Gulf of Mexico brought sounds that reminded us of the noise of a yoke violently shaken by a captive animal... of nervous laughter on lips about to cry. ... of the echo of a tomtom beaten by a native child in the tropical forest to announce jungle events to the tribes... This echo was in turn soft, sad, or violent. If the southern wind wasn't too strong, it made the cracks in the bark give off sounds like bare feet dancing on the grass to primitive music...like the rustling of a wreath of flowers placed on the chest of someone singing wild tunes... like the whisper of simple prayers uttered by sincere hearts, under the stars.

Like many trees in the tropical forest, a large number of the species in our collection bore flowers and fruit in the proper season. Beneath the trees of this enchanted forest, an infinite variety of wild flowers bloomed, one after the other, so that there were almost always flowers in our woods.

On the ponds, surrounded by protective nets made with steel mesh attached to wooden frames, regal white and black swans swam languorously. On the shores of the ponds lived numerous varieties of aquatic birds, like flamingoes with wings of fire and long, fine pink legs; cranes with white tufts; toucans with large red beaks; blue and white herons; red ibises; hoccos walking haughtily.

Other birds like cormorants, pelicans, sea gulls, and so on, fished for food in these miniature lakes.

In the groves and flowerbeds, about thirty types of hummingbirds darted so quickly that the eye could hardly follow their flight. The hummingbird that occasionally appears this far north belongs to this family. The hummingbird is the smallest of all birds. It prefers to live in and around gardens. It's not surprising that these pretty birds never thought of leaving our estate where they could find a profusion of flowers year round. These diminutive birds lay tiny little eggs that hatch in two weeks and the young ones emerge from these shells no bigger than a bee.

The tropical hummingbird resembles a precious stone that can fly, sparkling like a thousand flames in the sun.

The azure-bee hummingbird has two tufts of purple or bright green feathers on the sides of its head. The body of the ruby breasted hummingbird is covered with every imaginable shade of green, while the feathers on its chest are the color of fire and gold. The comet hummingbird's body is red, its wings are white and green, its head green and brown. The red feathers of its tail, when spread, look like the wings of an airplane. It's not surprising that my mother, who admired beauty in all things, made a point of acquiring every possible species of this delicate and marvelous jewel of the sky, the hummingbird.

Amid the tropical and semi-tropical vegetation, brightly colored red, green and yellow parrots and parakeets, along with their relatives the macaws and the cockatoos with white crests, hung from the branches with a single leg and amused themselves by swaying back and forth; or they would simply perch in the trees blinking their eyes and clicking their beaks in protest at the slightest noise. At other times you could see them flying heavily, two by two, searching for food, the brilliance of their plumage flashing in the shadows and the squawking of their discordant voices deafening the ear.

Green woodpeckers, with yellow and green plumage and long ivory beaks—one of the rarest bird species in the world—tapped on tree trunks, driving out bugs and snapping them up instantly.

Butterflies with broad wings of gold, fire, or azure, painted with more colors than an artist's palette, gathered nectar in the heart of the flowering bushes.

On sunny days, the light among the tree limbs shifted like theatre lighting: from green to rose, to mauve, to yellow. Under the thick foliage of some trees, the rays of the sun could hardly penetrate.

At night, the fireflies with their yellow, red and green lanterns, traced strange and wonderful patterns in the darkness.

When shadow enveloped the forest you could hear from a distance the piercing calls of the cicadas that reminded us of boat whistles; the pavas (from the pheasant family) sounded a discordant jingle; tinamous cooed like quails; hoatzins emitted strident calls and from the throats of the toucans arose a sound like a vesper chant.

On moonlit nights,—while my mother rested in her large colonial bed never dreaming that her son was still alive and very near her—I would spend hours strolling in the alleys and pathways of that magical forest. The calm and sweetness of the tropical night soothed the fever of my brow, slowed my pulse and numbed the aching in my soul.

I was familiar with all the sounds of the woods and I was not afraid. The only thing to fear was startling and provoking a rattlesnake. At night, when one couldn't see it, the sound of its rattles could cause a fatal misstep, but I had no fear of that. My mother had taken the precaution of obtaining a large number of the snake species that Americans call bull-snake which seem to have as their sole purpose waging a deadly war against all poisonous snakes. Bull-snakes are harmless to man and, with these protectors around, there's no need to fear the venomous species.

Hence, I walked fearlessly through the night, intoxicated by the scent of the orange, lemon and grapefruit blossoms that floated to me from orchards miles away, carried by the gulf breeze.

In the mysterious alleys, my practiced ear could recognize the different sounds made by the wind as it rustled the leaves of the many species of trees on our plantation.

When the long leaves of the coconut and palm trees rubbed together, they made a clacking sound like swords striking one another. The enormous leaves of the banana trees would groan when the wind picked up. The bamboos would creak as they bent in the wind and they would moan as if twisting in pain.

The constantly quaking leaves —wind or no wind—of the sacred tree called 'bo' or 'peepul,' the largest fig tree on earth, inhabited—according to Indian mythology—by the Gods of the Forest, whispered as if each leaf had a thought to share.

As for the filao, a kind of cedar that looks like a cross between a pine and a weeping willow with a head that reaches the clouds, its voice impressed me most. The bushy branches of this tree have long, thin leaves that look like hair and droop to the ground like the willow. At the slightest breeze, these strands touch one another and emit a plaintive sound that steals our souls and wrings our hearts. Perhaps the trees in the forest have a soul much like our own, a soul that knows how to sing, sigh, or weep for the ear that knows how to hear and understand it.

If I stress all these details this evening, it's because the glow of an internal sunset, low on the horizon, illuminates the night...and I'm seeing, or rather I'm reliving my past once again in all its detail...Perhaps it's the final scene before the curtain goes down.

What purpose would it serve to reveal the name of this enchanted place that was the delight of my childhood, the happiness of my youth, and the despair of my later years?

Let it suffice to tell you that about eighty miles away from our property was the town of Saint-Martinville where that unhappy Acadian, Emmeline Labiche, whose tragic story is known by every French Canadian, lived and died.

A little further on lies the cemetery of Baratavia where two graves were dug and on which no flower was ever planted, and no blade of grass ever cut... One of these graves holds the earthly remains of Jean Lafitte, the famous French pirate, while the other contains the remains of the emperor... NAPOLEON BONAPARTE!

In the old French parishes of Louisiana, you will be assured that the European conqueror was never taken to Saint-Helena but that a look-alike was escorted there. They will tell you that the Little Corporal sailed to Louisiana on one of the Lafitte frigates with the intention of first proclaiming himself Emperor of New France and then setting about to conquer the entire American continent. Unfortunately, he fell ill and died during the crossing. Instead of burying him at sea, Lafitte is said to have transported Napoleon's body to Louisiana and to have buried him at Baratavia. Who knows what the real secret is that sleeps in this abandoned tomb in a corner of Louisiana? In the realm of suppositions, any conjecture is welcome.

To return to the story of my life on our southern plantation, let me tell you that one morning, the woman who believed her son dead at sea, did not appear at the aviaries. That afternoon, a nurse came to get me and led me to the bedroom where my mother, who had been struck by a sudden fatal illness, brought each of her servants in turn to bid them farewell before taking her final leave...I stopped at the doorway of this room which I hadn't entered for thirty years, feeling overcome. My mother, from her deathbed, looked up at me at that moment. Was it the illusion of a dying woman or did she really recognize me just then? I'll never know, but she stretched her death-cold arms toward me and cried out: "MY SON!" An hour later, without another word, my mother died with her arms still around my neck.

After my mother's death, I could have invoked my rights, reclaimed my share of the inheritance, had the will annulled that left the plantation to certain charitable organizations, but why would I have done so? In the eyes of God and men I was guilty of having killed three people if I counted my father. My whole life wasn't long enough, nor any punishment harsh enough to atone for such a sin. My mother had included me in the yearly annuities she'd granted her servants. So I wasn't worried about my old age. All I requested and received from her estate was a darling little bird with feathers of fire, crimson and gold, that had been my mother's very favorite.

By way of atonement, since I loved freedom and space too much to shut myself up in a monastery, I became a wanderer. I left carrying a bird-cage and a duffle bag, practicing the trades I had learned in prison to earn my daily bread and the friendship of brave souls who didn't know about my past.

From the shores of the Gulf of Mexico, I set off for the 45th parallel where I knew I would find a strong young nation where they spoke the language of my parents, the sweet language of Old France. I traveled this way through the years, from village to village, from district to district, trying to find some semblance of peace for my tortured soul. In the season of bitterest cold, I would go back to the Louisiana plantation to spend the winter months and to weep and pray over the graves of my mother, my father, and my wife.

The bird that had been my mother's favorite under the semi-tropical skies, couldn't survive the cold winds of the north where I carried him. After a few months, he died. Since he was all I had left from my past, I decided to have him stuffed and to preserve his little heart with the help of a formula that an old prison companion had taught me.

Now I'm done shedding light on the mystery that shrouded the life of this Père l'Allumette whom you've known for twenty years. When God brings to an end my difficult pilgrimage on this earth, you can bury me wherever you wish. I don't deserve to be put to rest beside good, honest souls. Do what you will with this old body. You'll find a few dollars in my bag that will help pay for the cost of a simple funeral. I have no friends or relatives to notify nor any inheritance to bequeath. Over my grave, if they put up a cross, you can have them write: "Here lies Père L'Allumette, a wretched soul who paid fifty-five years of hell for a crime due to unbridled jealousy and rage. Reflect, passer-by, and avoid the same fate."

Madame Labranche had been deciphering these last lines written by the old man for several minutes, not realizing that tears were streaming down her cheeks and that all those who were listening raptly were as moved as she was. After uttering the last words, she closed the notebook with a sob and whispered hoarsely: "Dear friends, let's say the rosary for poor Père L'Allumette and ask this poor heart who suffered so much to protect our homes and our children!"

Madame Labranche decided to have the wanderer buried next to her husband and her son; those who had known one another here on earth would surely be happy to see one another again in heaven.

The night before the funeral, Alfred, the orphan who'd never known a mother's caress, took advantage of a few moments when those at the wake, in a pause between reciting rosaries, fell asleep overcome with fatigue, to slip into the shed. A few moments later, he returned concealing something in his vest. Stealthily, he went into the large bedroom where the body was displayed. He unbolted the casket, raised the lid, then gently, tenderly, piously placed on Père l'Allumette's chest the small ebony box holding the ruby heart and the stuffed body of the bird with feathers of fire, crimson and gold.

CHAPTER II

Good Fortune Falls from the Sky

It was June in the year following Père l'Allumette's death. One night, three weeks before Maurice's vacation, Vic, who couldn't sleep, got up and looked out her window at the semi-darkness that obscured the earth.

The young woman's room looked out onto the "cap," an immense stone cliff with sheer rock walls that rose at such an angle that even mountain goats couldn't have scaled it.

Since her return to the farm, not a week passed, winter or summer, that Vic—sometimes alone, sometimes accompanied by her mother and Maurice during vacation time—didn't take a walk on the "PALISSADES," as she called the top of this cliff. From a perch on its crest, one could see, on a clear day, the steeples of four churches.

When she made her pilgrimage alone, Vic would lie back against the rocks of the "PALISSADES" and, if no work at the farm had called her, she would have spent hours looking off into the distance. Sometimes, warm droplets welled up in her eyes, but she quickly wiped them away with the back of her hand and, tossing her proud head, she would retrace her steps back to the house. She wasn't unhappy, since she was devoting her life to her mother and Maurice, but she wasn't happy either. In the depths of her heart there was a deep empty space, like an abyss that she was afraid to peer down into.

This particular June evening the sky was cloudless but dotted with stars. "Well," murmured the young woman as she watched the sky, "There's a falling star. What wish could I make?" Captivated, her eyes followed the streak of light as it widened and then, frozen with terror, she saw a huge "ball of fire" strike the ground next to the "cap;" at the same time she heard an explosion like the sound of dynamite and the ground beneath her feet shook. The whole thing lasted only seconds. "Perhaps I dreamed it," Vic told herself as she got back in bed, "but tomorrow I'm going to explore a bit."

The next afternoon, once the chores were done, Vic went off in search of the meteor without saying anything to her mother, for she thought that it must have been a meteor that she had seen the night before, falling from the sky like a "ball of fire."

She headed for the side of the "cap" where she had seen the falling fragment hit the earth. She made a huge circle, searching in the weeds, the bushes, and the rocks. She felt sure that a meteor that looked like a huge luminous ball and that exploded with a sound like dynamite when it struck the earth must have left some visible trace.

At last she saw a freshly formed cavity in the earth with an opening about as wide as a well. Maybe it's the den of some wild animal, she thought to herself, but even if an animal can move the earth with its claws and its nose, it certainly can't pulverize rocks.

Vic carefully examined the upturned earth and the crumbled rocks but she couldn't judge the depth of the hole. Fairly intrigued, she made a kind of enclosure of rocks and fallen branches around the hole so that the farm animals wouldn't fall into it. Then she headed back to the house, not wanting her absence to be noticed.

During the days that followed, Vic felt herself drawn to the same spot but didn't dare climb down into the freshly dug hole even with the help of ropes or ladders. She was afraid; she didn't know exactly why and she didn't want to tell anyone her secret for fear they would laugh at her.

She poked, handled, and examined the rock fragments and the earth of indeterminate color that had surged up from the bowels of the earth and, in her mind's eye; she saw the many rich mineral samples in Raymond's superb collection. The collection was kept by his mother, Madame Fénélon, in her home, because Raymond was afraid that nighttime marauders, tempted by the lure of gain, might break into his office and steal it. He had often spoken on this subject to a fascinated Vic, for minerals were his life.

More and more intrigued as the days wore on, Vic, wanting to share her secret, decided to send the following telegram to Raymond: "If free, come to see me. Need to consult. If possible, alert me of arrival. Will meet at station. Vic."

When the engineer responded, Vic announced his visit to her mother so that she wouldn't be surprised to see her daughter go off in the buggy to the station to fetch their visitor.

When the train arrived from Lowell: a firm, direct handshake, eyes that hold one another's gaze like those lost reunited, a mist that obscures their sight...and that's all that passes between these two beings meant to love one another and find happiness.

Vic explains her telegram message and asks Raymond to keep her discovery secret until they're certain of its importance.

"I wouldn't be surprised," says the engineer, "if you've discovered a mine, for your farm is located in the heart of mining territory in this part of the country. I don't want to give you false hopes, but if your discovery has value I would be delighted for you. Life owes you so much that it will never give you enough to repay you.

Under the pretext of a walk on the "PALISSADES," Raymond and Vic make several excursions to the pit. Several days after his arrival, the engineer departs again, carrying with him a variety of rock and soil samples and promising Vic to have a prompt analysis made.

The analysis is remarkable, for among the samples submitted there are found to be traces of molybdenum in sufficient quantity to guarantee a rich vein. Molybdenum is a rare and precious mineral that is used principally to mix with steel to strengthen it.

Along with the analysis, the engineer sent word that he was planning a second visit to the Labranche farm to explain in detail the importance of the discovery. Vic now explained to her astonished mother that the impact of a meteorite had laid open a mine of molybdenum on their farm; she explained the purpose of Raymond's first visit and his forthcoming return to provide explanations, consultation and advice.

The train that brought Raymond back to the Eastern Provinces was the same one that delivered Maurice for his two months of vacation.

After a lengthy parley, it was decided that the engineer would oversee the necessary steps to interest investors in the purchase of the farm. Everything worked out splendidly. After only a few weeks, the farm was sold at a price that exceeded the family's wildest dreams and a generous royalty from the mine profits was accorded to each member of the Labranche family.

When the last formalities were completed, Madame Labranche, accompanied by Maurice and Vic, set off to purchase a magnificent residence on the banks of the Prairie River (la Rivière des Prairies) on the outskirts of Montreal, in order to be able to see Maurice as often as the Seminary rules would allow.

Before leaving the farm, Madame Labranche, listening only to her generous heart, made a gracious gesture that was certain to bring the blessings of heaven upon her and her children. In recognition of his faithful and devoted service, she bought Alfred a lovely farm, thus realizing the dream the orphan had held in his heart all these years.

CHAPTER 12

Vic's Final and True Romance

The day came when Maurice was to celebrate his first mass. A special invitation to the ordination had been sent to the engineer who was now considered a member of the family.

It was mid-October with a temperature as mild as June. It was Indian Summer. While the Lord's newly-elected chatted with his mother, Raymond and Vic went off to sit on a bench at the edge of the river to watch the sun slowly sinking over the horizon. Amid the tree branches, still partly covered with leaves, birds clustered together for the night and sang out, into the blue canopy above, their most fervent prayers. The sound of the crickets and the frogs blended with the music of their winged brothers creating, on this beautiful October evening, a hymn of praise to the Creator from all His creatures.

Raymond was the first to shake off the enchantment of the evening to ask:

"What are you thinking about, Vic?"

The young woman started as if awakened too abruptly and studied the engineer for a while before saying:

"I was thinking about the past, about my life in the mill, about little 'Canuck,' the butt of the teasing and taunting of the factory girls. I relived the moment when you appeared like a guardian angel to save me from the clutches of the girls who wanted to throw me in the canal. I saw again, in my mind, that saintly and noble woman, your mother. Then came my unhappy love affair with Jean when, for the second time, you saved me from despair." "Then," Vic continued, as if talking to herself, "in a flash, came my return to the farm, the day of the snow storm, then my father's burial, my life as a farmer with all the events that accompanied it and the sale, once again thanks to you, of our land at such a fabulous price. I was thinking about the past and wondering what tomorrow will bring...In two weeks Maurice will set out for Rome where he'll spend three years of study in the

Eternal City. My mother will accompany him in order not to be separated from him. Poor Mama, she certainly deserves the great happiness that is hers today. They're insisting that I should go along, too, but I haven't decided yet. I'm in a kind of stupor. I'm not dreaming and yet I don't feel like I'm really awake either. Raymond?"

"Yes, Vic?"

"During the greatest crisis in my life, you vowed that you loved me. Do you still?"

Raymond captured the young woman's hand in his own in a burning caress.

"After the death of my mother, don't you think, Vic, that I would have started a family if I hadn't kept, in my heart, a hope that refused to die? I condemned myself to a life of restaurants and hotels because, all these years, I kept hoping, I don't know why. Vic, do you still think about Jean?"

"Can one keep oneself from thinking?...Yes, I still think about him and I probably always will; but my thoughts of him no longer belong in the realm of dreams, but rather that of nightmares...I stopped loving him a long time ago and I wonder now why I ever loved him so much. I think it was more infatuation than love, and infatuation fades and disappears."

Raymond's fingers trembled on the wrist of his companion:

"Could you learn to love me a little, Vic?"

"A little, Raymond?...When I finally woke myself abruptly from my childish dream, my brain was spinning, my eyes opened and my soul slowly filled with a sweet, true vision: my love for the great and noble heart that is yours, Raymond."

The engineer gently drew the young woman's head against his shoulder and, leaning against each other, his cheek against her hair, he spoke to her tenderly:

"You're thirty-four now, Vic, and I'm about to turn fifty. We can both be happy if we build our happiness on a solid foundation. Don't think for a moment that I'm jealous of the past, but I do wonder if, in your heart, a spark would be struck if, one day after we're married, you find yourself face to face with Jean. I know enough of your honor to feel certain that you would be faithful to me all the same, but I want you to be completely happy. I don't ever want there to be fresh tears in your eyes and renewed tempests in your heart. Before joining our lives together, I'm going to put your love to a final test. Please understand, Vic, that, in doing so, I am thinking only of our future happiness together. You heard that Jean had married...To put your heart to the test where he's concerned, you need to go, as soon as you can, to the United States and arrange to see him...If this encounter revives the flame that you believe is dead, I know you feel enough loyalty toward me to admit it. In that case, I will say good-bye to the first and only great dream of my life, but rest assured, I would nevertheless remain your devoted friend as in the past. For you, Vic, I will always be like a good and faithful dog who is happy if he's given a friendly pat in passing... And you could go with your family to Rome. If, on the other hand, only ashes remain from your past love, then, Vic, we will set off in life together, shoulder to shoulder, trying to make up for all the happiness we've lost in these long years of waiting. What do you think, Vic? You're crying?... Come now, all I want is your happiness and all I've succeeded in doing is making you cry?"

"I'm not sad or hurt, Raymond. If I'm crying, it's because I'm so happy to be loved by a heart like yours. Since you want me to—and you think it's wise—I'll see Jean again. But I know in advance that I won't be going to Rome. If I go anywhere, it will be on a wedding trip with you."

In an office in the back of one of his stores, Jean Guay is re-reading, for at least the fourth time, the following few lines: "Jean, I'm passing through Boston and will be in the lobby of the Statler Hotel between four and five o'clock on Tuesday, the twenty-fifth of October. I would like to see you—VIC."

Jean, who has gotten from life what he gave, murmurs to himself: "Vic? Why in the world would she want to see me? Could she still be in love with me after all these years and after the shameful manner in which I treated her?"

Jean finds himself slightly moved, as one might be when opening a tomb, and he promises himself that NOTHING will keep him from being at the Boston Statler at the date and time indicated.

The afternoon of October 25th, Vic was not too surprised, as she entered the Statler, to see Jean standing there impatiently, watching the main entrance of the hotel. She hesitated slightly. Is this really Jean, "her" Jean, this man with white hair, wrinkles, and a heavy step?...He rushes to meet her as soon as he sees her:

"Vic!"

She looks at him and laughs:

"Well, yes, it's me, and not some ghost as you seem to think. I was passing through Boston and I had a fancy to see how life has been treating you, or rather how you having been treating life, for the past eight years. Let's go up to the balcony, if you'd like, where it will be more comfortable to chat."

The two take the elevator and Vic starts in surprise when she hears Jean say to the elevator operator, "Eighth floor, please."

The young woman's eyes flash and her voice is full of sarcasm when she says, "The eighth floor? The balcony of this hotel must be very high!" She isn't afraid, but she is stung by his audacity.

"We'll be more comfortable chatting in my room than on the balcony," Jean replies.

"In your room?"

"Yes, I reserved a room for Mr. and Mrs. Guay!"

Instead of getting angry, Vic bursts out laughing, to the astonishment of the other passengers in the elevator.

Jean picks up his key at the counter on the eighth floor and walks in front of Vic to open the door of his room. The young woman enters as calm and at ease as if she were in her own room; only there is a smile lurking at the corners of her mouth, and there is a mocking look in her eyes that Jean, preoccupied, doesn't notice.

As soon as the door closes, Jean comes toward Vic, his arms open wide, and tries to embrace her:

"Have you lost your head, Jean?! I came here to talk, not to commit some folly! Stop this right now or I'm leaving immediately!"

Stunned at having his plan of attack rebuffed, Jean takes a seat across from Vic. His hands are trembling and there is a bitter smile on his lips. This is not the avid soul, so sure of conquest, that the young woman once knew.

"Jean, do you know why I wanted to see you again?"

"I admit that I don't have the slightest idea."

"It was simply to see whether I was still in love with you."

"And?"

"And I realize that I no longer love you the slightest bit!...I am as calm and indifferent in your presence as if you had always been a perfect stranger. I don't even understand any more why I once loved you so impetuously. The infatuation of a twenty-year-old, no doubt...I heard about your marriage. Are you happy, Jean?"

Jean turns his head away to stare at the carpet and Vic sees his lips tremble,—those same lips that knew so well how to give the devil's kiss.

"What is it that makes you unhappy?"

"Oh, simply differences in taste, opinion, ideas."

"You're probably making a mountain out of a mole hill! Jean, you've been so spoiled by life, having always taken everything and everyone for granted. If only you would choose to look inside yourself a little, to learn how to listen to and understand the contrary whispers that come from there, you could probably find the remedy for what you BELIEVE to be wrong with you. Life as a couple, it seems to me, is a cocktail you need to know how to mix and be willing to mix correctly if you want be intoxicated by it. Your wife is probably as unhappy in her own way as you believe yourself to be in yours. And you probably both refuse to give up a single one of your own ideas. Each of you thinks you're right and that can't ever make for a good relationship. But I don't believe in minding other people's business, so let me get back to my own. Jean, I told you that I wanted to see you again to confirm whether or not I was still in love with you, but I also wanted to ask you a question that has been tormenting me for the past eight years. If I ask you, will you answer me in complete honesty?"

"I promise you I will."

"Jean, why didn't you marry me after asking me to be your wife? If I had yielded all reserve to you, than I would have understood that you had an excuse to shunt me aside, but apart from kissing you madly and snuggling up against you, I never allowed the slightest impure thought or gesture to tarnish the beauty of the noble feelings I had for you. So tell me, why did you cast me aside like a toy one is tired of playing with?"

With moist eyes and a muffled voice, Jean answered:

"The woman I took as my wife was in love with me long before I met you, Vic....I made a point of honor of marrying her...She said she was so unhappy. And I wanted to right the wrongs I had done her in making so many promises to her when I was carried away by my emotions."

"You made a point of honor for her; why didn't you make a point of honor for me as well? I was an innocent child when I met you. Why did you insinuate your way into my life when you weren't free? If you had another love that bound you, why did you cast your eyes on me? How could you have caused me all that useless suffering so thoughtlessly?"

"I was a cad and a coward, Vic! But whatever you may think, you were the great love of my life! I made you suffer terribly, didn't I? Well, if knowing this can give you any satisfaction, I'll admit to you with great sincerity and humiliation that life has avenged you, for today our roles are reversed. And you, Vic, are you happy?"

"Yes, Jean! But my happiness won't be complete until, a few days from now, I marry Raymond Fénélon."

"Raymond!...Ah, his is a noble heart that is certainly worthy of your love."

"Raymond is the one who urged me to see you again to determine whether there might still be some spark of flame smoldering beneath the ashes of the love I once held for you. He doesn't want the slightest shadow to obscure our happiness as a couple. That's why I came to find you today, in order to go back to him completely healed. I'm happier than I've ever been, because I'm loved by the greatest heart in the universe and I love him too! And to think that there was a time when, if you had wanted it, I would have been your life companion and the mother of your children. How strange life is...but everything happens for the best."

"When are you to be married, Vic?"

"As soon as we can get our marriage banns. Mama and Maurice are going to Rome, and Raymond and I are leaving, as soon as we're married, for Central America where Raymond hopes to spend several years exploring the ruins of pagan temples there and perhaps even discover buried treasure. I don't need to tell you that a life of adventure, in countries so different from our own in every way, will please me enormously. Not to mention that, wherever Raymond is, I'll always be happy...Now, give me your hand, Jean. I have to go, for I've lots of errands to do."

"Vic, will you give me a kiss before you go...a kiss of FORGIVENESS?...You're shaking your head? Why refuse me this favor when we'll probably never see one another again in this world?"

"Jean, I forgave you a long time ago...but I can't kiss you, because I give my lips only to those I love. Nevertheless, in spite of all the suffering you caused me, I pity you...I realize that there's a reason why your hair has turned white and your forehead is so creased with wrinkles, AT YOUR AGE...Life is a huge wheel that all of humanity clings to. This wheel turns very slowly, but it turns nonetheless. Those who shout triumphantly from the top of the wheel today, may find themselves on the ground tomorrow, crushed under the weight of this wheel that is called LIFE!...Good-bye, Jean, if you're in pain, try to bear it like a MAN! Married life holds a share of happiness for you, but to discover it, you'll have to be more flexible in your tastes, your opinions, your personal ideas. In the past, you've been too enamored of your "ME". In order to give and receive happiness, you have to know how to forget yourself. Take the first step by giving up what you believe to be your rights and reasons and you'll see that it won't be long before happiness takes solid root in your home."

Vic left, carrying away with her, in her soul, the image of Jean, a Jean she hardly recognized, a Jean with trembling lips and eyes filled with unwept tears.

The young woman took a taxi to Boston's North Station where she sent the following telegram to Maurice: "Delay departure if possible. Will be in Montreal tomorrow. Vic."

To Raymond, she wrote a night letter: "Arrange affairs immediately. Obtain wedding banns. Reserve boat passage. Meet in Montreal. Have requested Maurice delay departure to bless marriage vows. Yours for life. VIC."

These messages sent, Vic ran to reserve a sleeping compartment and, as the Pullman car was open for boarding two hours before departure, she sequestered herself inside. She didn't want to run the risk of encountering Jean who might be taking the same train back to Lowell. Her heart held no spark of her former love for him, but the pain etched in the face she had once so loved, hurt her like the sight of any human suffering she couldn't ease.

As requested, Maurice delayed his and his mother's departure for Rome so he could bless the union of Raymond and his sister.

When the ceremony was over, nothing further retained the travelers: Madame Labranche had given a three year lease to carefully chosen tenants who would live in her house during her absence. Raymond had placed his property in the hands of trustworthy friends who would sell it when the moment was right. His personal effects, mineral samples, books, etc., had been packed up and shipped to Montreal where they were stored in a locked room that Madame Labranche had held aside when renting her house in order to store her personal effects as well as those of Vic and Maurice.

In New York they bid one another farewell with a pang of emotion but without tears, for it was happiness that was to "fill the sails" of these ships about to set out to sea.

While Maurice and his mother sailed toward the Eternal City, Vic and Raymond set off, in several long stages, toward Central America. They would visit, in the course of their travels, several of the Antilles Islands and then they would go deep into the mountains and jungles of the tropics seeking the remains of a civilization that had been buried beneath the earth for a thousand years. Perhaps one day the story of the adventures of our travelers in these countries of buried temples, tattered mummies, and frowning idols will be shared with the public.

THE END

FRENCH WOMEN OF NORTH AMERICA

By Corinne Rocheleau Rouleau (1881-1963)
Translation by Jeannine Bacon Roy
Illustrations by Miss Albani Rocheleau

To my mother and her eight sisters, "the matantes," who, each in their own way, were my heroines.

CORINNE ROCHELEAU ROULEAU (1881-1963)

Born on April 3, 1881,in Worcester, Massachusetts, Corinne Rocheleau, at nine years old, lost her hearing after a brief illness. Having lost her hearing, she soon began to lose the ability to speak. When she was thirteen, her parents sent her to Montreal to follow courses at the Institution des Sourdes Muettes (School for the Deaf) directed by the Sisters of the Providence. She progressed so rapidly, that she was soon given private tutors, and upon her return to Worcester in 1898, she spoke English and French fluently and was also able to lip read without difficulty. She finished her studies in Worcester, and in 1909, brilliantly passed a Civil Service exam which allowed her to obtain a position in Washington D.C. at the Bureau of Statistics. At her brother's request, she returned to Worcester two years later to oversee the management of the family's business. A woman of letters and quite cultured, she toured Europe for eight months in 1921, and took advantage of this free time to visit schools for the deaf in France and Switzerland.

In spite of her numerous occupations, her literary tastes and interests in the cause of the deaf-mutes never ceased. Her numerous articles in *L'Union* of Woonsocket, *L'Opinion Publique* of Worcester, *La Revue Canadienne* of Montréal and later *Le Travailleur* of Worcester, revealed her as being a woman of great literary gifts. She founded a woman's literary circle, le Cercle Jeanne-Mance of Worcester, and her conferences were well attended and very much appreciated. In 1915, she wrote a series of dramatic scenes, *Françaises d'Amérique* for this group. This work was well received and had a great following. In 1927, she published her major work, *Hors de sa Prison,* a documented history of a blind, deaf-mute girl at the Institution des Sourdes-Muettes of Montréal. The French Academy praised this book, and in 1928, a larger second edition was released. Two years later, with Rebecca Mack, she published *Those in Dark Silence,* the first combined study of the deaf-mutes in America. That same year, she wed Wilfrid Rouleau of Washington.

In Washington at the Voltra Bureau and at Catholic University, she continued her studies and her conferences on the problems of the deaf mutes. In 1936, she moved with her husband to Montréal, where she prepared an educational methods course for the professors at l'Institution des Sourdes-Muettes. After the death of her husband in 1940, she retired at the Institution des Sourdes-Muettes, where she died on November 21, 1963.

In addition to *Hors de sa Prison,* (Montréal, 1927,1928, editions in Braille, Paris and Montréal, 1930,Montréal 1960), *Those in Dark Silence,* with Rebecca Mack, (Washington, 1930), *Une Vie Rayonnante, Mme Henry Hamilton,* (Montréal, 1948), and *Parler est Chose Facile, Croyez-vous?.* (Montréal, 1951) on the subject of the deaf-mutes, she also published a play,*Françaises d'Amérique,* (Worcester, 1915; Montréal, 1924,1930,1940,1955), historical texts, *Laurentian Heritage* (Toronto 1948) and *Mobilisons notre Histoire* (Manchester N.H. 1955). She left two plays still in manuscript form, "Les fêtes Chez L'habitant" written for the Cercle Jeanne-Mance of Worcester in 1925, "Deux semaines de Parloir," a comedy written in 1937 for l'Institution des Sourdes-Muettes, and an historical pageant, "Living the Mass for One Hundred Years," written in 1954 for the Sisters of the Providence of Burlington, Vermont.

FRENCH WOMEN OF NORTH AMERICA

Historical Perspective

Historical sketches and excerpts from the lives of the principal heroines of New France

Illustrations by Miss Albani Rocheleau

As performed in Worcester, Massachusetts on February 10, 1915

PREFACE

Some say that a happy people have no history. If this saying applies to individuals, we must believe that the first French women in America were happy for we seldom hear about them.

We have often discussed the major feats and accomplishments of the French colonists, but we have left their "better halves" in semi-darkness. I believe that it is time to introduce these French women pioneers. As a young lady once asked me, "Were there ever any?"

It is truly sad that so few details survive concerning these courageous women who confronted the dangers of long and stormy ocean crossings to establish themselves in a strange and foreign country. The centuries have practically erased all traces of their footsteps on American soil.

To find the names of these heroines, we must consult the old records of Québec, of Montreal, of Detroit or of New Orleans. If this proves to be too much, we need only to look in the monumental work "Dictionnaire Généalogique de Tanguay" which would prove to us that so many thousands of these pioneer women lived and died. A genealogical dictionary, however, does not tell their stories.

But, by studying the Canadian and American archives, these women appear—almost like magic—from their pages. Taken aback by their beauty, their charm and dare I say it, their French mentality, I have retrieved them—one by one—from the cloudy depths of history where they have been hidden—first of all for the sheer pleasure of admiring them like cameos from the past and finally for the greater pleasure of seeing them reborn as interpreted by the members of the "Cercle Jeanne-Mince."

No one asked me why I did not interpret Marie de L'Incarnation, Marguerite Bourgeois and the "Soeurs Hospitalieres." It is because these have been interpreted by others more capable than I. It is also because I thought it best to leave these religious sisters hidden beneath their veils, in their cloisters, relegating to those who worked alongside them—women such as Madame de la Peltrie and Jeanne Mance—the task of revealing the arduous life of these wonderful women.

Finally, I wish to thank those who have helped me with their advice. First of all, I'd like to thank my sisters. Secondly, the Belisle family and in particular, Anna Belisle who directed the first performance of "Françaises d'Amérique." Thirdly, the President and the members of the "Cercle Jeanne-Mance" who gave me "carte blanche" for the preparation of their first "soirée canadienne."

It is because of all of them that we were able to bring alive that which was but a fleeting vision. This play is dedicated to them as well as to all those American women who have but a drop of French blood in them.

—Corinne Rocheleau
Worcester, Massachusetts. August 1915

The first performance of "Françaises d'Amérique" was held on February 10, 1915 under the direction of Miss Anna Bélisle and under the sponsorship of the "Cercle Jeanne Mance." The roles, in 1915, were as follows:

CAST OF CHARACTERS

A Voice
Miss Annette Levasseur
Huron
Miss Eva Marchessault

HISTORICAL FIGURES
[*Original Cast*]

Mrs. Louis Hébert
Miss Anne Perrott
Guillemette, her daughter
Miss Angeline Racine
Mrs. Samuel [Hélène] de Champlain
Miss Beatrice Lariviere
Mrs. de la Peltrie
Miss Eva Gosselin
Mrs. de la Tour, baronne de St. Estienne
Mrs. Joseph Brunelle
Lady in Waiting
Miss Ida Granger
Jeanne Mance
Miss Eva Marchessault
Mrs. Jacques de Lalande
Mrs. Ovila Bousquet
Mrs. Louis Jolliet
Miss Albani Rocheleau
Madeleine de Verchères
Miss Lilia Viau
Jeanne le Ber
Miss Blanche Marchessault
Jeanne le Ber's cousin

Miss Dora Levitre
Mrs. de la Mothe-Cadillac
Miss Alida Granger

EPILOGUE

A Franco-American mother
Mrs. Regis Cloutier
Marie
Miss Louise Parrott
Françoise
Miss Estelle Lacroix

PRODUCTION NOTES: The Prologue is recited after the "Chant des Huronnes" and before the curtain rises. Once the curtain is raised, the back and sides of the stage appear to be draped in a second curtain of a deep purple which frames the stage. This curtain stands as a background against which the various costumes and accessories are portrayed. It also has the advantage of simplifying the various stage settings.

Before the curtain rises, a voice is heard singing Ernest Gagnon's "Le Chant des Huronnes" from the wings.

"The white warrior regains his land
The evening breeze stirs the rosebush,
And my canoe, on the silver wave
Leaps, light as bird.
Glide, canoe, glide
On the azure river!
May an auspicious god
Give to the girl of the woods, a sky always pure!

Out of the forest, a fresh breeze murmurs
Causing the moving leaves to sigh.
The echo is silenced, and from my head
My ebony hair flows at the whim of the wind
Glide, canoe, glide

On the azure river!
May an auspicious god
Give to the girl of the woods, a sky always pure!

I hear the footsteps of the timid doe...
Silence...Hurry, my bow and my quiver!
Fly! Fly! Oh my rapid arrow!
Cut down the queen of the forest!
Glide, canoe, glide
On the azure river!
May an auspicious god
Give to the girl of the woods, a sky always pure!"

A Huron

A HURON

Prologue

The prologue can be recited before the curtain rises. If so, then there is no need for props.

If one desires something more elaborate, the curtain will rise revealing a forest background. The Huron is sitting on the ground, in front of a wigwam placed in the background, somewhat off center. She is wearing fringed buckskin and moccasins. Her hair is braided in pigtails. She has a leather band encircling her forehead in which is stuck an eagle feather.

(Rising, she comes to the forefront. She speaks slowly, gesturing broadly.)

The Huron: As the soaring eagle raises its eyes to the sun, so a Huron is drawn to the white woman.

For as many moons as the trees have leaves, the Redskins alone have inhabited this earth...but suddenly, on the waters of our great river, large birds alighted...but these were not birds...they were huge canoes with no oars but with large wings and glided along the water by the wind.

It is thus that the Great Manitou sent us the Palefaces...

The Hurons lived in wigwams which they placed at times by the running waters and at others in the shade of the large trees which swayed and murmured...The white men cut these trees to build strange wigwams which seemed to take root as soon as they were built.

The whites do not cover themselves with buffalo robes, bearskin or beaver; rather, they wrap themselves in strange fabrics with colors as wild as the maple leaves in autumn.

And their words are even stranger still...they tell us that over the sea, ...where the sun rises...there are more white men. They number more than the stones by the river and their Great Spirit is greater even than our Great Manitou!

The heart of the Huron is very heavy indeed!!! Should she believe these tall tales as told by the white men????

The voice of the white woman is as soft as a mother singing a lullaby to her child...but the Huron hears other voices...

In the land of the spirits, the Huron Chiefs raise their voices...the Huron listens.

The Huron returns to her wigwam which she has placed near the hunting grounds. In her light birch bark canoe, her oars cut through the waters softly and swiftly. Her moccasins make not a sound as she follows the chiefs along the warpath.

The Huron needs the sound of the night breeze through the leaves... the clear murmur of the brooks...the voices of the waterfalls...She needs the sounds and sights of thunder and lightning during the dark nights...the whistling wind ...the hurricane unleashed over the lakes!!!!

The Huron needs wide open spaces!!!!!!

The Huron needs Liberty!!!!!!

(She exits)

Madame Hébert and her daughter Guillemette

MADAME HÉBERT AND HER DAUGHTER GUILLEMETTE

Québec—1617-1684

BIOGRAPHICAL NOTE: In 1617 the first family came to settle in Canada. They were Louis Hébert, his wife, Marie Rollet and several children. This Parisian pharmacist played a major role in the colonization of New France. Samuel de Champlain said that he was "the first head of the family who lived off his land." His land was near the fort and his house was the first building erected in the "Haute Ville" according to the historian Ferland. Louis Hébert died in 1627 and was buried in the cemetery of the Jesuits. In 1629, his widow married Guillaume Hubou—an honorable man—and continued to live peacefully among his children.

His daughter, Anne Hébert, married Etienne Jonquest in 1618. It was the first marriage celebrated in Canada. (It preceded by two years the first marriage in New England.) Another one of his daughters, Guillemette, married Guillaume Couillard in 1621. Like her mother, this daughter raised a large family and was identified for over a half-century with the life of the colony. She died in 1684 and was buried in the chapel of l'Hôtel Dieu.

SCENERY—A table with one or two lit candles. Two chairs, a spinning wheel and, if desired, a spool. As the curtain rises, Madame Hébert sits alone and is busy spinning wool.

COSTUMES—The mother (Madame Hébert) is wearing a black dress with a white scarf and white cuffs. Her graying hair is covered with a black silk scarf.

The daughter (Guillemette) is wearing a short-sleeved cotton dress. The bodice has a plunging neckline and is of a floral or geometric print. The skirt is ankle length, of a solid color and is gathered at the waist. She is wearing flat shoes, decorated with a leather or silver bow. Her head covering is of white linen.

Madame Hébert: Guillemette! I just heard the cannon!!!

(Guillemette enters, holding her knitting.)

Guillemette: It's a volley from the fort to welcome a ship arriving from France. Tomorrow we will have visitors and news from the old country. You aren't upset, are you?

Madame Hébert: You know very well that I'm not!!! This Canadian land has become ours over the years. Now that we have peace, now that the farm is prospering and the children are growing like weeds at our feet, I would not want to return to France. But, I still love seeing our countrymen. A lot has happened since we left Paris!!!

Guillemette: Please tell me about it!! Tell me each story so that I may later retell the stories to my children. All they know of our beloved France is its name and its flag with the "fleurs de lys."

Madame Hébert: You were but a child yourself when we left the old country!

Guillemette: Of course not!!! I was almost twelve.

Madame Hébert: That's true! but your brother was yet small. Louis Hébert your father—had Anne, the eldest; Guillemette and Guillaume. He loved to explore and, having already spent many years in Acadia, promised Mr. de Champlain to come to Québec. It is then that I decided to follow him to America rather than pass half my life alone in France. But, going so far away was no fun! I cried when I saw the coast of France disappear, and you, my children, were tugging at my skirts—faces filled with terror while your father's face turned somber in the anticipation of the dangers and miseries to which we would be exposed.

Guillemette: And the crossing lasted three long months! And it was almost always stormy!!! When the wind wasn't raging, the fog covered us... and out of the fog came large blocks of ice.....much taller than our ship ...and threatened at any moment to crush us!!! We would have thought they were cathedrals or castles -- crystal cities --- floating all around us and blocking our way!!!

Madame Hébert: Yes, it was a terrible crossing. But, finally we arrived in Québec, where only the fortified home of Mr. Champlain was still standing with the other few homes in ruins.

Guillemette: You forgot the Indian Teepees!!! And how many of those there were !!!

Madame Hébert: Yes, the teepees...more than we needed.. but nothing to make a home habitable. Your father with his bare hands, tore out of the side of the mountain each and every stone which was used to build our home. Louis Hébert who was a pharmacist by trade became a stonemason, a settler and a farmer.

Guillemette: How well he succeeded !!!

Madame Hébert: How true! But how we had to work during the short summers in order to prepare for the long winters! God protected us.

Guillemette: And so, the family grew.

Madame Hébert: Yes, the family grew. The marriage of your sister Anne to Etienne Jonquest was the first. Years later, Admiral Kirk laid siege to the city. We lacked provisions, and during the siege we had to help those colonists less fortunate than us. As long as these provisions held, we distributed seven ounces of these per day to each person.

Guillemette: And so, it was pea soup that saved the colony!!!

Madame Hébert: Perhaps it saved us from dying from hunger, but nothing could save us from capitulating. Champlain, the Jesuits, and almost all the colonists had crossed the seas under the French flag...and there, over the fort flew the English banner. Since we were farmers, we were given permission, with four other families, to remain on our farms. The French population of Canada was then reduced to twenty-two people.

Guillemette: However, our friends, the Indians remained. They came and went, entered the house and stayed, sitting on the floor, eyes fixed on the clock—always for them a living being that they named "The Captain of the Days." We would have been quite lonely without the Indians.

Madame Hébert: But at last, after three years, our eyes, often turned to France, one day saw a French ship on the horizon. We had saved one of our banners and soon displayed it on the hillside; Canada was French once again!!!! What joy as we welcomed our countrymen as they descended from the ship. We cried tears of joy as the Jesuit priests celebrated Mass—of which we had been deprived for three long years—in our home, the only one which was not in ruins. With great joy we intoned the "Te Deum Laudamus."

Guillemette: And since then, calm has reigned around us. But you, Mother, were not made to be sitting still. You have adopted who knows how many small abandoned Indian children and have become the honorary Godmother of all of Québec!!!

Madame Hébert: My dear daughter, what a privilege to have become the mother of a whole colony!!!

(CURTAIN)

Hélène de Champlain

HÉLÈNE DE CHAMPLAIN

Québec—1620-1624

BIOGRAPHICAL NOTE: Eight years after their marriage, Samuel de Champlain brought his young wife, twenty-two year old Hélène Boullé, to Canada. She was said to have been gifted with great beauty and charm -- impressing even the natives. Mrs. de Champlain spent only four years in Québec,—from 1620 to 1624. On her return to France, she founded a convent of Ursuline sisters in the town of Meaux. After the death of her husband- Samuel de Champlain—in 1635, she entered the convent under the name of Sister Hélène of Saint-Augustin. She died there in 1654.

SCENERY—This scene takes place in France, after the death of her husband and before she entered the convent. She is approximately 37 years old.

COSTUME—She is dressed richly. The dress has a long skirt which is quite full. The bodice is fitted and comes to a "V" where it is attached to the skirt. The sleeves are puffed and the dress is finished with a wide starched collar. She is wearing a gold or silver purse hooked to her waist and is carrying a fan in her hand. Her hair is done up in curls.

(She is speaking to herself, while sitting in an armchair or standing and walking slowly.)

Mrs. de Champlain: When I was living in my father's house, many came to visit my father, the Lord Eustache de Boullé—Secretary to the King. One day, appeared before me, a gentleman with a striking military bearing... This gentleman visited often. Finally, I was told that the Lord Samuel de Champlain, great explorer and geographer for the King had done me the honor of asking for my hand in marriage. As I was but twelve years old, my parents betrothed me to him with the stipulation that I was to remain a few years more in my father's house. Meanwhile, they delivered to the Lord de Champlain 4,500 pounds as part of my dowry, for the advancement of his colony in Canada.

(Pause)

The Lord de Champlain returned two years later, and we celebrated our marriage. But, he left me once again in France, to pursue his goal of colonization. I was quite saddened, wanting desperately to accompany him to Canada. Finally, eight years later—he took me with him to Canada.

(Pause)

There was quite a difference between the world to which I was accustomed in my father's house—a gentleman in the King's court—and that which waited for me in my husband's home as governor of the walled city of Québec, Canada.

(Pause)

Québec was but a village where there was nothing of substance but our home, crudely built, as well as a few other homes occupied by the Hébert family and a few other colonists. As the beautiful manors were missing, so too were the courtesans. In their place were many adventurers as well as many Natives.

(Pause)

In our fortified residence which was barely comfortable, I established our home with three servants whom I had brought with me. And there I faced exile in a strange country where danger was all around me. ...I voluntarily left the men to do their soldiering, but, one day, while they were all gone, I heard the war cries of the Iroquois natives just outside the fort and I saw women and children rush into the fort. I had to take up arms and take up the command in the absence of my husband, Mr. de Champlain.

(Pause)

I belonged to a Huguenot family, but the example and pleas of Mr. de Champlain, a fervent Catholic, convinced me to join the Catholic Church. Upon arriving in Canada, I devoted myself to the daily teaching of the Indians who gathered before my door, or whom I visited in their in their bark wigwams. The Natives were very docile and listened to me voluntarily. But, what seemed to interest them the most, was a small mirror suspended on my belt. In this bewitching object they could see their painted faces, their hair decorated with eagle feathers and their bear tooth necklaces. They said between themselves, "This paleface woman is superhuman, for she carries in her heart the picture of each and everyone of us." And, for the privilege of looking into this magic mirror, they promised me anything that I wanted of them.

(Pause)

But soon, the vigorous climate, the uncertainties, and the sacrifices took its toll on my health. In spite of myself, this life in isolation weakened me. After four years of this, Mr. de Champlain decided to return me to France. ...My husband, who was thirty years older than me, was, in my estimation full of goodness and kindness. However, the interests of the colony seemed to be first and foremost with him...Knowing that I would see him only upon his short stays in France, I decided to retreat from the world... Mr. de Champlain was opposed to this; but soon he returned to Canada, leaving me free to follow the dream I had of founding a Ursuline convent, and retire there far away from the noise and vanities of court life.

(Pause)

My husband, after having spent many years in the service of his country and after having crossed the Atlantic twenty times in the interest of New France, died in that far-off country where he rests.

(Pause)

Meanwhile, Hélène Boullé, widow of Samuel de Champlain, will give herself totally to her God...tomorrow I will take the veil...tomorrow there will be no one but Sister Hélène of Saint-Augustin.

(Pause)

Happily, I will rid myself of this reputation which weighs heavily on me; I look forward to the tranquility of the cloister...as welcome as the calm after a storm.

(Curtain)

Mrs. de la Peltrie

MRS. DE LA PELTRIE

Québec—1639-1671

BIPGRAPHICAL NOTE: A native of Alençon, France, Mrs. de la Peltrie was a rich young widow of a distinguished rank. In 1639 with the Venerable Mother Mary of the Incarnation, she founded the Convent of the Ursulines in Québec—the first house of study for young girls in America. Madame de la Peltrie lived with her servant in a house located on the grounds of the Ursulines, near their monastery. During the winter of 1641 she hosted Jeanne Mance and in the spring of 1642, she helped with the foundation of Montreal. She then returned to Québec, where she lived the rest of her life and where she died in 1671.

COSTUME—Dress of a dark velour with a wide floor-length gathered skirt and a fitted bodice, finishing in a point at the skirt. The dress has a wide starched collar with matching cuffs—preferably white. Her hair is worn in waves at the front and gathered at the back in a bun .

PROPS—An armchair and some needlework.

Madame de la Peltrie: Today, I let myself succumb to reverie and the memories came in droves, knocking at the door of my memory…begging to be let in. The present slowly fades away and the past emerges…I seem to be still in France, in my dear village of Alençon, where as a young girl I married Sieur de la Peltrie and was widowed after five years of marriage…I was rich, and some said that I was pretty. I was used to living in luxury, but having been brought up very religiously, I was looking to serve God and neighbor.

(Pause)

In the midst of a serious illness, I seem to have heard a divine voice saying: "I want you to go to Canada to work with the Indian girls. In return, I will grant you great graces in this venture." "Lord," I replied, "I do not deserve this honor." "That is true," replied the voice," but I wish to use you in this new country. You will go to Canada and you will die there."

(Pause)

I was resolved to listen to this supernatural voice, but the members of my family tried various ways to keep the fortune which was one day to be theirs, to be wasted by me on the Indians of the New World. Finally, after surmounting many obstacles, I left with a few Ursulines to go found a school for native girls in Canada. I had already revealed my intentions to Mother Mary of the Incarnation...Traveling with me, on the same ship, were Augustinian sisters sent by the Duchess of Aiguillon to establish a hospital in Québec.

(Pause)

Upon our arrival, the village declared a holiday. Work ceased, and the entire population came down to the waterfront to meet us. We were met by the Governor who was followed by his troops and greeted us with a cannon salute. Upon disembarking, we followed the lead of Mother Mary of the Incarnation, and knelt down and kissed the soil of our new country. Accompanied by the people from the village as well as a band of Algonquins, we then proceeded to the church where we sang a "Te Deum."

(Pause)

Our first house, which we called our palace, had but two rooms. It was a little house in the Basse-Ville. The St. Lawrence ran by our front door, and behind us rose the immense mass of the promontory. At a distance, lay the forest where we could see the wigwams of the Algonquins whom we visited in order to learn their language.

Soon, we started our work of teaching six young Indian girls and a few French students. Preferring to leave the scholarly education to the Ursulines, I devoted myself to the task of "civilizing" the young Indian girls. I dressed them in the Normand style, covering their dark tresses with a white bonnet and crossed a white cloth over their buckskin dresses. Their large dark eyes followed me continually, and they imitated me in everything. Often, they would surprise the colonists by bowing reverently like the rich ladies of France!

(Pause)

But, to my dismay, this wonderful task did not last long. The forest exercised its magic on its children and recalled them to its ways. Forgetting all the lessons that they had learned, they returned to the forest. However, if we failed in "civilizing" them, we could try to convert them...this reminds me of a certain Christmas Eve when I attended Midnight Mass surrounded by forty newly converted Indians.

(Pause)

Our students soon became too numerous, and soon Mother of the Incarnation had a convent built for the young French students. However, she didn't neglect the Indians. Often she served as an interpreter for the various tribes and always opposed the sale of liquor to the Indians. She studied their language and translated the New Testament into Algonquin. This remarkable woman seemed to be at the center of the everyday life of the small colony who often relied on her intelligence and administrative skills.

(Pause)

Two years after our arrival in Canada, Mr. de Maisonneuve and Miss Mance came to found a new colony on the isle of Mont- Réal. Being impressed by the virtue and courage of Miss Mance, I treated her like a sister during the winter she spent in Quebec. In the spring, I accompanied her to help her with the founding of Ville-Marie.

(Pause)

However, I was soon recalled to Québec to be near the Ursulines, whom I never left for this is where God wanted me to be. And the grace He had promised me and which He granted me was to be the right arm to His great servant in Canada, Sister Marie de L'Incarnation.

(Curtain)

Mrs. de la Tour and The Lady in Waiting

MRS. DE LA TOUR

Fort la Tour—Acadia, 1647

BIOGRAPHICAL NOTE: This valiant woman, Marie Jaqueline, was the wife of Charles de la Tour, Baron of Saint Stephen and Commandant of Fort la Tour. This fort, quite large and well built, was near St. John's Bay in Acadia. This colony, although quite prosperous, was always in a state of uncertainty. The de la Tour's had few friends in the French court since they were Huguenots. Although they were welcomed in England for this very reason, they were often looked at with suspicion because they were French subjects. And finally, they were looked at with jealousy by the New England colonists, for their land was disputed American territory. They went in turn to Paris, London and Boston to plead their case. But their worst enemy was Sir d'Aulnay de Charnisay, their neighbor from Port-Royal who for years fought them fiercely. Mrs. de la Tour strongly supported her husband, obtained much needed help for him and in his absence, twice fought off attacks by the numerous troops led by Charnisay. Finally, she was betrayed and died of sorrow ten days after the fort was taken in 1647. The historian Garneau says of her, "So much worry and sorrow, the atrocious death of her men, the complete ruin of her fortune—all these trials wore out and killed a woman whose talents and courage deserved a much happier life." At the end of these events, Mr. de la Tour traveled for four years throughout various parts of America. He was well received in Québec, but after the death of Mr. de Charnisay, he returned to Acadia, and married Charnisay's widow, thereby acquiring all his worldly possessions and reaped the rewards of his ancient rival.

COSTUMES—Mrs. de la Tour is wearing a solid colored wool or silk dress. The gathered skirt is quite long, covered by a long apron of the same material. The dress has puffed sleeves. The large collar and cuffs are made of fabric. Her hair, which is quite gray, is styled simply. Her companion, a younger woman, is wearing a variation of the same costume; it can be simpler but with a white head covering and apron.

PROPS—An armchair, and a chair on which rests a shawl.

(Mrs. de la Tour, overwhelmed and staggering, enters onto the stage after the curtain rises. She enters leaning on the shoulder of her lady in waiting.)

Mrs. de la Tour: It has been many years that the loathsome d'Aulnay de Charnisay has been tracking us like animals in the forest. Now that he has ambushed us, I look to death as my only deliverance and hope that it comes soon. Immense sadness overwhelms me...I am too exhausted to fight it and my courage is gone.

(As she finishes these lines, she collapses into the chair. She sits during the remainder of the scene with her lady in waiting standing near her.)

The Lady in Waiting: Perhaps we will soon see Mr. de la Tour...?????

Mrs. de la Tour: *(Interrupting her)* My husband! Ah! Let's hope that he doesn't show!!! This fort will be nothing for him but a trap where he will surely meet a horrible death!! I would rather die alone than to see him massacred before my eyes!!!

The Lady in Waiting: This Canadian land seems to bring much unhappiness to its inhabitants!!!

Mrs. de la Tour: It wasn't always like this. For a few years, peace and abundance reigned on Acadia.

The Lady in Waiting: But, it did not last.

Mrs. de la Tour: Alas, no! For many years now, racial and religious wars have raged without respite among us.

The Lady in Waiting: Your enemies are not fair. Although you are Huguenots, you have remained nonetheless faithful to France and to your king.

Mrs. de la Tour: In spite of our loyalty, we still have many enemies at the French court...My own father-in-law served the English, married an English lady from the Queen of England's court, and was sent here to Acadia to take over this fort!!! In the meetings which preceded the bombing, he ordered us to abandon, like he did, the French cause...My husband replied: "If those who sent you think me capable of treason, even under my father's orders, they are highly mistaken. The king of France has entrusted me with the defense of this fort, and if it is attacked, I will defend it to my last breath." Then ensued a battle between the fort and the English naval forces. The bombing was intense. However, my husband won the battle and took his father prisoner.

The Lady in Waiting: And finally, your neighbors at Fort Royal took their turn to wage war on your fort...But why did M. de Charnisay latch onto your loss?

Mrs. de la Tour: Because of envy, intolerance and sheer greed!!! At first, he was looking to ruin us simply because we were Huguenots; but since his accusations did not succeed to diminish us before the French king, he fought us because of boundary lines...as if Acadia was not large enough for him and for us!!! It was then that I decided to return to France to plead our cause before the French king...but Mr. de Charnisay arrived there before I did.

The Lady in Waiting: And did he succeed in his plot?

Mrs. de la Tour: He had succeeded so well in damaging my husband's reputation before the king that the king gave him permission to arrest Mr. de la Tour and to return him to France as a prisoner. Having learned of this, I armed a ship with provisions and war gear and returned to Acadia. During this time, my husband, always threatened on the Port Royal front, had obtained from Governor Winthrop of Massachusetts, permission to recruit volunteers. He then added 80 men to our small garrison. These reinforcements, and the provisions which I supplied, kept Mr. de Charnisay from seizing our fort.

The Lady in Waiting: And he was so upset, that he went to Boston to complain and then he started again looking for new ways to return vengeance on his rival.

Mrs. de la Tour: And then, taking advantage of Mr. de la Tour's absence, he came to attack us...
(Rising from the chair)

I had but fifty men in the fort, but I communicated the fervor which animated me...standing on one of the bulwarks, I directed the fire on our enemy's ships , who were obliged to retreat...to retreat before a woman!!!!!

(Pause)

Four days later, the implacable de Charnisay surprised us once again, this time by land...I was still alone with but a handful of men; for three days I pushed back de Charnisay's many troops...however, we had a traitor among us!!! Yesterday, on Easter Sunday, a sentinel betrayed us!!!!

(She starts shaking and covers her face with her hands.)

The Lady in Waiting: Please calm yourself...I pray you...

Mrs. de la Tour: How can I calm myself while I dream of the atrocities which were to befall my men!!! We were hiding in a part of the fort from which we could still defend ourselves. I begged Mr. de Charnisay to grant us an honorable surrender. He promised us the honors of war and liberty...Ah! Why did I believe the words of this monster? Disgraced at having been held at bay by a woman, and furious to see the small number of men who were there to defend the fort, he had the whole garrison hung on the battlefield.

(Shaking)

Not a single one of my brave soldiers escaped this monster who forced me to help with their execution by tying the noose .

(Pause)

I am still alive, but not for long. My husband, if he returns will find nothing but ruin and desolation.

(Still Shaking)

This Acadia is a land of Martyrs!!!

(The lady in waiting kneels near the chair and hugs Mrs. de la Tour, while the curtain falls.)

(CURTAIN)

Jeanne Mance

JEANNE MANCE

Montreal—1641- 1673

BIOGRAPHICAL NOTE: Jeanne Mance was born around 1606 in Nugent-le-Roi, France in a family renown for having provided France with many magistrates, men of letters as well as soldiers. Many of these men became nobles at the court of the King. After the death of her parents, she found herself in charge of her own life and found herself pulled towards working in New France. Without a personal fortune, but endowed with a strong spirit and high hopes coupled with a natural dignity, she soon interested many illustrious people to her endeavors. We are told that she was well thought of by the queen mother—Anne of Austria. Mrs. de Bullion, a rich widow, granted her quite a large amount of money to found a hospital in Canada. Jeanne Mance was received as a member of the Montreal Company and in 1641 embarked in New Rochelle on a ship owned by Mr. Maisonneuve. Miss Mance played an important rôle in the founding of Montreal, and there established the "Hotel Dieu" (a hospital) where she died in 1673. Her body, which was buried in the church of this hospital, was consumed by flames in a fire a few years later.

COSTUME—A dress of dark wool with a long full skirt. The bodice is somewhat covered by a wide white collar. The sleeves are full and long, ending with white cuffs. She wears a white bonnet covering her hair which is braided and tied in a crown around her head or in ringlets.

PROPS—A small table and chair. A variety of medicine bottles, small carafes of wine and pieces of linen for bandages are on the table.

(As the curtain opens, she is standing behind the table, counting the bottles, bandages, etc.)

Jeanne Mance: Now let's see, Sister de Brésoles told me, "Miss Mance, we need medicine for the dispensary, wine for the sick and bandages for the wounded." Did I forget anything? No, that's right. Now, I will roll these into bandages before I bring them to her.

(Sitting, she starts to roll the bandages, stopping often as she continues with her monologue.)

How quiet everything is today!! If only Mrs. de Bullion who sent me to Canada to open a hospital could see us now, I believe that she would be very happy with her project. The hospital of Ville Marie is finally firmly established...but, how difficult this project was at the beginning. They wanted to keep us in Québec and they blamed Mr. de Maisonneuve for exposing us to the dangers of such a faraway outpost as the Isle of Mont-Réal. To all their objections he replied, "Sirs, it is my duty and my honor to establish a colony at Ville-Marie. I will get there even if every tree I meet along the way turns out to be an Iroquois." Later, I remembered his words during the days of danger when it seemed that there was in fact an Iroquois lurking behind every tree!

(Pause)

Meanwhile, the settling of our people at the base of Mont Royal was concluded without incident. The excellent Mrs. de la Peltrie who accompanied us returned shortly to Québec with her lady in waiting. The first months were quite peaceful.

(Pause)

However, our enemies were watching us!!! Many of our colonists working out in the fields were surprised by Iroquois and put to death. They even succeeded in capturing one of our women, Catherine Mercier. They took her prisoner into their camps, where she died after being tortured mercilessly.

(Pause)

The colonists were then forced to live within the confines of the fort, only going out to the fields in armed groups and always surrounded by guard dogs whom they had brought from France...One of these dogs named Pilot could smell the Iroquois from a fair distance and often ventured into the forest to ensure that the enemy was not lurking there. If the Iroquois were in the neighborhood, Pilot would come running into the fort at full speed, barking loudly, letting us know of the danger menacing us. The garrison would then form a search party with either Mr. Maisonneuve or Major Lambert Closse in charge, each man waving a pistol in each hand.

(Pause)

As the danger increased day by day, I found Mr. de Maisonneuve and told him, "What good is a hospital if the Iroquois go about murdering all the colonists?" I offered him the 20,000 pounds which I had left and suggested that he recruit a regiment for the protection of Ville Marie on his next trip to France.

(Pause)

After a two-year absence, he returned with 100 soldiers, numerous colonists, and an enormous sum of money given to him by Mrs. de Bullion and which we used to fortify the city...At the same time, Miss Bourgeois arrived to take part in the everyday work and tribulations of the colonists. Marguerite Bourgeois dedicated herself to teaching. Having nothing but the dress she was wearing, she put herself to work and succeeded in building the church of Notre Dame de Bonsecours, which also served as a school for her students.

(Pause)

A strong friendship developed between us. Soon, no longer able to continue alone the tasks ahead of us, we returned to France. Marguerite Bourgeois went searching for teachers who would later form her Congregation of Notre Dame. I hoped to return with religious sisters to take care of the sick.

(Pause)

Three nursing sisters returned with me to Ville Marie. In charge was Sister Judith Moreau de Brésoles. Having studied Chemistry and medicine, she had many occasions to exercise her skills, as much for the colonists as for the soldiers and the Hurons, our allies who had been wounded or maimed by the Iroquois. Their war cries often resounded in our ears!... With each alert, Sister de Brésoles and another sister climbed the steeple to sound the alarm and to warn the colonists working in dangerous areas.

(Pause)

During these days of continuous alarms, the women faced danger with extraordinary courage. One of the most courageous was Mrs. Duclos. One winter day, while looking outside, she spotted a cloud of Iroquois attacking a number of unarmed colonists. Mrs. Duclos grabbed an armful of rifles and braving the Iroquois all around her, began to distribute these to the colonists. While she was doing this, the alarm sounded from the steeple of the hospital, bringing with it more reinforcements.

(Pause)

The Iroquois were forever stalking us. They even spent entire nights, hidden in the courtyard of the hospital, beneath our windows, waiting to capture us.

(Pause)

Finally, Dollard des Ormeaux, with sixteen brave colonists, knowing they were going to their death, went down to Long-Sault and there during many days of fighting hundreds of Iroquois, finally died to save us.

(Pause)

Their sublime sacrifice was not in vain, for it inspired a tremendous fear in our enemy. In the forests all around us, we no longer heard the war cries.. Ville Marie no longer feared the Iroquois.

(Pause)

But, in this barbaric land, there are often squirmishes...In our hospital, we have many wounded,...there is always plenty of work for Jeanne Mance.

(Pause)

All right!! The bandages are ready.

(Rising.)

Let's bring this to Sister de Brésoles.

(CURTAIN)

Mrs. de Lalande and Mrs. Jolliet

MRS. DE LALANDE AND MRS. JOLLIET

Québec, Approximately 1692

BIOGRAPHICAL NOTE: Marie Couillard, daughter of Guillaume Couillard, was born in Québec in 1633. Her mother, Guillemette Hébert was the daughter of the first colonist in Québec. Her first marriage was to François Bissot, a rich fur merchant from Québec. After his death, she married Jacques de Lalande. Her daughter, Claire-Françoise Bissot, was born in 1656 and in 1675 wed Louis Jolliet, who discovered the Mississippi River and was a cartographer for the King. Louis Jolliet died in 1700 and his wife died in 1710. Among their descendants are a number of famous individuals, one of whom was the Cardinal Taschereau.

COSTUMES—Both women are wearing dresses made of rich materials such as silk or velour. The mother's dress is a bit more somber; that of the daughter more sophisticated. In general terms, the bodices are fitted, open-necked, following the styles of the day. The skirts are long with large pleats opening onto an underskirt of a contrasting color. Their hair is in curls. (Mrs. de Lalande's hair is either quite gray or white.) One can add a long, full dark colored cape with or without a hood to the costume.

(There are no props. As the curtain opens, they are walking along, quite slowly and talking to each other.)

Mrs. de Lalande: I am very willing to accompany you, dear daughter, wherever your husband's travels take you; but, since we must leave tomorrow for your husband's township of Jolliet, this evening let us stroll along these ramparts...This city of Québec is very dear to me, and I love to gaze upon my grandmother Hébert's old home up there by the fort...Who knows when we will see her again...

Mrs. Jolliet: Hearing you speak like this, Mother, you would think that this new township was in China!

Mrs. de Lalande: It is not that it is so far, but will we be quiet there for a long time? Your husband is quite an adventurer!!! Happily you are well suited to this life! When you married Louis Jolliet you knew what to expect.

Mrs. Jolliet: *(Smiling)* Yes, luckily I have the gifts to meet these challenges.

(More animated)

But, don't I also have the right to be proud of his exploits? To think that he is credited with having discovered the Mississippi River accompanied by Fr. Marquette. Also, was it not my husband who pushed his frail canoe on the somber waters of the Saguenay all the way to Hudson Bay? Often his adventures took him to regions where no white man had yet set foot!

Mrs. de Lalande: And as a reward for these exploits, he was given the Isle of Anticosti, where there is nothing but ice and cod!

Mrs. Jolliet: This land, however, was not to be scorned. For nine years we lived in the fort at Anticosti, and as you know, we were in the midst of making a fortune in fishing when Admiral Phipps and his ships from Boston came to destroy our fort.

Mrs. de Lalande: And as if that wasn't enough, he kept us prisoners while he went on to lay siege to Québec.

Mrs. Jolliet: Do you remember his anger when the officer whom he had sent to seek the surrender returned with these words from Mr. de Frontenac: " Go tell your master that I will answer him through the mouths of my cannons!" Immediately, the batteries opened fire and the first volleys took down Admiral Phipps' flagship. Soon after, a few Canadians jumped in the water and went to retrieve parts of the flagship in spite of heavy fire from the rest of the fleet. As prisoners on the ship, we watched the battle and we were overwhelmed with worry.

Mrs. de Lalande: Finally, after being under attack for many days, the Bostonians gave up the siege. I then asked Admiral Phipps to let us propose an exchange of prisoners to M. de Frontenac. The admiral agreed. And after M. de Frontenac met favorably with our demands, the exchange of prisoners took place the following day. We were free!!! And the enemy ships were raising their anchors!!!

Mrs. Jolliet: And, in joy and happiness, we processed solemnly to the new little church in the Basse-Ville which was later named Notre Dame de la Victoire. Soon afterwards, my husband joined us and he was named a royal guide. After this, he went on to explore the shores of the Gulf of the Saint Lawrence and of Labrador.

Mrs. de Lalande: And he learned that Admiral Phipps' fleet had met with violent storms while at sea and that one of the ships was shipwrecked on the shores of your Isle of Anticosti. On this island, which they had ravaged and which was now deserted, the majority of them died of hunger and thirst. Revenge was ours!!!

Mrs. Jolliet: Quite sweet revenge! But now we will finally be able to establish ourselves. Since my husband has become Lord of Jolliet, his lands will tie him down.

(Smiling with conviction.)

You'll see that we'll be well established on our lands!!!

Mrs. de Lalande: *(Shrugging her shoulders.)*

Ah yes, like birds on a branch...

(CURTAIN)

Madeleine de Verchères

MADELEINE DE VERCHÈRES

Verchères, Québec—1692

BIOGRAPHICAL NOTE: François de Jarret, an officer in de Carignan's regiment, settled in Canada, wed Marie Perrot and became the Lord of Verchères.

The fort of Verchères was a dangerous post, directly on the route traveled by the Iroquois to reach Montreal. They had already laid siege to this fort in 1690, during which Mrs. de Verchères, alone with but a few men, valiantly defended the fort. Her daughter, Madeleine, followed her example when, in 1692, while both Mr. and Mrs. Verchères were away, the Iroquois attacked the fort once again.

History tells us that a few years after her heroic defense of the fort, Madeleine Jarret de Verchères, once again saved a gentleman from the Iroquois. This gentleman, whom she later wed, was Pierre Thomas de Tarieu de la Naudière.

A descendant of Madeleine de Verchères, Lieutenant-Colonel de la Naudière, left Canada as commander of the 22nd Canadian-French regiment. He is presently (1915) stationed at a training camp in Shorncliffe, England and was recently promoted as Commandant of this regiment.

COSTUME—She is wearing a solid colored calf length dress of rough linen. The bodice has a square neck and is laced in the front. Her hair is braided and falls across her back. She is wearing a simple white cap and shoes with flat heels.

(As the curtain rises, Madeleine enters, examining a rifle—preferably an old musket.)

Madeleine de Verchères: I was examining my rifle...Alexandre, as he came in, said to me while laughing..."You dream, Madeleine...There are no more Iroquois..." Hmmm. does my little brother think that we will no longer see any Iroquois at Verchères? Personally, I think that we would do well not to let our rifles rust...

(She pauses, during which time she places her rifle upright on a nearby wall.)

It was not all that long ago that they very nearly massacred us all. My father was in Québec on military business and my mother was visiting in Montreal. Our colonists were working in the fields. Within the walls of the fort, the women and children moved around freely, visiting with one another.

As I went down to the river accompanied by an old servant, I heard a strange noise coming from the fields where the men were working...I told the servant, "Run to the top of the hill, Laviolette, to see what's going on." Soon, the terrified voice of Laviolette yelled to me, "Run! Miss, Run! The Iroquois are coming!!," as I spotted a band of Iroquois who were descending upon me...Fear gave me wings, as I ran toward the fort yelling," To arms! To arms!"

(Pause)

In front of the entrance to the fort, I found two young women who had just witnessed their husbands being killed by the Iroquois. They were running here and there, crazed with fear, their hair blowing in the wind... Ordering them to come into the fort with me, I closed the barriers behind them. Running to the blockhouse, I spotted two of our soldiers, Labonté and Gachet, ready to ignite a keg of powder to destroy the fort and its inhabitants rather than let them fall victim to the Iroquois. Pulling the flaming wick from their hands, I extinguished it with my feet and ordered them to leave.

I was but fourteen years old...my two brothers were even younger. I called to them and said, "Let's fight to the death! Remember that our father often told us that a gentleman is born to shed his blood for God and Country!!!!"

(Pause)

First, replacing my white cap with a man's hat, I armed the small garrison and I had a breach in the fort wall repaired. Then, I had the men fire the fort's only cannon, to warn the men in the fields of the danger. The noise scared the Iroquois, who retreated, but succeeded nonetheless to overcome some of our colonists! We could see the massacre!

(She covers her eyes momentarily.)

The women and children filled the fort with screams and lamentations. I made them understand that they needed to overcome their pain in order to hide from the enemy that we were defenseless.

(Pause)

I then remembered that I was awaiting visitors from Montreal...their canoe was on its way to our fort at Verchères. How was I to let them know of the danger facing them? Since the two soldiers refused to risk their lives by going outside the fort, fortified with courage, I left the fort and went down to the river. The Iroquois, fearing a trap, did not dare put themselves in the face of the cannon .. I returned from the river with a relative, Marguerite and her husband Pierre Fontaine.

(Pause. She then retrieves her rifle.)

At dusk, I told Pierre Fontaine to take the two soldiers and to retire to the most secure part of the fort, also taking with them the women and children. I kept guard with my brothers and Laviolette...the night was glacial...complete with sleet and snow.

(Walking)

The only noise was the sound of our steps and our "Who goes there?" which was answered by the two soldiers patrolling the most secure section of the fort. The Iroquois thought the fort was filled with soldiers!

(Pause)

The long night progressed very slowly. After the dawn came the day, and then it was night once again. Bravely, we guarded the fort. Patiently, the Iroquois waited to attack.

For forty-eight hours I had neither eaten nor slept, staying by the ramparts, watching the Iroquois, or going to the secure place in the fort, encouraging the women and children. But, after these first few days and these first horrible nights, I was able to sleep a little, sitting at a table, my rifle before me with my head resting on it.

(Pause)

On the seventh day, just before dawn, as I was resting so, my little brother Alexandre who was guarding the side of the fort facing the river, thought he could hear the cadence of an oar against the water. "Who goes there?" , he cried. I jumped, and upon rising, ran to the fortifications, not knowing that an alarm had been sounded in Montreal, and fearing more enemies. "Who goes there?," I yelled in return. A voice answered from the river, "We are French! It's de la Monnerie who is coming to your rescue!"

(Pause)

Finally!! My, God!!! Finally! This siege of six days and six nights is finally over!...Finished are my deathly fears and worries!!!

(Pause)

Letting the soldiers guard the front of the fort, I went down to the river. Dawn was breaking on the horizon...The canoes bearing our friends were reaching the shore...Mr. de la Monnerie disembarked first, getting there before me.

(Pause—She salutes.)

Saluting him in a military manner, and standing quite erect in spite of being exhausted and carrying my rifle, which suddenly felt quite heavy, I said, "Sir, I surrender my arms!"

"Miss," he answered," they are in excellent hands!"

(She exits.)

(CURTAIN)

Jeanne Le Ber and Cousin

JEANNE LE BER

Montreal—1662-1714

BIOGRAPHICAL NOTE: Jeanne Le Ber was born in Montréal in 1662. Both of her parents were natives of Rouen, France—in Normandy. She was the goddaughter of Jeanne Mance and was entrusted to Marguerite Bourgeois, then later sent to the Ursulines in Québec, where her aunt, Marie Le Ber was a nun. We are told that the journals of the convent where she lived record many acts of penitence which she inflicted upon herself. A self-proclaimed hermit, she isolated herself first in her father's house, later in the convent of the Sisters of the Congregation. She lived 35 years in absolute isolation, and which is even more remarkable, she did this as a lay person, never taking the vows of any religious congregation. She died in 1714.

COSTUMES—Jeanne Le Ber is clothed in a simple gray dress, quite full, adjusted slightly in the bodice but with the back and sides quite loose. The sleeves are quite wide, and turned over to the elbows revealing a white linen lining. Her hair is covered by a small white square of lace or other fine fabric. On top of this, she is wearing a small black lace mantilla, tied at the neck. Her cousin is wearing a solid colored dress with white cuffs and a white cap.

PROPS—A kneeler, a chair, a book, a crucifix.

(The role of Jeanne Le Ber is a non-speaking role. It is her cousin who speaks for her. As the curtain rises, Jeanne is kneeling on the kneeler which is placed at center stage, towards the rear. Her cousin is sitting to her left , slightly closer to the front and is holding an open book in her lap. She seems to be distracted, and is speaking to herself, opening and closing her book, looking toward Jeanne Le Ber who is kneeling without moving and absorbed in contemplation.)

The Cousin: For fifteen long years, I was my cousin's faithful companion. But now, she very seldom lets me approach her, only when she is too exhausted to serve herself...While she is absorbed in meditation, let us wait for her...

(Pause)

How she has changed!!! She is still beautiful, but her penances have left her frail...It seemed that she was born to live in luxury...She was the daughter of Jacques Le Ber, one of the richest merchants of New France. She was the goddaughter of Jeanne Mance, a student of Marguerite Bourgeois.

(Pause)

While still quite young, she showed a propensity for solitude and silence, and yet she was quite gracious and well-mannered, talking quite easily with a charm and grace which is still being talked about with admiration by those who were privileged to hear her...She scorned the rich toiletries and the fine garments of France, and while she was dining, she was extremely solemn.

(Pause)

She had no sooner left the convent, that she found herself surrounded with an entourage of young people who were among the most brilliant in Montréal. Anxious to see her daughter well established in this country, her parents found her a suitable husband, but Jeanne Le Ber refused to see him and expressed to her parents her desire to live in solitude. After much reflection, they consented to this experience in the hopes that she would soon tire of it and renounce this project.

(Pause)

Jeanne started her life in solitude by locking herself in her room, where during fifteen years, she lived without any communication with her family except by using me as an intermediary. She left the house only to attend daily mass every morning at five. I accompanied her every day.

(Pause)

During Mrs. Le Ber's last illness, Jeanne never once went to her mother's bedside although she loved her mother very much. She also never left her room when they brought her brother, Jean Le Ber, home—mortally wounded in a battle against the English at Laprairie...After he died, Marguerite Bourgeois hurried to assist the family and to offer her sympathies. Suddenly, she whom we called the holy recluse, appeared among the mourners, giving to Miss Bourgeois what was needed to bury him, prayed for a moment before the corpse, and returned once again to her room.

(Pause)

Although she succeeded quite well at living as a recluse in her father's house, she aspired to a life where she would no longer need to leave the house to attend daily mass.

Marguerite Bourgeois and her newly established Congregation of Notre Dame were looking to build a chapel for their convent. Jeanne Le Ber offered to build the chapel at her own expense as long as they could attach an apartment for her where she could spend the rest of her life, close to the tabernacle and the sanctuary lamp.

(Pause)

The project was undertaken...Directly behind the altar an apartment was built which was divided into three small rooms. In the first, she worked, embroidering chasubles and altar cloths for she was quite gifted. In the second room, she had a bed made of straw. Finally, in the third room, separated by a grill from the chapel , she could attend mass without being seen.

(Pause)

Jeanne divided her time between work, meditation and prayer. Each evening, at midnight, she would open the grill and enter the chapel, alone, to pray before the altar.

(Pause)

In a solemn ceremony, she made a vow of perpetual solitude. This sacrifice was quite difficult for Mr. Le Ber; however, he consented and to the end he remained profoundly attached to his daughter. As long as he lived, he took advantage of the privilege which was given to him to visit his daughter twice a year. Although Jeanne did not leave her cloister to help her father at his deathbed, she did attend the funeral mass while seated behind the grill in her room.

(Pause)

Although living quite apart from the world around her, her example nonetheless was felt far and wide...Two Protestant ministers, while passing through Montréal, saw her shadow through the grill, and having heard her story from our beloved bishop, were so impressed that upon their return to New England, one of them renounced his religion to convert to the religion which so inspired Jeanne to her life of sacrifice...It is not in vain that she is called, "...the saint recluse of Montréal."

(CURTAIN)

Madame de la Mothe-Cadillac

MADAME DE LA MOTHE-CADILLAC

New Orleans—1717

BIOGRAPHICAL NOTE: Marie-Thérèse Guyon, daughter of Denis Guyon, a member of the middle class, was born in Québec in 1671. At sixteen years of age, she wed Antoine de la Mothe, Lord of Cadillac, Launay and Montet, a son of a wealthy family of Gascogne, France. In 1694 Mr. de Cadillac was sent to Machillimackinac by Frontenac, as commander and in 1699 became captain of the troops. He established Fort Pontchartrain, in Detroit, in 1710 and was governor of New Orleans from 1713 to 1717. His wife accompanied him on many of his expeditions, and followed him on his return to France where he died in 1718. Of their ten children, we know that Antoine, the eldest joined the Navy as an Ensign. Marie-Thérèse, the fifth child was the first child born and baptized in Detroit.

COSTUME—Mrs. de la Mothe-Cadillac is wearing an opulent dress of fine silk, satin or velour. The bodice is quite fitted. The skirt falls in layers. She is wearing high heels. Her hair in curls, is gathered high on her head. The costume may be completed with the addition of a long and ample cape. There are no props.

Mrs. de la Mothe-Cadillac: The thought of our leaving shortly for France fills me with both joy and sadness. I never dreaded the dangerous and fitful life in the various forts where my husband was posted in this New World—where I was born and where for the past twenty years I have followed my husband who served the King.

First as a Captain in Acadia, then as commandant at Machillimackinac, Mr. de la Mothe-Cadillac then went on to establish the Fort Pontchartrain, in Detroit. It is there where we spent our best years. There were many colonists, and the fort prospered.

Our small manor house, surrounded on all sides by a porch, faced the river on which the canoes and river barges traveled back and forth continuously. We lived peacefully with the Native Americans, who erected their wigwams all around us at the edge of the forest.

Each year, during the summer, the beautiful green grass which surrounded our manor was a backdrop for some delightful scenes.

Within these beautiful groupings, we saw colonists wearing bright blue shirts with fringed deerskin pants and a bright red sash belt from which hung a long hunting knife encased in a silver sheath; soldiers in their blue and white uniforms and officers with gold braids wearing flamboyant hats who in all their finery resembled peacocks.

(Pause)

Proud and happy, I moved about these groups, my husband at my side and accompanied by my son Antoine, a young man of 15. Mr. de Cadillac, would walk up onto the porch, and holding his silver goblet high, proposed a toast to the King followed by responses of "Long Live the King!," and "Long Live Lord Cadillac of Detroit!" followed by a verse sung in unison:

"Great God, Save the King!
Great God, Revenge the King!
Long Live the King!
May always glorious,
Victorious Louis
See his enemies,
Always submissive!
Long Live the King!"

And to this roaring chant, was added the sound of trumpets, the beating of the drums and a volley of artillery fire which echoed over Lake St. Claire.

(Pause)

But, alas, my husband's strong personality created enemies. Forced to go to Montreal to defend himself in long and expensive legal proceedings, he then had to sell his lands and manor house in Detroit in order to pay the legal fees.

He was then named Governor of Louisiana. Our four years in New Orleans were quite tempestuous! The Natchez tribe warred against us and the Spanish from Mexico caused us all sorts of problems.

(Pause)

Finally, our mission in the New World seems complete. Knowing that we contributed to extend the French regime throughout this region consoles me and fills me with a legitimate pride in our accomplishments!

Who knows? In our Castle Sarrazin in Gascogne, we will perhaps enjoy a bit of calm that we did not know in New France.

(Pause)

But always my thoughts, as in previous days did my feet, will follow the banner with the Fleur de Lys...in the forts of Acadia, on the heights of Québec, on the isle of Montreal, on the Great Lakes, the happy fort at Detroit, along the rolling Mississippi, all the way to the Gulf of Mexico... And there, as here, my wishes will unite themselves with the prayers of so many valiant women, and rise to the heavens so that this land known as America will always keep its French mark, like soft wax maintains the seal of the King.

(CURTAIN)

A Franco-American mother, Marie, and Françoise

EPILOGUE

One evening on June 23rd—the eve of the feast of Saint John

NOTE: The scene represents the main room in the home of a well-to-do colonist living on the shores of the St. Lawrence, before the English conquest. The songs, which were chosen, are all still quite popular and quite old. They can be sung in their entirety, or but one or two verses to shorten the scene. The main idea of the Epilogue is to introduce a few mannerisms and costumes of "le Bon Vieux Temps."

COSTUMES—The mother is wearing a simple skirt—soft wool or cotton—with a simple cotton top with long sleeves. She has gray hair, tied back in a bun and covered with a starched white bonnet tied under her chin. The two young girls are wearing dresses of soft wool or cotton, with fitted bodices, tied to the chin. The skirts are gathered, calf length. They are wearing bright colored striped stockings, with low-heeled shoes. Their hair is braided, or hangs loosely curled around their shoulders.

SETS/PROPS—The scene takes place in a large square room. The back wall has one or two shuttered windows. At stage right is a spinning wheel; at stage left, near the wall, a simple long table is covered with a checkered tablecloth. On the table sits two copper candlesticks and a folded quilt placed inside a workbasket. A number of chairs with straw seats are arranged around the room. On the wall is an antique mirror. The set can be altered somewhat, keeping in mind the time frame and locale.

(As the curtain rises, Françoise is sitting in one of the chairs and the mother is walking in the room, holding her knitting. She stops from time to time at the open window all the while singing:)

"A Saint-Malo, beau port de mer
Trois gros navires sont arrivés.
Nous irons sur l'eau,

Nous y prom, promener,
Nous irons jouer dans l'ile..."

Françoise answers with the 2nd verse:

"Trois gros navires sont arrives
Chargés d'avoine, chargés de blé."

(She is interrupted by Marie who enters onto the stage, wearing a large cape with a hood over her dress.)

The Mother: Ah, Finally, there you are...

Françoise: Here you are. What's going on in the village?

Marie: A lot of comings and goings. The carriages are arriving, and standing outside the windows of the church you can hear the choir practicing for tomorrow's Mass.

(She sits. The mother sits in the middle with one girl on either side. One of the girls is spinning while the other is piecing together the squares of a quilt which are three-quarters completed.)

Marie: *(Continuing)*
The pastor sent me to bring a letter to the Lord, and they showed me the holy bread.

Françoise: Oh! Is it beautiful?

Marie: It is brown and golden, and it smells as wonderful as a cake. It is formed into a crown and garlands, and it is as high as this!! The Lady of the manor said that it was the most beautiful holy bread that she has ever offered for the feast of Saint Jean-Baptiste.

Françoise: And who will do the begging during the High Mass?

Marie: The lawyer and his wife, and the doctor's daughter with a gentleman from Québec.

(The sound of bells ringing in the distance is heard.)

The Mother: The Angelus, my children!

Marie and Françoise: Already!

(They rise, and remain standing in silence for a minute, heads bent, then sit down again.)

The Mother: Our guests will be arriving shortly. Is everything ready for them Françoise?

Françoise: Yes, the food is ready and the soup is warming.

Marie: *(Humming, teasingly)*

C'est la belle Françoise, lon gai
C'est la belle Françoise
Qui veut se marier, ma luron lurette,
Qui veut se marier, ma luron luré!"

Françoise: *(Answering)*

"Marianne, s'en va-t-au moulin,
C'est pour y faire moudre son grain,
A cheval sur son âne,
Ma p'tit mamzell' Marianne,
A cheval sur son âne Catin
S'en allant au moulin"

The Mother: Enough, enough, no more teasing!

Marie: Where are Antoine and Pierre?

The Mother: All the men went to the woods to cut pine and cedar branches for the bonfire that will be lit in the village later.

Marie: Oh! I forgot—The fire for the St. Jean celebration.

Françoise: It is quite entertaining and quite nice, these fires that we light in each village on both sides of the river...But why do we light fires for this feast day?

The Mother: It is a tradition that we took with us from Normandy.

Françoise: From the old country? France must be beautiful...How sad that we are no longer there!

The Mother: But, my daughter, we are there yet! Look around you... France is wherever there are French people!!!!

(In the distance there is the sound of many voices singing "A la Claire Fontaine." The mother and daughters leave their work and run to the window(s). There they stay as the voices get closer and closer. After two or three verses of "Claire Fontaine" the curtain falls.)

THE END

PRINCIPAL WORKS CONSULTED [AS LISTED IN THE ORIGINAL, SEE ADDITIONAL INFORMATION BELOW]:

Histoires du Canada, Garneau.
Histoires du Canada, Ferland.
Dictionnaire Généalogique des Familles Canadiennes, Tanguay.
Œuvres de Francis Parkman.
Relations des Jésuites.
Vie de Mlle Mance, Publiée par les Religieuses de l'Hôtel-Dieu.
History of North America, University Edition.
Louisiana Under French Rule.
The French in the Heart of America, John Finley.
Legends of Le Détroit, Hamlin.
Maids and Matrons of New France.
Le Costome Historique, Racinet.
Encyclopedia of Costume, Planché.
L'Oublié, Laure Conan.
Articles et brochures sur l'Acadie, publiés par l'abbé Azarie Couillard-Després, de la Société Royale du Canada.
Ainsi que différentes brochures publiées par Georges Montorgueil, l'abbé Albert Dion, la Commission des Champs de Bataille Nationaux, etc., etc.

Histoires du Canada, Garneau.
Garneau, F.-X. (François-Xavier), 1809-1866
Histoire du Canada
Publisher Paris : F. Alcan, 1913-1920
Edition 5. éd., rev. / annotée et pub. avec une introduction et des appendices par son petit-fils, Hector Garneau ; préface de M. Gabriel Honotaux

Histoires du Canada, Ferland.
Ferland, Jean Baptiste Antoine, 1805-1865
Cours d'histoire du Canada

Publisher Québec, A. Coté, 1861-65

Dictionnaire Généalogique des Familles Canadiennes, l'abbé Cyprien Tanguay.
http://www4.bnquebec.ca/numtxt/tanguay.htm

Œuvres de Francis Parkman.
The separate volumes, and the dates of first publication, are:
Pioneers of France in the New World (1865)
The Jesuits in North America in the 17th Century (1867)
The Discovery of the Great West (1869)
The Old Regime in Canada (1874)
Count Frontenac and New France under Louis XIV (1877)
Montcalm and Wolfe (1884)
A Half-Century of Conflict (1892)
http://www.gutenberg.org/browse/authors/p#a510

Relations des Jésuites.
http://www.collectionscanada.ca/relations-des-jesuites/index-f.html
http://www.collectionscanada.ca/jesuit-relations/index-e.html

Vie de Mlle Mance, Publiée par les Religieuses de l'Hôtel-Dieu.

Vie de Mlle Mance et histoire de l'Hôtel-Dieu de Villemarie dans l'île de Montréal, en Canada, Villemarie : chez les soeurs de l'Hôtel-Dieu de Villemarie, 1854.

History of North America, University Edition. No other reference found.

Louisiana Under French Rule.

Wallace, Joseph, History of Illinois and Louisiana under French rule, etc. Cincinnati, 1893.

The French in the Heart of America, John Finley.
STATE EDUCATION BUILDING, ALBANY, N. Y.
Washington's Birthday, 1915.
http://www.gutenberg.org/etext/7147

Legends of Le Détroit, Hamlin.

Legends of Le Detroit, Marie Caroline Watson Hamlin; Illustrated by Miss Isabella Stewart, Detroit; Thorndike Nourse, 1884.

Maids and Matrons of New France.

Maids and Matrons of New France, de Mary Sifton Pepper. Toronto : George N. Morgan & Co. Limited, 1902.

Le Costome Historique, Racinet.

Auguste Racinet, *The Complete Costume History*

Tétart-Vittu, Françoise / Haslam & Whiteway Ltd, 1876 and 1888.

About 120 illustrations from Racinet's *Le Costume Historique* are posted among the NYPL 'Picture Collection Online'.

http://digital.nypl.org/mmpco/browseSTresults.cfm?trg=1&sourceid=301

Encyclopedia of Costume, Planché.

An Illustrated Dictionary of Historic Costume

James R. Planché, Dover Publications, Mineola, NY.

ISBN: 0486423239

Unabridged republication of *A Cyclopaedia of Costume or Dictionary of Dress,* originally published by Chatto and Windus, London, 1876.

L'Oublié, Laure Conan.

(Marie-Louise-) Félicité ANGERS {CA} (F: 1845 - 1924 Jun 7)

(&ps: Laure CONAN) L'Oublie [Fr-1900].

Articles et brochures sur l'Acadie, publiés par l'abbé Azarie Couillard-Després, de la Société Royale du Canada.

Couillard- Després, Azarie,_"Histoire des seigneurs de la Rivière du Sud et de leurs alliés canadiens et acadiens," Saint-Hyacinthe, [Que.] : Impr. de *La Tribune,* 1912.

La première famille française au Canada, ses alliés et ses descendants, Corp Couillard Després, Azarie (1876-). Publication: Montréal, Imp. de l'École catholique des sourds-muets, 1906.

Le parchemin, Corp Association l'Espinay, Couillard, Després (alliés). Publication: Montréal : L'Association, 2001.

Ainsi que différentes brochures publiées par Georges Montorgueil, l'abbé Albert Dion, la Commission des Champs de Bataille Nationaux,

LIST OF ILLUSTRATIONS

by Miss Albani Rocheleau

Illustrations appear before each segment of the play.

French Women of North America

Dear Ms. Robbins,

It is with pleasure that I give permission for the reprints of the sketches that appear in the book *Françaises d'Amérique* as drawn by my mother, Albani Rocheleau-Brodeur. I wish you success in the endeavor.— Madeleine Brodeur Westerback

THE YOUNG FRANCO-AMERICAN

By Alberte Gastonguay, (1906-1978)
Translation by Madeleine C. Paré Roy

To you, beloved parents, who are no longer with me, with my affectionate remembrance, the first work of my hands.—1931

THE BEGINNING

For a long time now the very soul of Mr. Carignan had been preoccupied. The land that his ancestors had sown with their labor and their love was very dear to him. During those evenings spent gathered by the fire as the wind shook the hundred year old maple trees, the Carignans chatted about the United States, that country streaming with gold. Peter's son had already left, and when his letters arrived, Peter seemed happy and satisfied. Carignan wanted to tempt his own fate. After deliberating the possibility for a long time, the day came when they packed their belongings and the family made their way to the then nearly uninhabited town of Lewiston, Maine. There already were a few American families who held the high ground of the town, such as the Garcelons, the Grays and the McCarthys, those proud descendants of the early Colonists. The Carignans built their home near the Androscoggin River, whose waters even today flow into what is called the 'canal' and are essential for the functioning and productivity of the mills. It was a very modest house. Since they had no electricity, candles and later on lamps provided a great service. The father and mother based their happiness not in material goods, but rather in watching their many children, who were close in age, grow up. They worked the farm and loved their adopted country.

A few weeks went by when other families originating from 'la Beauce' came to join the Carignans. They were the Casavants, the Marcottes, the Paradis and the Joncas. They formed the first nucleus of French-Canadians in Lewiston. They spoke their native tongue and even today, many members of the older generation don't speak a word of English. This small core of Canadians evolved, were faithful to their language and their principles, so much so, that the land they trudged since their arrival has traditionally become known as 'le Petit Canada,' 'Little Canada'.

After a hard day's work, in the evening after the chores were done, families gathered to talk about the land they had left behind; the progress that their present life afforded them and their ambitions for the future. Sitting together around the wooden table where many generations before them had gathered, they enjoyed a glass of wine or beer that had been brought from their homeland with great care. And, to complete the evening, they sang the sweet songs of their motherland together. A final echo resounded with a decrescendo accentuating the last words of the popular song, "*O Canada.*" It was only after the family gathered to recite the evening prayers, a custom that even in 1932, still prevailed in a large number of Franco-American families did they retire for the night. The mother then blew out the lamp and the angel of sleep hovered in the shadow of the night. The following day, they resumed their labors and time passed. There had also been a few families of Garcelons who descended directly from France, but within one generation of mingling with the English-speaking Colonists, they had lost the characteristics of their nationality.

Carignan's oldest daughter was named Eulalie. She had her father's dark complexion and proud demeanor and her mother's keen mind and alert spirit. She was sixteen, it was time to think about marriage for her. For a while now, Jean, the son of Antoine, had been Eulalie's beloved. Under the vigilant supervision of her parents the courtship was carried out and in the spring of the following year, a wedding was celebrated. Glasses were raised against each other in a toast and everyone was in good spirit, while the bride, beautiful under her lacy veil and puffed up sleeves, fluctuated between laughing and crying. A pink blush colored her youthful cheek and her eyelids lowered over her beautiful eyes when someone begged her to sing her favorite song. The festivities lasted all day. It was a day of uninterrupted laughter, with no worries and preoccupations. The following day, everyone resumed their work and the couple's new life began, for in those days, honeymoons were unheard of.

Jean, Antoine's son was an ambitious man blessed with practical qualities. The first years of their marriage were spent in virtually perfect happiness. After a few prosperous years, Jean became a merchant. Later, when his employer had died, he purchased the business and worked with even more diligence. He was loved by the public in general. Many were the Canadians who had left their country to establish themselves in the United States; so much so, that the majority of the population to this day is Canadian. The young couple thought it would be good to mingle and to catch a glimpse of the American spirit and often mused about this. In the evening, when Jean returned home tired but completely content, he would relate his concerns of the day to his faithful wife as their two hearts beat as one, and in the shadow one could see two heads leaning over the side of a crib, because their union had been blessed, and baby Jeanne had been entrusted to their devoted care. What wonderful dreams surrounded that little bed. They would teach the child to know God, to remember her forefathers, to respect authority, to sing the sweet songs of the motherland, to let her heart vibrate at the memory of the Canadian blood that flowed through her young veins.

The adoptive land progressed; commerce prospered. The Canadians rendered themselves indispensable. Courageous, diplomatic, they managed to obtain public positions and showed themselves worthy of them. Jean, due to his loyalty and his know-how gained the esteem of his fellow countrymen. One clear spring morning, our young man announced to his friends his candidacy for mayor. One had to fight against the hostile elements. Would his friends support him? Need he not be concerned about a bit of jealousy and envy on their part? The big day was here and somewhat worried, Jean counted the hours. That night, as dusk approached, in the mist of joyous acclamations, he learned that he had been named mayor of the town. The Canadians were in the limelight and one of their own occupied one of the town's most important offices. At that time, Lewiston consisted of 32,000 inhabitants.

By an ill-fated stroke of luck, one that doesn't want happiness to be perfect, the grim reaper was prowling around the happy home. It was spring, the season when nature smiles and clothes itself with greenery; when the blond strands of new wheat sway to the symphony of sounds created by the cold North winds. Unexpectedly, the roguish wind caressed Eulalie's shoulder with its deadly breath. A few days later, tears were shed in the happy home over the loss of the one who thus far had been its soul and support. It was the first stone to crumble from the structure... how many more would crumble in the future?

JEAN

Jean, now alone with his daughter shook off the grief that overtook him, by immersing himself completely in his business. Public life monopolized his time and he willingly allowed it to. He'd return home in the evening just in time to say a few words to the child that was doubly dear to him since his delicate wife's death. Jeanne, already a young lady attended High School. She was fifteen.

She had inherited her mother's fine spirit, filled with goodness and integrity. Her open-mindedness and seriousness derived from the Latin blood that flowed in her veins. Born on American soil, she had grown up with a certain freedom and despite her flightiness and inattention to social conventions, there was an air of unadulterated pride about her. Jeanne had a lively and active friendship with young men, enjoyed her studies, and was especially fond of sports, for which she had a passionate affection. Her father, who nevertheless loved her dearly, would sometimes express his surprise at the way she got carried away. Surely, he thought to himself, she would become more serious as she matured and in the light rings that are shaped by smoke, he once again saw the beloved wife that Jeanne reminded him of, and so his memories of her passed before him as if in a hazy dream.

Our young Franco-American, returned from a stroll, made her way to her father whom she charmed with a caress. This caused him to forget for a moment the many worries that were consuming him. Sitting at his desk, he saw his childhood days pass before his clouded eyes; he saw the days when he was courting Eulalie, and the era in which his beloved daughter was living. The world had changed, he mused, and maybe his daughter, whom he found to be somewhat volatile, was not completely to blame. His mind wandered and wondered...would his child, through her exposure to foreign nationalities, lose the distinctive charm of the race of her forefathers? He was proud to be of the French race, to be able to tell his Canadian brothers that he was doing his part to preserve the maternal language and that he had succeeded in climbing the political ladder in a land that wasn't his. He was respected everywhere; his name was proclaimed from every mouth, and back home on his native soil, people loved to mention his name. Would his daughter keep the mentality of her ancestors or would her integrated and cosmopolitan education transform her to the point where she would forget her ancestors and their noble deeds? Such were Jean's thoughts on this November evening when the rain battered the windows of his apartment.

II

The hall of the amphitheater was artistically decorated in celebration of the triumphs of the youthful students. All their young, happy faces radiated life and the future. Jeanne was ravishing in her ball gown, her arm leaning on that of her strong and vigorous father's. Jean was happy and smiled at everyone. The President of the University had expressed words of high praise for Jeanne as he eulogized the graduates.

At the start of the opening ceremony, a religious service had been held in the college chapel. The young girl had been there often, but tonight, the songs took a new meaning. Besides the enthusiastic lyrics that she usually sang with so much fervor, what surfaced for her were the soothing songs that her Canadian mother used to sing and the breeze gaily carried throughout the house. That memory was short lived. Once the President recited the prayer, the graduates exited from the chapel and made their way towards the amphitheater.

During her years at the University, Jeanne had formed a bond of friendship with a young American named Carl. He was upright, from an honest family, and he loved the young girl very much. She was his first love. His ambition was to become a chemist, to get married and to live happily. His parents were Presbyterians. His father, a descendant of the first Pilgrims, was a broad-minded man who had given his son full freedom in regards to religious matters, and the son had not chosen any religion. His mother's opinion in this matter was not even considered. Carl grew up.

Since their first encounter one night at a dance, their young hearts had been smitten. It was in September when the moon flirts with the tips of pine trees and spreads her golden robe on the neighbor's rooftop, whispering so low that one can barely hear the murmur of the leaves answering. And love, slipping in on the half-closed roses, came and agitated their young hearts. Thereafter, people often saw them together and it was good to see them resplendent with youth. Sporting events found them together, and when the holidays came, Jeanne invited Carl to her home. Her father protested somewhat, but eventually gave in and welcomed the young man. The trusting father was completely unaware of the drama that was unfolding. Jeanne had explained to her father that she and Carl were just good friends, that it was simply the college atmosphere that was conducive to this type of friendship, and that this was the way things went between young men and women. The father had faith in his only daughter.

One night, all three were found together once again after the graduation ceremony. In a lively bound, Jeanne left her companions and quickly was at her father's side. Looking at him straight in the face, she tells him: "Since you love me very much, listen to what I'm about to tell you. In three days, it will be my birthday and on that day I'll become engaged to the one that I have chosen for a husband, for I love him with all my heart." At these words, the father grew pale, the lights lost their glow, his hands trembled, he was thunderstruck. His Franco-Canadian blood boiled within him. He was tempted to annihilate this stranger with no particular religion, who was coming to take away the beloved daughter that he worshiped. No, no, none of this would happen. Reflecting, he knew that Jeanne was independent, capable of resisting all opposition. And he, her father, had blindly welcomed this young man in to his home; the door to his home had always been open to him and he had never given any thought to the consequences. What to do now? His daughter would not bear a Canadian name such as his. In the presence of people of his race, he would swear that he didn't have a daughter. And on this child so many wonderful dreams had been based. Gently he would remind her of her mother's name, of her God, for though Jeanne did not give the appearance of being pious, he believed she was. His thoughts were jumbled, none of them offering any solution. With a grief stricken face and a broken spirit, the father stared at his daughter for a long time without saying a word. "Well father," said Jeanne, "Don't you share my happiness and aren't I giving you the son of one of our most noble American families as a son? Just the other night, you were saying that your right hand man was really Mr. Smith, Carl's father. He'll help you even more now that his son will become your son-in-law." But her father, with a deep frown in his brow, did not answer.

Near the two of them stood Carl, observing the two's body language without understanding any of it.

"Let's dance, my dear," said the young male voice.

"Yes, let's dance, let's dance until we're dizzy," answered Jeanne.

"What's wrong with your father? He's all-sad when he should be thrilled at seeing your successful accomplishments. You're now ready to become a business person, and most of all my darling, you will be the most beautiful of all fiancées."

Jeanne smiled and scrutinized the look on Carl's face. Well before the last dying chords of the orchestra echoed, Jean, son of Antoine, was sitting at his desk, his head in his hand, immobilized, searching the recesses of his ingenious mind, without finding an answer that resolves, an answer that calms.

A light breeze floated through the air that had suddenly become cool. Carl wrapped Jeanne with his cloak and held her pressed against himself. These last words were heard "See you soon my adorable Jeanne." Holding her in his arms, the future fiancée placed a kiss on her flushed lips.

Two strokes rang out on the grandfather clock. In the wink of an eye, Jeanne was at the top of the stairs. A few minutes later, through the door that was ajar, against the pale wall, could be seen the silhouette of the young girl kneeling by her bed in the silence of the night.

THE AWAKENING

The wind fluttered with gentle wings in the folds of the pink curtains while the sun's warm rays played in the young girl's room. The night had been troublesome, a restless sleep and an overactive imagination had somewhat shaken the young girl's nerves.

Her eyelids opened lazily. She felt happy but something in the air seemed to warn her that this happiness could not last. Carl was the object of her dreams, she appreciated his kind heart and his love assured her of a most wonderful existence. Together, they had put together so many wonderful plans; life is so beautiful when one is in love. Hugging the soft pillow, she closed her large eyes and sleep overtook her.

She was then transported to a scene in a theater. There she saw a young couple whose happiness was to be envied. They were happy. All of a sudden, the scene changed. At the foot of a small bed, the young woman was crying. In a corner of a room, the father stood staring without saying a word. The young woman mumbled prayers asking the God of her youth for the balm of consolation. In her agony, she threw an anguished glance towards the husband who could not unite his prayers to hers. They were at a turning point in their life's path and they could not relate to one another. In the heart of the distressed young mother, the anguish was immense, her very soul was suffering. The curtain fell. The nine strokes that rang from the old clock awoke Jeanne. Still emotional and confused over the image in the dream, she gazed with joy at the flowers that gracefully bent their heads towards her, greeting her with Carl's love. No, she loved Carl and Carl adored her. Her father would consent to her marriage...had he ever refused her anything? Happily she got up and went down to her father's office. She straightened out his papers, took care of the most pressing correspondence, looked at magazines, entertained her father with her girlish and teasing ways, who in one kiss forgot the concerns of the previous evening. Then, adjusting her beret and having put a rose in her lapel, she cheerily said: "Good morning father dear. Carl is waiting for me and we're both leaving for the country in his new Nash. It's the latest model to come out. Come see it." In a whirlwind she was outdoors and Jean, looking at the car that glistened under the sun's rays thought: "When we were young, we didn't think of leaving by ourselves like this, but today, it's the style and Jeanne is so lovely, it's no wonder she causes such a furor. She is of Canadian blood despite her little American airs. Ah! She's the true picture of her mother." Jean rubbed his hands as he smoked his pipe. He threw a last glance at the young travelers and heard only the loud, majestic roar of the machine in the morning's pure air.

The country on that day was delightful; the warm breeze that sweetened the ripened wheat was an invitation to love. As they rode along, Jeanne kept close to Carl, snuggled against his shoulder, their gentle warmth mingled while he once again babbled sweet nothings; French words babbled from the beloved lips, letting their joyful youth throw to the wind a defiance that sustained the strength and the health of their young bodies. Under a linden tree the young lovers intertwined. In a short while, they would live only for one another. They spoke about preparations. Jeanne expressed to her lover that their union would be blessed by the priest, a friend of her father's. Carl, in turn declared that a minister would be more than happy to unite them. A light cloud obscured their beautiful blue sky and disturbed the pure harmony of this summer afternoon. "Carl dear," she said, "you love me very much, surely you would not refuse me. We will marry before the priest. Besides, that would be my father's advice." And, headstrong, she caressed him.

"My minister would marry us just as well, my darling Jeanne."

At these words, the young Franco-American felt her heart tear to pieces. The blood of many generations, the blood of the proud heroes who died for their faith stirred within her bosom. Looking intently in the face of the one who was before her, she said: "No, we are already starting to disagree with each other. The faith of my forefathers has awakened just in time. We don't have the same beliefs. The two of us will make our way in life, we will be friends and we will remember the happy days." She suppressed the other words that came to her mind." "You will meet the companion that suits you, and I, I'll follow my destiny." In a loud voice she said: "Goodbye and good luck, Carl." Jeanne disappeared leaving the young man dumfounded. The pebbles along the route gathered the tears of the wounded swallow. Step by step, one by one, she dropped the pearls of her youthful love, weary and suffering in her passionate soul. From above, her ancestors must have smiled to see how the grandeur and honor of their blood caused the emancipated and modern young girl's brow to redden, yet, how strong and filled with grace and beauty she was.

That night when Jean returned home, he found Jeanne at work. Her livid face alone revealed her pain though it was shaded by the pale glimmer of the amber light.

A NEW PAGE

Twelve strokes resounded from the old bronze clock. Jeanne got up, donned her velvet beret and went out. At the bottom of the oak stairway was her employer. For several months now, Jeanne, confused, disturbed, sick at heart, had found refuge in her work and that's how she had come one warm afternoon in June, to ask for a job from attorney Flaherty. After an intense exam, he hired her. In Jeanne's country, work was highly considered among the young women and many pursued it as a healthy distraction, while others attained the desired goal of their ambition. Besides, Jeanne was an excellent secretary. Her work was without reproach, and voluntarily she overlooked her employer's obstinacy, would brush off his coat, would never let the thermometer rise above the degree desired by the master, she would keep his desk in order; in short, she did her best to be liked, and the attorney did like her.

"Wait for me Jeanne, I'll drive you home."

Nimbly, Jeanne jumped into the car as it started running. Many times already he had gone out of his way to accommodate her, his advances were frequently repeated, until eventually Jeanne became fond of this devoted companion Flaherty who had a wife and child. How passion intoxicates!

One night Jean did not return home. The hours rang mournfully across the somber atmosphere that surrounded the young Jeanne. Without a doubt, her beloved father would not be much longer before coming home. Some urgent business must be keeping him. What to think! Suddenly, footsteps resounded on the damp pavement. It was him. The man entered looking upset and without saying a word. The frail, courageous girl stood near him. He looked at her for a long time, then two tears streamed down the cheeks of the dejected man. A dead silence reigned, only Jean's breathing could be heard. His hand fell heavily onto the mahogany table. Somehow, he had to talk. So, looking at his beloved child, panting in_monosyllables the father related that he had lost everything. That due to dishonest transactions he had in the interval of twenty-four hours became a poor man. They had mocked him, his franchise, his credibility, and today every thing was handed into strange hands, leaving him alone and poor. They would come in a few days to seize his goods, practically taking his heart and soul, for what he owned, he had earned himself and at such a price. Could he at this cruel moment rely on material help from his daughter, at least on her filial affection? The man wept.

Jeanne had listened to her father's moving account without making the least movement. When he was done, she took his head in her hands and gave it a long kiss. She was ready to face life's struggles and she was not afraid to work. Had she not found a job willingly and without any obligation to do so? She would keep on working and this time, it would be her turn to spoil her broken and burdened father a bit. She would make his life so pleasant that her presence would be indispensable. She would surround him with all her warm affection.

A struggle arose in her soul. Had she not recognized feelings of love for her employer, who was a husband and father, and in her soul had told herself, "I will leave my position. I'll go somewhere else to look for work." But, today, now that she knew that they were poor and that surely her salary was necessary, could she quit her position? After all, it was not easy to find work. Would she be strong enough to triumph over the struggle, because if her frivolous ways had occasionally compromised her, in the depth of her soul, integrity and sincerity still vibrated. It is difficult when one loves not to give in, and Jeanne knew this. Would she have to mask her feelings and keep her distance from the man with whom she was smitten? Would she reveal her painful situation to her father? Would she return to Carl to let him know of her distress and misfortune? These were the many questions that troubled Jeanne and caused her anxiety and restlessness. Each day brought its pain and one would see her at night after work caressing her father's brow where a few silver strands now adorned his temples, with her gentle hand, warmed up by her generous nature.

It was therefore the ultimate tête-à-tête, when there are no secrets, when one can confide with no afterthought and the air itself echoed the delightful sounds produced by words of consolation and sympathy. It was always late into the night when they separated. For one, the day had been painful, for the other it was filled with struggle.

At work one day, Jeanne learned that her employer was asking the courts for a divorce. Things were becoming more complicated. For a few days now the attorney was worried but had said nothing. One night when he was getting ready to leave, he came to sit near the young girl and said: "Soon I'll offer you a much more advantageous position." With these words he left, leaving Jeanne to ponder this riddle.

FLAHERTY

Born in Louisiana, Flaherty had come to visit Maine with his sick father. The father, a politician and diplomat, had lost his immense fortune. His wife had died when his son had reached the age of ten. Since then, the child had followed his father in his diplomatic pursuits and had received his most recent degree from Harvard College. He was therefore very much in demand. Blessed with a splendid physique, enjoying an intellect open to all the arts, alert and accomplished, he was loved capriciously and often. Already he had broken many hearts. More than one college girl had fallen for his charms, until one night at a ball, he met a charming young girl, the only child of a rich banker. Madeleine was so smitten with the prince charming that a year later she married Flaherty. Beautiful, likeable, rich and very intelligent, she could have made a man who would have loved her for the sake of love very happy. But that was not the case. Flaherty especially loved money. He loved greatness and wealth. The first months of their marriage flowed smoothly. There were no children to strengthen the material bonds, so, slowly the two spouses drifted apart. And behold, now large clouds loomed over the horizon. They would burst soon.

One night, Flaherty returned home and found his wife sitting in her boudoir. After exchanging the usual greetings, he arose and announced to her in a brusque voice that he would not be home for dinner. He went to the Club to rejoin his friends. His wife said not a word, but she turned as white as a ghost. He had offered this excuse many times already and she suffered from his abandonment, for she loved him so very much. Little by little he smothered the fire of love and soon there would be nothing left but smoke. In a heated moment, she got dressed and went out. Her legs trembled as she tread the cobbled sidewalk. The wind lashed at her pale face. Her brisk steps led her to the judge of the Superior Courts, an intimate friend of her father. The judge received her and the session lasted for three hours. A full moon followed her as she returned home. Perhaps it reproached her haste, suspended above her blond head, a silent witness to her nocturnal excursion. But its wrinkled face did not seem astonished, it had witnessed many others. Its years of existence gave it the right to be blasé.

The young women went up to her room. Her husband arrived late into the night. Only the wind playing in the curtains broke the silence. At the dinner the next day, they saw each other again. A sealed letter, folded in three, lay under the porcelain plate in front of which sat Flaherty. It was the legal action furnished by the judge the night before during Madeleine's unexpected visit. Their separation was then underway. This time it was decisive from both one and the other. Dinner was silent and it was that night that Flaherty had told Jeanne at the office, "Soon, I'll offer you a more advantageous position."

He left alone for the route that outlines the lake. His steel blue eyes were almost black. His pride bristled against the one who had dared defy his will. Today, she was removing herself from his domination, asking the law to justify her cause. Now, the law would follow its course and Flaherty would be dragged before the tribunals. Nevertheless, he would regain his original freedom. And so, the scene changed. Jeanne appeared to him to be so gentle, so beautiful, so attractive. And, he was not someone to reject and he knew it very well. He'd know how to conquer her. She was young and she needed her employment. He'd be obliging, attentive, and in a few weeks, her heart would be subdued. A new perspective offered itself. How long had he been meditating? He looked at the time, it was eleven o'clock. One could not hear anything but the waves of the agitated lake as they crashed on the silvery rocks. The city lights brought him back to his senses. He entered the Club where his friends greeted him with their half full glasses.

AT THE COUNTRY CLUB

For many days now the heat had been intense. Today, the air was limited and rendered the body less active. Leaning on the side of the desk, Jeanne, staring straight ahead, was thinking pleasant thoughts when Flaherty, entering quietly placed his hand on her shoulder. The young girl shuddered and blushed.

"You were far away," said Flaherty "Would I be indiscrete if I asked you what you were thinking about?" Jeanne did not answer but looked straight at him.

"Tonight," he said, "at the Country Club, there is the famous golf tournament between Boston and Portland. Would you do me the honor of accompanying me?" After a short reflection, Jeanne answered with a smile.

In approaching the Villa, Jeanne saw the large crowd that had already gathered. For this event, the master decorator had surpassed himself, for from every angle one admired the play of lights that gave the Villa the aspect of a lordly house. A red light reflected its glow on Jeanne's gilded brown hair. Her eyes seemed larger than usual and her slightly flushed cheeks made her the living portrait of the woman poets dream of. Flaherty only had eyes for her, so much so that he almost forgot why he had come. Regaining his self-composure, he gave a meticulous explanation of the comings and the goings of the tenacious players. The crowd was in a frenzy as they were at the last stage of the game. Portland came out victorious and the cheering of the crowd was overwhelming. Eagerly, Flaherty seized Jeanne by the arm and led her away from the crowd towards the Villa, that Villa that would have caused envy among wealthy lords. Because it was built amid the pine trees, resting in discreet shadows, the warmth of its intimacy invited hearts to love. So it was that on this warm September evening two souls with little in common broke loose from the intoxicating crowd and walked alone in the narrow path that led to the open fields. Only the stars in the sky whispered. Flaherty wrapped his arm around Jeanne's slender waist and together they strolled for a long time without speaking under the discreet gaze of the sparkling canopy.

At a detour on the path, Flaherty's sedate voice filled the air and Jeanne listened. He was saying: "Your religion, Jeanne, does it forbid a young girl to join her life with a divorced man?" Because Jeanne sometimes spoke to him about religion.

"Yes," answered the young girl.

"Then your religion is not one of love?"

"Our religion doesn't forbid us to love, but it doesn't allow divorce."

"Aren't you free to organize your life in a way that seems best for you?"

"At birth, we received principles of law that we must follow until death. The home is founded on solid basics that no human being can alter."

Flaherty remained quiet. He couldn't understand Jeanne's mentality. For him, every living being was free and his behavior did not depend on any authority, but deep down he admired the young Franco-American who was able to talk about her religion and to stand behind it against multiple attacks from one of a different race. Since he would not be able to conquer her with the strength of his reasoning, he would attempt to conquer her with love. Coming nearer to her he said: "Let's forget all worry on this calm night; all sorrow, all laws, and give our hearts up to love. I love you Jeanne and I have always loved you. I am free and I offer you my life. Let's travel the path on rose petals whose perfume will intoxicate us till the very last day." He attempted to kiss her. The young girl got up and briskly took a few steps away from him. Her soul had been captured it is true. Not trusting herself she ran into the night. When she came near the well, she stopped. Something very painful and indefinable tugged at her heart. The principles of uprightness instilled in her since her youth tormented her mind. The spirit struggled with the flesh, and the spirit came out the victor. She came back towards Flaherty who stiffened and looked at her without saying a word. Both re-entered the Villa where the many joy-filled dancers twirled on the waxed floor. They joined the others and mingled with the crowd. Portland celebrated its magnificent triumph and you could see the cars of jolly fellows file by one after the other. Two o'clock rang out when Flaherty returned home. Returning from the Club, neither he nor Jeanne made any allusion to what had transpired a few hours earlier. Jeanne had appeared gracious. She laughed readily and as she left him, she smiled a big smile as she said: "See you tomorrow." Flaherty didn't expect such a difficult struggle. Tonight he was defeated, but tomorrow he would be in charge again and this time, Jeanne would give in. After all, she had whims that he would soon make her forget. She was still a child, impressionable, who had kept all her candor, but he would know how to make her listen to reason regarding her childish ways and show her life from a new angle. In his heart he told himself, I love her and she will be mine.

The smoke from his cigarette rose up in spirals tracing the name of his beloved in the air. The future was promising and since he had not been able to find happiness with Madeleine, well, he would ask another for his share of joy and pleasure. Don't we create our own happiness, he thought to himself. It was with this thought in mind that Flaherty fell asleep. The night was warm, the wind made an almost noiseless noise in the leaves; the perfume of roses wafted mysteriously; all of nature was at rest.

The following day when Jeanne returned to work, she found a bouquet of roses on her desk. She loved flowers, especially roses. Flaherty knew what made her happy, but the courageous girl did not want to completely reveal her joy for fear of attracting even more the one that hereafter she must separate from her heart and her life. In the morning's mail, one letter was addressed to her. She opened it and read with great surprise and a deep happiness that an intimate friend was soon to arrive as secretary to the President the Commercial Bank. She was due to arrive that very evening and Jeanne would go to meet her. Now, she would not be alone anymore and her soul thrilled with joy. She could see her now, tall, chestnut brown hair and very attractive, with lively blue eyes. She had known her in college and after her studies were terminated, she had moved to another city to pursue her private studies. And today, after a five-year absence, they would be reunited once again. They would chat with open hearts, and Jacqueline, whom she loved and cherished so much, would pour her soul out into hers. During this charming daydream, Flaherty entered and drew Jeanne from her pleasant reverie. He smiled as he saw the open letter on the desk. Without a doubt a letter from an admirer, he thought. However, as he wasn't sure, he said: "You were lovely, so wrapped up in that cloud of thought. Could I ask who is the principal object that is the cause of your happiness?" Overcome with joy, Jeanne declared that her favorite friend had just been hired as secretary of Commercial Bank and would be there in a few days. That night Jeanne left work earlier than usual. Making her way, she remembered that Flaherty had made no reference to the previous evening. Would he by any chance abandon his quest? Facing Jeanne's sincerity, had he understood that it was futile to pursue the battle? Or, was he keeping quiet to resume it with more strength and cleverness? Jeanne feared him. He attracted her despite her better judgment, but she wanted to be true to her religion, to her noble destiny. And in a silent prayer, she confided the difficult challenge to the Almighty in heaven.

Midnight rang out and the two young girls chatted ceaselessly, illuminated by the faint light of a boudoir lamp. It was a fairly cool night, the kind when one loves to sit by the fireside to listen to the first crackling of the wood in the hearth. Their soft voices mingled with the fire's first songs. If one were to judge by the harmonious exchanges, their two souls shared very similar opinions.

Jacqueline possessed a ravishing personality and her genuineness blended with a great simplicity attracted everyone's sympathy. Full of ambition, she rejoiced in her new position as well as the pleasant reunion with a dear friend. Her heart, still uncommitted, delighted in stealing from this one and that one, the_ardor of their young love. Oh, it was only in passing, she would know how to avoid the traps; she was reasonable and she could allow her youth the pleasure of a flirtation without consequences, she told herself. Born of a father who had converted to Catholicism, Jacqueline had inherited by birth the very fibers of religious freedom, and besides, she had been brought up in a milieu that was foreign to her beliefs. The young girl did no more than she had to. Innovative and resourceful, she managed to get out of all kinds of situations. At the thought of the new position that was assigned to her, Jacqueline was overwhelmed with joy and legitimate pride. She would go though life smiling, with her head held high, and a sincere heart, asking life to offer her the best it had and in return giving the total earnestness of her youth.

"Come in," said a male voice, and Flaherty continued his task without lifting his head. Jacqueline took a seat and waited. Lifting his eyes, Flaherty looked at the new visitor as a smile of admiration livened his thin lips.

"Without a doubt you want to talk to Miss Lacombe? She has already left and will not return this evening. May I help you?" Those few words spoken in a very warm tone of voice captured Jacqueline's attention. This employer was definitely interesting and pleasant.

Several months had gone by since Jacqueline's arrival. Since then, she had met Jeanne's employer, sometimes with Jeanne, sometimes without her. And it seemed that Flaherty enjoyed her company, so much so, that one night the two left to celebrate their youth and their freedom. It was a night when the moon seems to lose itself beyond the black, round clouds, while a gentle breeze caresses the face, murmuring love songs that the birds in the woods echo joyfully. The young man was handsome in his sport clothes, Apollo claimed him for a son. His sweet words were all characteristic of the sentiments that aroused him. She, she was seductive in her thin dress, so flimsy that it seemed as if a bird could carry it off to other skies on it's wings. And so, the man became the fallen angel and suffered all the shame and tyranny. Large black clouds became more numerous above their heads; large tears fell as if to wash with a single stroke the sin that had been committed.

The night was without sleep and the following day without sun. For a while now, Jeanne noticed that Jacqueline retreated and that while Flaherty maintained the same kind attention toward her that he had in the past, little by little he reclaimed the piece of his heart that he had given her. Jeanne suffered in her human heart, but her moral core rejoiced at the triumph she had won at such a high price against the struggles that she had had to uphold, to prove to her father and her God that their faith was still alive in her young Franco-American heart. Her task was becoming difficult. Her father noticed her pallor and worried about her, but Jeanne pretended not to notice. What if by virtue of kindness she managed to convert Flaherty? At this new thought, her heart became enthusiastic and as Christmas was approaching, she would invite him to Midnight Mass with her and Jacqueline. She ignored the deep intimacy that already existed between him and her dear friend, and made plans to attain the goal that she had set for herself. Christmas arrived and all three attended Midnight Mass. Jeanne was happy to have been able to bring him with her. Jacqueline was happy to be by his side, feeling however, the cold-heartedness of her betrayal towards her childhood friend. He, half serious, half curious, listened with noticeable attention to the hymn, "O Holy Night," and with a placid expression followed the ritual at the altar. What was going on in his soul at that time, no one ever knew.

And life went on. A few weeks later, one night when Jeanne was alone, she opened the evening newspaper and learned about Jacqueline's engagement to Flaherty. Her soul was distressed and big tears flowed down her thin cheeks. It was as if a part of her heart had died. She then remembered having suffered a similar sensation after she had left Carl. This time she suffered doubly, because Flaherty had seduced the heart of her dearest friend and in losing the affection of one she had lost faith in the other. She then mustered all her courage and all her energy. Later, when the wound would be healed, would she understand what she had been shielded from? But at this moment, her soul was too crestfallen, too crushed. Her head buried among the divan cushions was heavy, so heavy that she could barely lift it up. A force compelled her. She looked up and saw the picture of her mother that a ray of light coming from the neighboring apartment illuminated. She was smiling and the child looked at her for a long time. A silent conversation took place between them, and when Jeanne sought forgetfulness and rest in sleep, her eyes bore only traces of having wept. Tomorrow she would have to once again make her way to the office and greet the employer's clients with a smile, to say nothing of the employer himself.

Time is a great healer and the passing days would dull her pain. Happy days would return and with them a gentle smile would return to her lips. Jeanne needed rest. For a while now her father was doing well in his business. He resumed his trade and prosperity once again became a part of the home that for so long had known misfortune. Fatigued, Jeanne gave her resignation and left for a respite by the ocean. Flaherty was sorry to see her leave because down deep he valued the young women even if he did not understand her. He thanked her for her services as a gentleman would, and Jeanne disappeared from his life.

Jacqueline and he left for a long voyage but it is said that Jacqueline always avoided making eye contact with people, and that her eyes were always red rimmed.

THE ROSSIGNI HOTEL

The ocean beat its waves against the fine sand; a golden sun warmed the blond earth with its strong rays, while a gentle breeze softly sang the refrain of the active sea in Jeanne's unheeding ear. Yes, for two days, Jeanne gave her body and her spirit a restorative rest. Bathers, up since dawn chatted near the window. Jeanne listened. They were men's voices. One was saying, "I have traveled far and wide and I have never seen the ocean so beautiful." "I remember," said the other, "having seen the ocean as beautiful as it is today, last summer, when we took a trip to Bermuda. We were four, my sister, my friend and her sister and myself. I had offered her a position in our company, but she refused. Oh! She was charming. I never really knew the reason for her refusal. We had had a very pleasant time the night before...it's true that many toasts had been raised, but anyway, that young girl disappeared from my life completely. I've seen her brother since then, he has never given me any information about her goings on. The ocean is rising, come, the open sea beckons to us." The voices diminished bit by bit and Jeanne got up. She went out and ran on the shore that was so warm. In an instant she was under the water. The waves were strong and carried away the light weight that had been entrusted to their care. A scream rang out through the morning air. The two young men, expert swimmers, brought the young girl back to the shore. There, they lavished emergency care on her, and that night when Jeanne awoke, an elderly woman was at her bedside. She then learned about the danger she ran into, the name of her rescuers and the problem they had in resuscitating her. And now, the good women begged her to remain very calm so as to regain her compromised strength as soon as possible.

It was not until the next evening that Jeanne reappeared in the dining room. From a distance she smiled at her rescuers, who down deep really wished to meet her close up. It was a custom at this hotel, in the evening, when the weather was bad, to gather the guests and to organize an improvised concert between them. The best talent of the season, according to the judge's approval, was offered a prize at the house's expense. Since it was raining torrentially, that night they organized an intimate get- together where everyone joined the competition. As Jeanne was a musician, her turn to perform came. Keeping her charming simplicity, she made her way to the piano and with all her soul played "Liszt's Liebestraum" and as an encore played "Paderewski's Waltz" Jeanne won the contest. Her heart pounded very hard and after gracefully thanking everyone, she was making her way to her room, when the two young men, who for a while now had wanted to approach her, expressed their congratulation in perfect French. The three made their way to a favorable corner where they could talk with ease. One of them was of German origin and was presently the manager of a large factory in New York. He had grown up on American soil and all he retained from his ancestral line was his robust stature. Two piercing, dark blue eyes were so deeply set that he seemed to look at you from a distance. His rugged features softened under an honest and spontaneous smile. He had been deeply in love with a young woman from a noble family, but she had been mercilessly taken from him by a ravaging illness just a few months before their wedding. Since then, he had remained single and had never met another girl capable of making his aching heart quiver again. He loved work and was totally devoted to it.

His companion, of average build, and a wide forehead and dark eyes was an untiring and industrious man who rummaged through every library, looking for a new or old book to complete the list of volumes of one series or another, for he especially enjoyed searching for ancient manuscripts and the antique books for the collection of New York City's Museum. He was twenty-eight years old. His father was American and his mother French. He inherited his father's independence and from his mother, his enthusiasm and lofty character. He had murmured his first French words on her lap, and since then he had broadened and maintained his mother tongue. That was why now he was a distinguished linguist after successfully undergoing the final exams in this subject at Colombia University. "You play marvelously well, Mademoiselle," said the younger of the two, who besides being a linguist possessed a poetic tone of voice. "Your magical fingers allowed us to hear an angelic melody." Jeanne smiled and was pleased with the flattering compliment. The other, whose name was Ludwig, and who also spoke French, although with a bit of foreign accent, added: "Frau, I most certainly prefer the sweets sounds of the piano to a factory's infernal noise. Tell me, do you play often?"

"Especially when I'm alone," answered Jeanne, "only I should learn not to swim alone, and I owe both of you a very sincere thank you because it is certainly thanks to you that I am still very much alive."

"The main thing is that we reached you in time," answered Ludwig.

"It seems that the waves were determined to hold on to you, in order to keep their treasure, for we had a very difficult time returning you to shore. But, all this is part of the past and we were so happy to become your saviors." "He deserves all the credit apparently," said Jacques laughing.

"Now that we told you about ourselves, and what we do, tell us in turn how you spend your time." Jeanne said: "I have just left my job, and for now I'm only thinking of getting a good rest and in a few weeks, I hope to be blessed by fate and enjoy a great windfall." This, she said in a half-serious, half-mocking tone, intriguing the young German. He looked in the shadow, he looked at the pale face that was putting up a front so as not to let them see her real feelings. A long silence prevailed between them.

Having risen, Jeanne approached a magnificent painting that had drawn her attention "Oh," she said, "it's a painting by the artist Dyer, a very famous painter, renowned for the beauty of his landscapes. This one of the Alps is breathtaking don't you think?" The two young men got up and together they admired the work of art. The clock in the lobby struck twelve. It was time to part company. Jacques, the youngest of the two said to Jeanne "Have sweet dreams, but leave them open to your Prince Charming." "You don't know that I am a new Blue-beard Mr. Jacques," and she disappeared up the winding staircase.

"It's promising," said Ludwig "She's certainly interesting and for you who's interested in psychology, she really is the next subject for a new book."

"She is unemployed," thought Jacques, "and we would need an assistant at the International Library. We'll see tomorrow."

The next day was a splendid one. There were many bathers and the ocean was calm. Jeanne, sitting on the sand, lost in thought observed the small and agile sea birds that flew over the ocean, when the parasol that shaded her, suddenly lifted up and our two young men sat down beside her. The sun had already tanned their skin, they looked like ancient Greek statues.

"What was Mademoiselle Jeanne thinking of when we arrived near her? She had such a far away look, so lost in space that we were reluctant to draw her out of such a beautiful reverie."

"I was admiring nature," Jeanne answered, "and each time that a wave came up and vanished at my feet, it recalled, and repeated to me, the name of loved ones." Abandoning her reverie, Jeanne got up quickly and ran towards the ocean. The young men followed her. Refreshed, she returned to the sand.

"We have a proposition to offer you Mademoiselle Jeanne," said Jacques. "At the International Library we need someone capable of being both a secretary and a librarian. We're offering you the position. You may think about it and give us an answer in a few days."

Jeanne couldn't believe her eyes. For a long time, she'd dreamt of a position away from home. This very day, she'd write to her father sharing her happiness with him. He would stay with his sister and Jeanne would go to New York to live out a few moments of merriment. She would close the door of the painful past behind her and throw away the key in the abyss of forgetfulness.

"I accept your offer Mr. Jacques. When will I start?"

"In three weeks if that's convenient for you. I'll see that you get a suitable apartment and that you won't be too bewildered in that big city." And together they worked out the final details. Overjoyed, Jeanne went up to her room. She packed her trunks and returned home to announce the wonderful news to her dear father. He was happy about her good fortune, but a small corner of his heart was troubled. The few days that remained were spent in a thousand tasks while Jeanne filled the house with her beautiful contralto voice. Her father hardly spoke. He regretted seeing his only child leave. Although the fortune that pursued him left him no choice but to accept his beloved child's new work, he regretted seeing her leave lest she forget her God and her roots.

NEW YORK

It was seven o'clock in the morning when Jeanne descended at the Pennsylvania station. Jacques was there to meet her. He thought she looked lovely in her brown beret, and her laughing eyes under the golden fringe of her long, thick eyelashes captivated his heart. He immediately led her to her apartment where a young Scottish girl already lived and who, like her, worked at the International Library.

"Make your way to the library by two o'clock," Jacques told her as he left. In a bound he was in the taxi that left with great speed. She's charming, thought Jacques. But, I must find that volume of mine today. Forgetting the young woman, he thought only of his books.

Two o'clock rang when Jeanne met Jacques on the winding staircase. He led her to the cloakroom and then to the large public room. Many people were standing before the high cases; some in search of a romantic book, others wanting books on art, others historical books, bibliographies, etc...

"Mademoiselle, you will be at the counter starting tomorrow morning. Here you will find all the information about which you may have questions. Miss Carroll will be in charge of you." At those words, Jacques returned to his office. The afternoon went by without difficulty. Miss Carroll turned out to be very kind and Jeanne was so vividly interested that the hours went by swiftly.

That night when she returned to her apartment, she settled in and looked at New York through the half-opened window. It was continuous commotion, the throngs passed this way and that, and in such hurried steps. The tall buildings and many skyscrapers drew her attention. Broadway, lit up seemed to be a fairyland. Her young heart smiled at life, she felt happy.

Around ten o'clock, Jacques telephoned her. It gave her great pleasure. She felt less alone in such a large city. Before going to bed, she wrote to her father. And, when came time to seal the letter, she sealed it with a long kiss. She once again looked at the window, and this time, she discovered a cross glimmering in the distance among the fairly-land of lights. She gathered her thoughts for a few moments, then lay down to rest her weary body.

Jeanne was at the counter for a few hours when a man of about fifty presented himself. He wanted a certain book, a bibliography concerning one of the prominent Russian families. Jeanne attempted to find it for him and after several attempts could not satisfy the gentleman. He left grumbling between his teeth. He had barely taken three steps when he returned.

"Here is my card," he said, "call me as soon as you have found the book in question. Thank you."

Confused, Jeanne nonchalantly took the card and read: Baron Kenovitch.

"Oh - oh," said Jeanne, "here is someone whose dignity we must not offend. Very well, let's hurry up and locate this precious volume."

That said, she began searching all the old archives. Around three o'clock the following day, Baron Kenovitch came to pick up the book he desired so much.

"Thank you, Mademoiselle, and may I ask the name of the lovely assistant?"

"Jeanne Lacombe," she said simply.

"You are French Mademoiselle?"

"I am Franco-American and I have only been working in New York for a few days."

"Perfect," said the Baron. "We must meet again." At that, he left, but not without smiling at her, with a wily smile. Jacques arrived in a hurry and happily told Jeanne: "The Metropolitan Museum of Art is opening its doors next Sunday after a complete renovation. If you'd like to accompany me, I'd be delighted."

"With pleasure. For a long time I have wished to visit that museum."

"I will come pick you up around three o'clock Sunday." Assuming a serious air, he continued towards the main library where the whole of a new edition had just arrived.

Under the guidance of Miss Carroll, Jeanne was making considerable progress and loved her work more and more. Once in a while, a remote image of Carl lightly skimmed her soul, reminding her of dreams of long ago. But, when the thought of Flaherty and Jacqueline came to cloud her thoughts, she pitied their fate and remembered with gratitude the privilege of which she had been the happy beneficiary. Little by little she would forget, especially she would forgive, for she was good at heart. Life was offering new horizons and Jeanne would plunge into them heart and soul. She too would have her share of happiness, and so she smiled at the future, at the unknown. What a delightful age is that of youth!

Jeanne was in dreamland. For tonight, being very tired, she could not read. The sandman teased her so badly; she gave in to his charm and left for the land of the spirits.

II

It was raining when Jacques came to pick up Jeanne. A fine rain fell slowly and the sky was so gray that the skyscrapers were lost among the clouds. Jeanne, dressed in black took her place near Jacques in his small 'Roadster.' They traveled down Fifth Avenue, up to the museum, in considerable traffic. They entered and visited the department devoted to sculpture. There, the works of art were numerous and the beauty of the marble and the figures completely captivated the attention of the young couple. As they came around a corner, Jeanne bumped into Baron Kenovitch. He wasted no time in greeting her and took her by the arm. Jeanne freed herself, but the gesture did not go unnoticed by her friend, Jeanne, who frowned as he looked at the Baron.

"My apologies," said the Baron, "if I had not supported Mademoiselle, she would have hurt herself on the pavement."

Jeanne blushed, resenting the insincerity of his words. Jacques seized Jeanne and they moved away.

"How long has it been since you've known this man?"

"He's come to the library three times since I've been there."

"He's a troublesome person. He's educated and of noble blood, but he also has a disturbing boldness."

"What a magnificent painting," exclaimed Jeanne, "it's a reproduction of the Virgin, by Fra Angelico. Look, Jacques."

Jacques looked at something other than the painting. The Baron Kenovitch was standing just a short distance away. A sarcastic smile lightly touched his pale lips. When Jeanne looked up in that direction, the crowd had closed in around the Baron and he was out of her sight. Next they visited the Egyptian exhibit. They alluded to their bizarre traditions and costumes. For a long time they discussed the Egyptians' methods and their ornaments as well as their science. It was already dark and they had visited so little. The young couple postponed their visit to the other departments till another day.

"Here now, at this rate, we'll be going without supper," said Jacques laughing. "However, that was not in my plan."

When they left the museum, the rain had stopped. Jacques suggested they go to the theater as soon as they were done dinner. They made their way to the Roxie, where they were offering one of their most beautiful programs that night. Jeanne was happy and began to appreciate Jacques who was so good to her. The performance over, they considered returning home. On their way, Jeanne learned that Jacques very seldom attended Mass. Oh, just negligence, without a doubt. He remembered having gone when he was young and even lately he had gone, but circumstances were no longer the same. He had omitted that precept, and today, he exempted himself from it without any guilt. He had read so, so many books, that they had practically become his religion. His mother was certainly a saintly woman, but she had died so long ago. Since then, he had roamed here and there, but his innate pride has served as his safeguard, and at thirty, he was a gentleman, wholesome in body and spirit and above all, he would be a model husband. That is what Jeanne was thinking, but one question presented itself. What was the depth of his feelings and his principles? She would soon know.

"She is charming," Jacques told himself returning home alone. He was surprised to see how quickly the time passed when he was in her company. He had escorted many other young women, he knew about love without having taken advantage of it, but Jeanne had a certain "je ne sais quoi," a little something that pleased and kept one interested. Whistling a familiar tune, Jacques opened his new book and became absorbed in his reading, so much so that he almost forgot to go to bed.

It was six thirty when Jeanne opened her curtain. "It's raining," she thought, but no, the sun rays were stretching between the tall buildings, but rarely did they ever reach the ground. "To work, this morning," said Jeanne talking to herself. The echo of her voice kept her company and she felt less alone. The morning air was fresh. Alert and lively, Jeanne wove her way among the throngs that already crowded the sidewalks. In the wink of an eye she had made her way to her work. Today, she had to research scientific books, first medical discoveries, for Mr. the Baron who seemed to delight in the company of antique things and ancient books. Jeanne had a rather vague recollection of him. She found him to be both impudent and a bit amusing.

In the afternoon he visited her. He was attractive and very well dressed, and had a gallantry beyond compare. They spoke for a long time and, among other things, he informed her that he owned a magnificent library and that he would be very honored if she would do him the honor of a visit to his ' land of books.'

"Here," he said "I will expect you, or rather, I will go next Thursday night to pick you up for dinner." At this, he took his books and disappeared in the shadow of the corridor. Jeanne was speechless, here he had left without even waiting for an answer. What would she do? She would go, she thought simple-mindedly. He was a gentleman and without a doubt he wanted to see her alone to provide her with a wholesome distraction. Nevertheless, she did not whisper a word about this to Jacques. Moreover, she knew that Jacques did not especially like the Baron. His attitude the other day assured her of that. Maybe Jacques was a bit jealous and was falling in love with Jeanne? She kept her secret and that night when Jacques came to meet her after work, her lips parted as if to let her secret escape, but no, her lovely mouth closed again and that evening, late into the night, she mused about it.

Jeanne looked at herself in the mirror one last time and seemed satisfied. Her long, pale green velvet dress brought out the sparkle in her dark eyes, sculpted her young body, and draped it like a Greek statue. Dressed in this fashion, without jewelry, except for an old necklace, a last souvenir from a first love, she waited. A few minutes later, the Baron himself presented himself at her door and the two left.

As they made their way, he threw an admiring glance towards Jeanne. She was so beautiful and so attractive. His perceptive eyes did not deceive him. He had found a pearl and he promised himself that he would capture her.

"How quaint your beautiful living quarters are," said Jeanne after having given a quick glance around the room, "It is a corner of paradise on earth, and this carved chest is an object of art."

"Yes," replied the Baron, who enjoyed Jeanne 's spontaneity, "this chest comes from old Europe. It belonged to my uncle who they tell me had received it from the grand Czar himself for having performed an act of bravery. My uncle having passed away, it was willed to me and I brought it here with me, and I take care of it as I do the pupil of my eye. I store my most precious souvenirs in it along with the trinkets of my first love encounters. Mademoiselle Jeanne, I hope one day to confide my secret and permit you to see down to the bottom of this chest." Jeanne smiled, and a young Japanese, with an inscrutable air about him, announced dinner. The Baron led Jeanne to the dining room where she was served the most delicious cuisine. They talked, they laughed and Jeanne rejoiced over having accepted the invitation. She enjoyed herself tremendously.

They proceeded to the library where a quantity of books, old and new, lined the walls. The room was spacious and offered to the visitor a warm and congenial atmosphere. At the end of the room a golden brown divan clearly stood out in the shadow. A small window let in the light of day. A soft velvety carpet showed wear and tear, while a barely perceptible light lit up the room. A single door gave access to the interior. The other panels of the wall were covered with books of all sorts. Sitting on the divan, the two of them sipped the black coffee that the Japanese brought them. And together, they smoked a cigarette while they discussed literature. Jeanne felt overwhelmed. All these books, to her were souls who had thought, who had lived and who had left the best of themselves for prosperity, and who now, after hundreds of years saw their names reflected on the honor roll. They were not completely forgotten and from the grave were they rested, their souls arose victorious. She found herself filled with admiration for the man who had known how to appreciate them, and turning towards the Baron, she smiled at him tenderly.

He looked at her and became aware of the various feelings that arose in him. His body trembled, he almost lost his head. He left the room. Jeanne followed him and both of them descended into the parlor. The Baron became animated and talked extensively about his voyages, about his tastes, about his active life. To please him, Jeanne played the "Liebestraum" by Liszt, so well, that she had to play it again at the request of her amiable host. It was late when she realized what time it was. Whoever would have seen the Baron on his return to the parlor would have been able to see a smile developing at the corner of his lips. What was going on behind that smile? No one knew, not even the Japanese.

III

"Everything went well," Jeanne told herself upon her return. "There was no reason to worry. The Baron is definitely a true gentleman. And his library is most interesting. Tomorrow, I will tell Jacques about my visit at the Baron's and his irreproachable conduct. That will probably convince my dear friend that he is jealous, and she laughed. I have five hours to sleep. Quick, let us give ourselves up to slumber."

"Yes, Jacques, I went to the Baron Kenovitch's home and I had a wonderful time. He owns the most interesting library in the world." While she spoke this way, Jacques looked at her, astounded. Was she telling him everything or just part of it? Had he respected her or was Jeanne playing a game? His temples throbbed and his lips did not dare question her. She looked so sincere that he allowed himself to believe her, but doubt teased his spirit. "As long," he thought to himself, "as she does not go back without telling me."

"I was just coming to ask you to accompany me to my friend Ludwig's next Sunday, if you are not busy with the Baron," said Jacques spitefully. Jeanne looked at him without saying a word. She understood all the irony he put into his words. She turned away and remained thoughtful.

"Forgive me, Mademoiselle Jeanne. So, you will come?" he said in a semi-endearing tone.

"Yes," said Jeanne, "on condition that in the morning both of us go to Mass together."

"Understood," answered Jacques smiling a broad smile.

That night, Jeanne wrote a long letter to her father. She told him about her daily life, how New York agreed with her. She talked to him about Jacques and the Baron, of Ms Carroll, and ended it all with an affectionate kiss that her old father surely savored. A few days later, she received a note from her father. In his turn, he told her that financially he was doing very well, that her friend Lucienne had wed a wonderful boy from town, that Georgette was making a new home for herself, and finally, that the aunt who lived with him was good and kind. He added a few words saying: "Be a bit leery of your Baron. Lastly, I have faith in you. Remember your

God and forefathers." A thousand and one details followed all this. Jeanne felt a tear roll down the length of her pink cheek. Her dear father loved her so much and she adored him. It was especially for him that she struggled. She wanted to relieve him, she wished to give back a bit of devotion and tenderness to the one who had done so much for her.

They were pleased with her at the library. They had let her know that she would soon be promoted. So, her salary would increase and it was towards her paternal home that her noble ambitions and ardent affection were directed. And life in the big city provided a very soothing balm on a still very raw wound.

Sunday arrived. The temperature was ideal. Early on, Jeanne and Jacques had attended Mass at the small chapel of the Adoration Fathers. They then made their way to the Port to view the Statue of Liberty and the new transatlantic ships that were docking. They spent agreeable hours together. Jeanne took in everything and wore Jacques out with her endless questions. He laughed and was amused to hear his companion talk without stopping and wanting to know everything at once. Finally, it was two o'clock when they decided to leave the area. Ludwig lived with his married sister just outside the city limits, in the Bronx. He was hardly ever free. By a stroke of luck, he had been able to get this time off and he was glad to make the most of it with Jacques and Jeanne. Ludwig's sister had a charming, five room house. Alone with her husband, she enjoyed receiving her brother and his friends over, and at her house there was always a bit of that marvelous German beer that as it warms the stomach, gives the spirit an edge of both happiness and mischievousness. For Jeanne, it was quite a revelation. The sun beamed its strong rays on the myriad of flowers that all came from the homeland. Flowers of a remarkable shade, of rare shape, with delightful perfumes, adorned and enhanced the colonial structure of the home. Another surprise awaited Jeanne inside the house. A rather small parlor represented a completely German parlor. All the furniture, paintings, draperies, even the windows reminded one of German art. In a shaded corner, a magnificent tapestry woven in 1793 attracted one's attention and admiration. The design was a familial scene and the figures were ravishing. Jeanne admired it for a long time and it was Ludwig who interrupted her thoughts.

"I would really like to also show you the factory where I work. I am sure that you would both enjoy seeing it."

So, all three went on their way. The factory that was managed by an important corporation was located in the lower end of the city. It would have taken many days to visit it all, but in a few hours Ludwig hoped to have them see the most important parts of the establishment.

"It is here that are manufactured every imaginable and necessary parts for the functioning of all known automobiles. We pack them and ship them to each manufacturer according to the brand of automobile that they deal with."

While Ludwig was explaining and Jacques was attentively examining, Jeanne felt Ludwig's arm wrap around her waist. She did not move. She heard the young man tell her: "I have to see you alone. Tell me when I could do that."

"Come tomorrow after seven o'clock."

"Thank you," Ludwig said simply. He removed his arm and continued his explanations. Jacques, who was genuinely interested, had not been aware of the situation. He was very enthusiastic about what he willingly called the "cream of genius." He asked himself why he had not undertaken this trade rather than the one of librarian. He felt an urge to revolutionize the world. In the wink of an eye, he was on the second story of the building. Jeanne followed him, but her mind was distracted. What could Ludwig possibly want? She hardly knew him. In the few months that she had been in New York, she had only caught a glimpse of him three times. Was he ill, or did he want to confide some secret problem to her? His large, deep-set eyes were spirited yet revealed a character capable of conquering the obstacles met along life's path. Or, did he want to offer her a more advantageous position, or again, was he assuming the role of steward for Jacques, did he have a role to fill? Oh well, she would know soon. But her curious mind kept wondering. Every once in a while, she would hear the voice of Jacques, who was going from one amazing thing to another, so she got a hold of herself and with an air of indifference asked Ludwig about the operation of the different machines. He eagerly answered her, but not without casting a scrutinizing glance her way Jeanne laughed and the original conversation continued.

The young couple returned home in thick fog. The lights of Broadway had lost some of their radiance. The lights seemed to be wrapped in angels' hair, while a gauzy veil floated and waved through the haze. The hurried crowds piled on to the sidewalk. Jacques ended the evening at Jeanne's. It was the first time that she invited him to come up. He had hinted to her about this, but Jeanne had apparently not understood. But tonight, she knew that she would have the enjoyable company of the young Scottish girl, who in turn eagerly wished to meet the friend who was so good to Jeanne. It was under these circumstances that the three chatted for a long time.

"What do you think of Towle's recent book, *The Abnormal*?"

"I think," said Jeanne, "that book is crude, besides being immoral."

"It speaks in favor of science, since soon the scientists will attempt to create a body so perfect that it will be able to reproduce itself."

"I believe that only God can give life," replied Jeanne. "What is missing from your perfect body is the breath which gives it life and which it cannot produce on its own."

"I believe in the evolution and the progress of science. And no matter how incredible this reasoning may be to us, I wonder what the future holds for us."

"Are you not just a bit of a materialist? For me, man, as clever as he might be will never be able to perform a divine act."

"But in the end, this book speaks about the future, it is only a preamble to scientific progress."

"For me, the author has succeeded in forging a monster with a criminal mind. You remember the results? Three murders, and the monster was even going to kill the fiancée of he who had created it. Luckily it was destroyed, because it's ravages were many."

"Jeanne, I believe that you strongly hold onto your principles and that amidst life's occurrences you see the finger of God. Myself, I forget a lot of that."

"Come Jacques, do not be so spineless. We would think that you were a rogue."

Getting up, she lit a cigarette and from between her long, curled eyelashes, she examined the young man's features. He had stopped talking and seemed to be in deep thought. What is he thinking about, Jeanne asked herself. Had she opened a new horizon for him? Or, did he think she was naive and judgmental?

"*The Two Loves,* is playing at the Paramount this week, will you come with me?" He asked as if to change the subject.

"Not tomorrow for sure," quickly answered Jeanne. "I am seeing someone." Having said too much, she bit her lip and her dark eyes sparkled. Jacques left without saying another word except goodnight. But as he went down the stairs, she could hear him humming the sentimental tune of "Goodnight Sweetheart."

It was nine o'clock sharp when Ludwig arrived at Jeanne's. He had some serious plan in mind, for he looked anxious and his movements were nervous. What was the matter, wondered Jeanne. Has something bad happened to him? He settled himself in the living room and without preface or form said: "I am leaving in two weeks for the American West. I need a private secretary and I thought of you." And then he was silent. Dumfounded, Jeanne looked at him "But Mr. Ludwig, this is a proposition that demands consideration. I love my position and I was not thinking of making any changes at the moment."

"Take it or leave it," said Ludwig sarcastically.

"Let me think about it."

Having come nearer to her, in a flattering voice, Ludwig said: "It is you dear Jeanne that I want. Come out there with me. Life will be good to us and you will learn to love me so much that a day will come when you will not be able to do without me. You stirred the very fibers of my heart."

"No," said Jeanne, getting away from him. Gathering all her strength, she returned an instant later and staring at Ludwig she said: "I can not accept your proposition, you had better look elsewhere for your affections." She turned around and locked herself in her room. Footsteps resounded on the damp pavement. It was Ludwig who had left the house without saying a word and hastily walked away into the bustling crowd.

Alone in her room, Jeanne wondered: why did this good friendship turn into something painful? If only Ludwig had been polite, maybe she would have agreed to accept this new position that as a whole would have been advantageous for her. She did not like his rudeness. What if in a moment of weakness Ludwig lost himself because he lost her. Then, she remembered that in her childhood, she had learned that one must give to others what is due them. Her righteous soul did not want to think the worst. She struggled and understood how sometimes it is difficult to live up to one's beliefs. Her own experience led her to be indulgent towards others, and towards Ludwig, who was filled with passion; she felt a kind forgiveness and gentle understanding. She would soon forget the incident. Letting her arms fall from where they had been shielding her delicate face, two wet streaks appeared the length of her pale cheeks. Often she wondered if she should not return to her father. But then, knowing that her help was indispensable to her dear home stimulated her and filled her with courage for the next day's struggles. A day would come when love as she understood it, would be part of her life, for her dream man was the man on whom she could lean her head and he would be so good, that at his side she would feel very small, so small that he would capture her whole being and would quickly conceal her within his heart. Jeanne began to laugh at her own thoughts. Getting up, she once again went to scrutinize her mother's eyes, who against the gold background, seemed to follow her every step and to grasp all the emotions of her young heart. For a long time, she looked at the picture, for so long, that after a while she believed that it was speaking to her.

"Remember that in your veins flows the purest and most noble blood, and that it is not up to a young Franco- American girl to defile it. It is the blood of valiant heroes and martyrs."

A SECOND MEETING

The following day started out wrong. On her arrival at the library, Jeanne found a small note on her desk telling her to immediately go to her employer's office. This could not be good news. A first cloud arose in the morning's atmosphere.

Around eleven o'clock, Baron Kenovitch presented himself at the counter. After politely greeting him, Jeanne asked him what he wanted. "Mademoiselle, I would be delighted if you would agree to come have dinner with me next Thursday at seven o' clock. I have received some books from Europe that would capture your interest for long hours on end. Besides, I wish to introduce you to a charming and very distinguished young man who would be delighted to make your acquaintance. Therefore, Mademoiselle, I will expect you at seven o'clock on Thursday." Then turning back towards her, "It is a surprise that I am reserving for the most beautiful of fairies. Let us keep it secret."

His eyes became soft and enveloped her whole being with a passionate look. The Baron was still agile despite his portly build and so nimble that he was sometimes the envy of adolescents who looked at him with spite. He had seen much and lived much. Human love was his idol and he lived strictly for pleasure. His life had been one long romance and at fifty years old, the demon of mid-life was starting to torment him. He wanted to attract hearts, to attach them to himself with strings of tender affection, so that later, at the end of his life, he would remember the happy hours of years gone by.

The following Thursday, Jeanne, looking like a painting in her rose garnished, black tulle dress, rang the Baron's doorbell. The always-impassive Japanese led her to the main parlor. As she made her way there, Jeanne wondered whom the young man she was to be introduced to could possibly be. She was anxious to see him. As she entered, she found the Baron by himself. Without a doubt the stranger would not be long in coming. Jeanne went to sit on the couch next to the Baron who informed her in a slightly concerned voice that the young Ducles, at the last minute had not been able to accept the Baron's invitation, and he begged Mademoiselle to excuse him. Jeanne frowned, wondering if that were really the truth.

During dinner, in an intimate tête-à-tête, the Baron told his guest about his voyages, his brave deeds, and even a little about his love affairs. He was charming with his eloquent words, and his keen mind captivated Jeanne. He looked at her intensely and observed the spontaneity of the expressions on her youthful face. He had traveled to Bengal, had hunted tigers, and willingly he embellished the adventures which gave more valor to his actions. He recalled how once a tiger had come sniffing around his tent, and bravely reaching out, he had seized his gun and with just one shot downed the ferocious animal. He went on to tell her that he had wed a charming young women of noble birth and after three years of married life, while she was horseback riding, she fell and died as a result of the accident. He had suffered terribly from the loss, but later on, he met a charming heiress to the king of steel. Her millions could buy him a title, and besides, the young girl was ravishing. So, he joined his life to hers, but after a two-year union, they separated. Paris allowed them to divorce and today, the Baron was back in circulation. At one time he had known more affluence then he knew today, but having the most charming of young girls by his side, he felt perfectly happy, he said smiling. Rising, he took Jeanne by the arm and led her to the library.

Only a large sofa stood out against the somber wall. The Baron closed the door and put the key in his vest. Seizing Jeanne by the waist he pulled her towards the sofa. Jeanne objected but to no avail. The Baron pressed his moist lips on the helpless young mouth. Then Jeanne had an inspiration from above, for in her heart she was pleading for God's help. The Baron persisted in his disastrous pursuit and the poor girl regretted her lack of prudence. No, she would not give in. She remembered her God and His commandments. She had kept her heart and her body intact up to now, she was ready for a fight; she would resist with all her heart and soul. The fear that had appeared on her face was replaced by an extraordinary calm. Coming closer to the Baron, she studied his impassioned expression. She became cajoling and in an attempt to gain time to think, she pretended to fix her hair. The Baron seeing such a submissive prey did not force himself on her. Calming herself a bit, she said: "You are a first class lover and I can see that you are not a beginner in these matters. You must have ravished many a heart."

"Yes," said the Baron proudly, "many women remember me. I pleased them. But, come closer to me, you beautiful little flower."

Jeanne approached him and said: "Is there anything more wonderful than love, than the union of two beings?"

"I see that you understand me, my adorable Jeanne." He brushed the nape of her neck with his seductive lips. On contact, Jeanne bristled with disgust, but containing herself she said with a childish pout, "But, dear Baron, this sofa is far from comfortable enough for making love and since we have reached that point, a bit of your cognac would put us in better form." With this insistence, the Baron got up and ran to his splendid reserve.

Jeanne, freed from the Baron's grasp for an instant, for he had had to open the door to make his way to his reserve, quickly went down the stairs and ran out on the sidewalk without her cloak. She hailed a taxi and returned home half crazed. It seemed to her that the Baron was pursuing her, that each car that she encountered harbored the insolent man whose toy she would have been if she had not been fortunate enough to get away from him. Paralyzed with fear, she climbed up to her apartment and throwing herself on her bed she sobbed. The hours slipped by and Jeanne cried the whole time. Why was she still so afraid, she wondered. She had been wrong to accept the Baron's invitation. She had taken a huge risk. Luckily she had not lost everything. Wanting to tempt fate, and not fearing danger was her weakness; but then, resisting all that attacked her honor and her race was her strength. Many others give in to temptation, she told herself, and then rise above it. No, I will not let myself succumb; my principles, the blood that flows in my veins and the blood of heroes do not allow me to. With a proud look on her face, Jeanne picked herself up and faced life with a serene heart. She went on and put the maddening episode behind her. Allowing her lofty ideals to soar, in the future, she promised to adhere to what was right and to be faithful to the traditions that come from a beloved father.

The following day, Jacques said to Jeanne: "Baron Kenovitch has just obtained the position of head master of the library's rare books department. He is to take charge in a few days." Jeanne grew pale. Jacques continued, "Some say it is just a fantasy on his part, he will not stay. I tell them that he is tenacious and very well versed in this matter, for he is well read. What displeases me most is that I will have to follow his orders, and you also," he added as he looked at his companion. Jeanne said not a word.

Things were becoming complicated. Would she reveal to Jacques what had happened, or would she confront the battle as a brave solider. If she told him, he might doubt her word. Would he lose faith in her or admire her courage and honesty? She wondered why the Baron had worked so hard to obtain this position. He would now have the right to let her go or to impose too heavy a load on her. The poor girl thought of Ludwig. What if she wrote to him that she was ready to accept his offer? Surely, he would be happy to have her return, for she had seen in his eyes the great love that he had for her. Deep in her heart, she preferred Ludwig to the Baron. She would write to her father to ask for his advice. But, no. She was independent. It was not so much that she did not want any advice, it was just that the battle seemed challenging and she wanted to have the satisfaction of solving it herself and in the most favorable way possible. Color returned to her cheeks as her ideas multiplied, but her mouth did not betray the secret in her soul.

"How lovely you are tonight Jeanne," said Jacques tenderly "I feel that there are so many things that I want to tell you only, will you listen to me? I've often thought of establishing a home where among the flowers of a perpetual garden, the most beautiful would be the wife of my choice. I've met many lovable young persons, but because I am a bachelor and selective, as a consequence, I still have not met she who would suit me."

Jeanne laughed wholeheartedly. Jacques immediately added: "The present company is always excluded of course." In, turn, a knowing smile caused his crimson lips to open, reveling two rows of beautiful, white teeth.

"Jacques, you are a big child. Sometimes I am tempted to let you rest your head on my shoulder as do little children who are unsure about the affection they need."

"I would not ask for any better," he said half seriously. Then, turning around, "Jeanne, does Baron Kenovitch mean anything to you? A while ago, you grew pale when I mentioned his new position to you." "No, Jacques, he means nothing to me. I had given him my friendship and he abused it. Today, I am withdrawing it. We do not share the same principles, our souls do not speak the same language." A pearl shaped tear sparkled under her black eyelashes. Jacques understood that she was suffering.

"Jeanne, why not just follow your first impulse and let your heart dictate your line of conduct."

"Because in this case, my head must guide my very human and too sensitive heart. It would have very easily attached itself to this Baron whose intellectual qualities captivated and took hold of me, but who is deprived of moral qualities. I can no longer put my heart at risk."

"So, he was insolent towards you?" said Jacques. Jeanne did not have an answer. She was called to the phone. When she returned, the conversation turned to another subject. They needed to discuss the events of the day that had unfolded at the stock market. The decline in stocks was being felt more and more and Jacques, who owned shares, was becoming concerned. Jeanne helped him with her encouragement and the young man told himself that he had before him a pearl of great quality. So, his expression became very gentle, and his whole being betrayed the state of his idealistic soul.

"Jeanne, do you believe in love?" It was the second time that this question was posed to her. Pondering the question, she suddenly lifted her head and said with a smile, "Yes, I believe in love. When two beings unite to support each other in their walk towards their ideals; when goodness blends with indulgence in an effort to soften the difficult journey; when on thick reeds the flower of devotion sprouts; when the dwindling courage of one is sustained by the other; when at last their hearts merge together in one belief, I believe in love." Jacques looked at her for a long time.

"It is late," he said "Jeanne, I will think about what you have just told me."

He left, but not without placing a respectful kiss on her curly hair. Never, he thought, has anyone ever talked to me this way before.

That night, the sky offered a ravishing spectacle to the observant eye. In the heavens a star brighter than the others wrote Jeanne's name with its luminous rays; or depending on whose eyes were looking, the name of a dear friend.

"Mademoiselle, we need this classification for four o'clock today," said the Baron.

"I will try, Baron Kenovitch sir, but it is a long project. I will do my best to satisfy you."

"There is a way to shorten it. It all depends on you."

Jeanne understood. Without flinching, she said: "You will have it."

What an enormous task! Her tired eyes were red-rimmed. She had hardly reached the halfway mark of the imposed task when two o'clock rang out. If only I were very simply accommodating I could diminish my burden. Immediately, she retracted. No, I must not. She returned to the difficult task. There was a knock at the door. It opened immediately, allowing the Baron to enter. At a glance he became aware of the strain that Jeanne was undergoing.

"Oh, I see that all is going well thanks to your skills and intellectual capacities," he told her sarcastically, "I knew that it was not a task above your intelligence." Jeanne blushed and continued her work.

"Do not forget that everything must be ready at precisely four o'clock," and smiling, he left the room.

He will have it, thought Jeanne, and once again, he will not have conquered me. In fact, at the appointed hour, the Baron came to get his order. The work Jeanne delivered to him was impeccable and complete. The Baron remained mute and was somewhat surprised. He had expected that the young girl would come to plead with him to delay the time of delivery, but instead, she had made a superhuman effort and had handed it over at the assigned time. Decidedly, he told himself, I will have a difficult time subduing her.

"Thank you, Mademoiselle. I am happy to congratulate you on your efficient work. Tomorrow we will have special research to do and I am counting on your good will and your kindness. By the way, tonight we are organizing a theater party and I feel sure that your presence would be appreciated."

Jeanne threw a quick glance his way and coldly answered: "I am sorry, I have an engagement tonight, and the person who will accompany me is a young man whom I can trust," she added in a whisper. The Baron pretended not to hear. Sharply he said: "As soon as you come in tomorrow, come to my office. Do not worry about anything Jeanne, I am here to protect you."

"Or to dishonor you," Jeanne muttered between her teeth.

When she arrived home, Jeanne found a letter whose handwriting she could not recognize. Without any rush, she opened it. Her heart beat faster as she proceeded to read it. Carl informed her of the sudden death of his dear mother. He was seeking a bit of consolation from she who had been his friend in happier times. Since they had left each other, he had suffered and wanted to renew their former friendship. He needed her so much. Jeanne felt her heart break. Her love for Carl was evidently not totally dormant and at this emotional time, it abruptly reawakened. In a humble prayer she would ask the Heavens to give her best friend the balm of consolation and to shower him with the penetrating oil of courage that creates a race of the strong. In spontaneous haste she started to write to the unhappy young man. However, she could not renew a friendship that she had such a difficult time breaking because she had summoned her most deeply anchored principles and her vibrant Franco-American faith. Her letter, however, was one of tender sympathy that deeply touched his burdened heart. She let him know that she could not entertain a regular correspondence with him, and that in New York, she had fallen in love with a young man who spoke French. She wished for him a wife that would know how to make him perfectly happy by brightening the many years that were ahead of him, with her smile and her goodness

That night, Jacques, beaming with happiness came to pick up Jeanne. The Knights of Columbus were having a fantastic dance uniquely for its members and their companions. They left together. Jeanne surrendered to the "joie de vivre," all the while keeping the image of the afflicted Carl in her thoughts.

"Jeanne, in two months, I am leaving on vacation, but this time, I will not go to Old Orchard, for I know full well that I will not meet you there. I thought of heading towards the lakes and forests of Maine. For a long time now, I have wanted to take a trip in that part of the country. And do you know who would make the voyage even more enjoyable? I will let you guess."

"It would be for you to have a male friend with you," said Jeanne teasing him.

"Oh! Oh! I believe that I would prefer a lady friend, someone who looks like you," said Jacques.

"Well then, let us make our vacation plans."

And like two children, they chatted about their trek across the open country; of their trips on the water, under a blue sky and a restorative sun or the waning eye of Phoebe, singing Irving Berlin's latest ballad.

In the dark sitting in a tall, stuffed arm chair, his head thrown back on its high back, one leg dangling over the arm of the chair, a half-lit cigarette in his mouth, and in the shadow, to the radio playing "*Make me Dream,*" one of Jacques's favorite pieces, the young man day-dreamed. It was time to establish a home, and more and more Jeanne seemed to be the ideal candidate. At her side, he could undoubtedly see himself obligated to observe the religious duties that he had somewhat neglected. This would not confine him too much he thought, and he smiled. Besides, his loved one would know exactly how to satisfy even his slightest whims, and in the shadow of the apartment, little angels with blond and brown hair fluttered about. Jacque's sleep was haunted with angelic visions.

II

"Good morning sir," said Jeanne as she presented herself to the Baron in his office. She looked at him without flinching.

"Come, my darling," he said coyly, "sit down near me." Jeanne sat down without saying a word.

"Today, I will have the great pleasure of having you near me. How seductive your independent attitude makes you." And his large hand stroked Jeanne's hair. She moved away from his caress. A bit offended, he added: "In the future, you will need to be more agreeable, because my dear Jeanne, do not ignore the fact that I practically have the right to life or death over your beautiful brown head. But, have no fear. I would not want to abuse that right. Only, do not be so cowardly, it is as if everything frightens you, although I realize that the first visit to my house did not do anything to remove any sentiment of fear from you." He laughed diabolically. Jeanne blushed at the allusion, but contained herself. Then she opened her mouth and said: "What is the work that I must undertake?"

"Oh. I forgot. Your eyes are so charming that they made me lose my memory. Here."

Surely, Jeanne would be busy all day. She regained control over her agitated nerves, and without enthusiasm and always on the alert, she got to work. The Baron, on his end seemed to busy himself, but his inquisitorial eye did not let Jeanne out of it's sight for a minute. In the afternoon, Jeanne felt tired. Her face became pale and her hand trembled. She fainted. The Baron ran to her side immediately and transported the young girl to his private suite. He poured a few drops of cognac on her discolored lips and revived her. In the main office, a young man had been waiting for a few minutes. In search of the Baron, Jacques unexpectedly opened the door. He appeared angry, concerned and upset. Leaning on the Baron's shoulder rested the young women he loved. So, she was deceiving him! Shocked and furious, he looked at one and then the other and his eyes hurled lightening bolts. She, whom he thought was sincere, who so many times had told him about her struggles with the conservation of her faith and her morals; she whom he admired for her honesty and filial love; she whom he thought he would make his wife, she was there in the arms of the Baron, an impostor and a disgrace to manhood.

No, this was too much... all his illusions crumbled. He could see his most beautiful dream disappear under the shadow that clouded his eyes, for big tears flooded his defeated face like a waterfall. Before so much pain, the Baron felt moved. Taking Jacques by the arm, he led him to Jeanne's side.

"Watch over her," he said "and continue to pour the invigorating cognac between her bluish lips, then you will understand why her listless head was resting on my old shoulder."

Like a sleepwalker, Jacques did as he was told and when Jeanne opened her eyes a second time, the face she glimpsed was the face of the young man who had become calm due to the sincere words spoken by the Baron in a half-saddened tone of voice. The door closed once again and the Baron took over the work where Jeanne had left off.

Youth laughs at pain. The following day, Jeanne was on her feet and had forgotten the incident of the previous day. She reread for the third time a long letter from Ludwig who was telling her about the success that enveloped him. He was perfectly happy, all that was missing was Jeanne's presence. There was still time for her to come and join him, but, being so far away, how could he compete with her friend Jacques. He kept his hopes up and fantasized that he would convince Jeanne and have her share his philosophical ideas. He had included a small booklet of his own composition containing diverse philosophical ideas that really amused Jeanne. Surely, he would have been mortified to see her having a good laugh at his expense, but it was done with such spontaneity that he would not have been able to hold a grudge.

"Dear Ludwig, he will never change. He imagines that things would always be wonderful if I was there, and besides that, he hopes to win me over to his way of thinking."

That night, when Jacques came to pick her up, she showed him Ludwig's letter. He was a bit disturbed. It seemed to him that Jeanne had seen on his face all the sentiments that had invaded his soul, as he stood dumbfounded, before yesterday's scene. What would she tell him? Would she be hurt to see that he had been able to doubt her even for an instant? Each sentence that Jeanne uttered seemed to him to be an accusation. All evening, he expected some kind of reproach, but the incident was part of the past, and Jeanne loved the future. Her broad mind willingly forgave and gave her deeper understanding of human nature.

"Jeanne, would you like to go to a night club?"

"Yes, that would make me very happy. When will we go?"

"Halloween night."

Jeanne very honestly had no qualms about it. She would voluntarily accompany Jacques and would know how to keep her head. Moreover, since she was young, she had been used to working her way out of difficulties on her own just like any of her sisters, if once in a while a few of them had the misfortune of falling, a great number of them were immunized against the excess of pleasure, thanks to the struggles that they have had to endure against the storms that life offered. Jeanne, who loved pleasure, was excited at the thought of her next evening outing.

For several days now, the Baron appeared distant and independent. Jeanne worked more at ease. Still, she mistrusted his new attitude somewhat. Did he have some secret plot or was he simply abandoning the game? These peaceful days restored the calm to her soul, for her, the sun seemed more glorious and its rays were warmer.

One night as she returned home from work, she found a very formal letter on her desk. She recognized her aunt's handwriting. Without delay, she opened it. With a lot of tenderness, the aunt announced to her that her dear father had suddenly become blind. She had delayed telling her about it, hoping to have better news to give her.

The doctors had done all they could to prevent this sad ending. The poor father had not wanted them to tell her earlier, he always hoped for some noticeable change. And, the aunt continued, telling Jeanne not to be alarmed, her dear father had a devoted and loving support in her, and that with only the two of them, with their debts paid, they could manage without too much money. Her stricken father was Christian, and his deep faith helped him to accept the cruel ordeal. For her part, the aunt was very good and Jeanne knew that her devotion was incessant. When she was young, she had benefited so much from this. This time, Jeanne felt her courage almost vanish. Her dear father was so sorely tested. She doubled her tenderness and respect towards him. She would write him longer and more cheerful letters so as to break up the monotony of the hours that must all seem the same. Now, she was anxious for summer so she could go home and curl up next to him and feel the gentle warmth of his aged hand.

But, that night her soul was troubled. So she told herself, "I will work even more and save more so as to offer all the luxury possible to he whom I love." The following day, she wrote her saddened father a long letter filled with warm, filial affection.

The Baron, encountering Jeanne in the corridor noticed that her beautiful eyes had cried. Sympathetically, he inquired about the cause of these red circles. Jeanne related to him how her father had become blind. Very affectionately he wanted to console her and offer her some diversion. For a moment Jeanne almost accepted his enticing offers, but remembered the dangers she had encountered and, she thanked him resolutely letting him know that it was impossible for her to accept his generous offers. A bit annoyed, he added: "I thought of offering you a more lucrative position than the one you occupy at the moment. I would hope you would be reasonable enough to accept this. After all, I am doing it with your interest in mind."

"May I know what this new position consists of?"

"Yes, Mademoiselle. You would have the honor of being my private secretary at $ 100 a week. Is it not appealing?"

The Baron left, but not without bowing deeply before Jeanne, who was left stupefied at the unexpected offer. If I accept, thought Jeanne, I could help my father much more and accomplish my goal of lessening his unhappiness. Her heart jumped for joy. But, looking at the other side of the coin, she saw how she would be at the mercy of a shrewd man for whom ' living ' meant the satisfaction of a being's every desire. Caught in this situation, it would be difficult to get out of it. Could she rely on an invincible strength without the intervention of Providence? Big dark clouds surrounded her and melancholy filled her heart. The struggle continued. Up to now, she had not soiled the pure blood of her race and its traditions echoed very clear and vibrant in her young soul. She quickly reached her decision. She would not accept the Baron's offer. Without a doubt, as a dominating authoritarian man, one who always got what he wanted, he would be offended. And then, maybe he would rebuke her for having scorned what in his view was so advantageous an offer. She thought of all this in just a few seconds.

"Well Mademoiselle Jeanne, this morning you are bringing me an affirmative answer," said the Baron scrutinizing the lovely face that leaned towards him.

"I owe you my sincere thanks Mr. Baron, but after thinking about it, I prefer to keep my present position."

Furious, the Baron got up and grabbed Jeanne by the shoulders, and said: "Idiot," and left the room.

Jeanne returned to her task shaken and nervous. She expected to get fired. Mustering all her courage, she continued the research that she had undertaken that very morning. The day proceeded without any serious incidents. That night, it was to Jacques, her friend in good and bad times, that she relayed the vicissitudes of the last few hours and the gnawing worry she had that she might lose her position.

"Have faith Jeanne, keep up your courage, and have recourse to God," said Jacques.

It was the first time that Jacques mentioned the name of God, that he seemed to think about Him. Had she awakened both himself and a latent religion within him in these distressful hours when he had thought of summoning the help of a Supreme Being? Oh!, how that word spoken by Jacques drew him closer to her. This was a healing balm that spread smoothly on her wounded heart. She felt his sincere sympathy and the desire that he had to help her.

"Look here," said Jacques, "today, Mr. Stewart, one of the Library's trustees, received a letter from an old friend asking him if he could recommend a good man who could begin to do ground work for a public library in Rumford, Maine. This city is in your state is it not Jeanne? So, he talked to me about the project and frankly, it appealed to me. Only, I would be leery about leaving you because I love you so very much, much more than you believe." Softly, he stroked the girl's fine hair. "And," he added immediately, "it is a worthwhile undertaking. I will be able to save enough money to build myself a very comfortable little nest. There now, I am straying from my subject...and I would leave in two months. I have to terminate my term here and then, I need to collect the books necessary for the founding of the new library. Jeanne, what do you think of Jacques and his aspiration?"

"I am very happy for you," said Jeanne "I cannot help but feel the sadness that your departure will cause me, for you have always been so kind to me. Your future comes first, and I believe Mr. Stewart could not have made a better choice," she added with a sincere smile. Jacques looked at her lovingly. He was happy to see that she shared his enthusiasm. Inwardly, he wondered, "Does Jeanne really love me?" And while he was staring off into space, daydreaming about the future, Jeanne drew him out of his dream, saying "Jacques, you will make your way to Lewiston on your way to your new post. I will have so many things to tell them that I wish to confide only to you." This was said with a note of sadness in her voice, something that did not go unnoticed by her friend. So, without saying a word, he took both her hands in his, and each understood the other.

"In two months I will be gone," he said in a whisper. Then, turning his head towards the half-opened window, he clearly and honestly evaluated the future.

"Jeanne," he said, "will you come join me one day?" Not daring to look at her, he waited for an answer.

"Jacques, I will give you an answer tomorrow, after I have reflected before the statue of the Virgin."

As they parted, a ray of hope animated the young man's being, while Jeanne's eyes betrayed an indescribable joy.

The following day, Jacques came to seek an answer. He longed for happiness and to feel loved by Jeanne would give him courage. What if she were to disappoint him, even hurt him?

"Come on, quit the idle chatter, and go in."

"Well, then," said Jacques without preface.

Jeanne smiled and said: "Jacques, I value your friendship and one day my faithful friend, I will come."

He embraced her in his strong arms. A long silence followed, for two hearts understand each other better in the absence of words and sound.

The time to leave arrived. Jacques, entrusted to transmit a million things to Jeanne's father, found the burden light, for she held him in her loving heart. Traces of black smoke were barely streaking the skies and Jeanne remained behind in the bustling crowd.

THE MAJOR CONFLICT

For three days now, Helen Smith occupied the room next to Jeanne's. She was the young, worldly type and despite her thirty years, her face, lit up by large dark eyes, had that certain freshness of twenty year olds.

Evenings flowed one into the other. Jeanne and Helen had met at the communal table and after only a few hours of meeting each other, Helen took an interest in Jeanne. One day, on one of their holidays, Helen invited Jeanne to accompany her to one of her friend's house. Jeanne refused. She found Helen a bit difficult to understand, her secretive lifestyle repulsed her. Yet, she exerted a certain kind of magnetism on Jeanne towards which the young girl was not indifferent. She later learned that Helen had lost her mother at a young age. She was American and had been brought up by an elderly aunt who had never understood her, so that what happened was that the growing child gave in to all her tendencies, both good and bad. Today, she believed in living lavishly and for her, perfect happiness consisted of having absolutely no boundaries, no restraints. What would be Jeanne's attitude towards this new school of thought?

Helen had red hair, what we call "auburn." Tall and lean, her dark eyes deeply set, her nose curved, her mouth a bit large, she was attractive. She especially possessed a striking magnetism. It was hard to resist her.

"Almost always," she said one day as she smiled, "I get what I want." She went out night and day and seemingly had no specific job. Rarely did she speak about her past. She knew how to be pleasant and I will add that she certainly was a psychologist. She was really taken with Jeanne. But, she would go slowly and would try to catch the bird unaware. One night, at supper, Helen was missing. No one was worried about her. Around eleven o' clock, they heard moaning coming from the stairway. Jeanne got up and imagine her surprise when she found Helen crouched at the bottom of the stairway, bearing a gash on her forehead from which there gushed young, vigorous blood. Quickly, they carried the young girl to her bed, giving her emergency treatment. When she opened her eyes, she smiled, but her eyes seemed to be reliving the scene, and deep into her eyes one could see an expression of sadness and vengeance mingled together.

Jeanne sat near the injured women and waited for her to speak. But the words did not come and Helen once again closed her large eyes. Many hours went by and Jeanne did not leave the room. Maybe her friend would need her. Surely a horrible episode must have taken place because even in her sleep, the wounded women fidgeted and grimaced, articulating incomprehensible words. Around three o'clock, Helen opened her eyes and looked at Jeanne.

"Are you feeling better Helen?"

She smiled and said not a word.

"What can I do for you?"

"Nothing," answered the wounded one. "You can leave, and thank you, I prefer to be alone. Thank you."

Jeanne left.

Without a doubt it was a lover's quarrel, Jeanne thought. She would get over it. She had barely closed her door when she heard these words: "No, Richard, not her, not her." Jeanne ran over but as she got there, nothing struck her as abnormal except that Helen was rambling on. Knowing that her presence was useless, she returned to her room and went to bed.

Before leaving for work, she went and softly knocked on her friend's door. As she received no answer, she entered. The bed was deserted and the bird had flown away. No doubt it seemed a bit bizarre, but it really was not any of her affairs. Jeanne left.

They met at supper. Helen's face bore no serious effect from yesterday's accident, however, she was silent and did not speak except to respond to the polite attention that was given to her. She smiled at Jeanne, but avoided speaking to her. So, Jeanne understood that she needed to let the past take care of the past.

The days seemed long to the child who was far away from home even if Jacques was writing to her regularly. His letters, full of affection and enthusiasm, warmed Jeanne's heart, but his absence caused her to suffer. The Baron, at his end, seeing her alone and suspecting that she was lonely, conducted himself in the most likeable manner and sought to attract her by his endless kindness. Jeanne always resisted him, but her courage was sometimes tempted to give in. It was at those times that she would walk into a church to restore her strength in the saving water of fervent prayer. She remained kneeling for a long time and it was only after having prayed that she once again made her way to work or to the house. She was often lonely, despite the fact that New York offered so many distractions. In the midst of so much glitter, she remained indifferent. Her soul hovered beyond the skyscrapers.

For a week now, Helen had not returned to the house. Oh, there were many other boarders, but Jeanne did not feel drawn to them. Helen had left without saying a word. No one knew where she had gone. Would she come back soon, or was she on a long voyage? Her room was not for rent, which meant that she was thinking of coming back. One evening, when Jeanne returned from an outing, she found Helen sitting in the parlor. She was smartly dressed and with her was a tall, elegant young man. Just as she attempted to walk by without looking in, Helen called Jeanne.

"Jeanne, I would like you to meet someone. He is one of my good friends. Mr. Russell, Mademoiselle Lacombe."

"Very happy to meet you Mademoiselle," said the young man speaking French with a bit of an English accent.

He is superb thought Jeanne, with his little brown mustache and his dreamy, gray eyes. He looked at Jeanne with interest and with an air of approval. Helen smiled. Jeanne left and Helen continued talking with Russell.

"Yes," she was saying, "we will have to win her over. She is lovely and would be very suitable." He gave a wink that Helen easily understood.

"Let me approach the skittish bird. The magnet always attracts and you know that none got away."

"I will invite her to a dance. You will keep me updated so I know what kind of an effect I produced with her. Then I will act accordingly."

Around midnight there was a knock on Jeanne's door.

"Come in," said Jeanne.

Helen opened the door slightly and sidled in.

"Do you know," she said, "that you captivated Russell's heart tonight. After you left, he did nothing but talk about you. I am becoming jealous," she said laughingly. "And you, what do you think of him?"

"Oh, he is charming and I love his gray-green eyes. He certainly is a handsome type."

"He asked me tonight if you like to dance. He is like that, he moves very fast in a relationship, but he is a gentleman."

Jeanne did not answer right away. "But isn't he your friend?"

"Yes," said Helen, "but one can loan a friend, especially to you. Besides, I prefer someone else. So, feel very at ease with him."

"We will see," added Jeanne "And now run along so I can sleep, as the night brings wisdom." The room was quiet again and Jeanne consulted with the angels.

Helen shut herself in her apartment and telephoned Russell saying: "The answer was not positive, however it was not negative. So, I believe that we will succeed in reaching her." Russell added a few words that Helen did not repeat, but a smile caressed her crimson lips.

"Jeanne, I have an invitation to convey to you. Next Thursday night, we are having an intimate get together at my friend's Russell's house. You understand that he would be very pleased at your presence, for you pleased him from the first moment he saw you. We are counting on you. Make yourself attractive for that night; it will be an evening that you will remember for a long time."

At those words, Helen left the room with a bound, not without noticing Jeanne's penetrating stare. Jeanne continued to put her apartment in order, all the while thinking about the disturbing invitation she had just received. In a haze, her heart saw Jacques. Time, he assured her, passed quickly despite their separation. He certainly missed her presence, but he was so busy that he had soon overcome loneliness. And Jeanne thought, his love is no longer as intense; his soul is losing some of its generous spirit; he is withdrawing step by step. Why at my end should I keep an irreproachable faithfulness to him? The devil of loneliness was sowing the seeds and captured the shaken soul of the suffering child in its strong claws.

The pages of past years unfolded slowly and she once again saw herself in her first struggles, and a crown of laurel adorned her righteous head. Her will was yielding to temptation. So, she would give in completely to the pagan influence that surrounded her. It was a struggle. In the better part of her soul, she saw the straight and narrow path that led to the horizon where were seated the strong leaders of her race and her language. Would she follow their eloquent example or as a child of a mixed education, would laxity swallow her up? She was a Franco-American, but she was also a human being.

"Jeanne, do not forget to prepare a few pieces from your repertoire for next Thursday, for there will be a man there named Craft, who is the director of the Metropolitan Opera House. I am sure that your voice will interest him. It would probably be a good opportunity for you. He is always looking for some kind of a star. I can see you playing the role of Marguerite from Faust. You would be ravishing." Those few sentences convinced Jeanne that she would accept the invitation. Music was her dream. What if by chance Helen was predicting a happy event? So, filled with happiness, she chose the best known numbers of her repertoire. She spent at least an hour making her choice. Then she went to the parlor and sat at the piano. There was no one there at the moment and Jeanne, full of enthusiasm sang: "*Do You Know The Country,*" [1] and saved for last Gounod's "*Ave Maria.*" It was not only a song that her versatile voice intoned well, it was a prayer from a humble heart, one whose echo gently transported one to heaven.

[1] From the opera, "Mignon" by Ambroise Thomas, 1811 - 1896.

II

A letter from Jacques arrived Thursday morning. It was filled with plans for the two of them. Soon, he hoped to be able to build the house of his dreams so as to settle in with the fairy princess who had ravished his heart. He often saw Jeanne's father and together they talked about the one who was far away...The old father let flow from his blind eyes the last tears of his paternal love and in a spontaneous impulse, he squeezed Jacques' hand without saying a word. So, Jacques delved into his imagination and his memory in order to relate a pleasantry that brought a smile to the elderly man's lips. Jacques met many girls who had eyes for him. Once or twice he had accompanied one or the other, but his heart was tied by stronger bonds than those formed by the caprice of a fleeting passion. He was waiting for Jeanne to join him. It would soon come to pass that he would be in a position to marry, because, although Jacques came from a wealthy family, he had squandered much, but today, he thought more and more about saving. He was barely twenty years old and life was good to him. Today, his soul was filled with ambition and he envisioned life under a cloudless sky since love had bloomed in his young masculine heart.

Jeanne felt renewed with this breath of friendship. Her whole being glowed and when Helen came to ask her if she was ready, she found Jeanne giddy, sitting, holding Jacque's letter.

"Why, Jeanne! You are not ready," said Helen astonished.

"I will be in ten minutes."

"Russell is waiting for us and because of a letter, you are keeping everybody waiting," added Helen in an offended tone.

"I am ready, I am ready!"

A few minutes later, Jeanne, all flushed with excitement in her haste, walked towards Helen and Russell. She was very pretty in her pale, yellow green dress that contrasted and brought out her dark eyes. Russell could not help but cast an admiring glance towards the new arrival. The three of them left. Jeanne knew that she was going with Helen and Russell to meet friends, but that was all. For a long time they traveled through the city and finally they stopped in front of a large brick house. The house was dark. Only a streak of light revealed the fact that it was occupied. The car stopped and Helen walked ahead and lightly pressed the doorbell toward the stone wall, three times. Immediately, a valet appeared and without saying a word brought the small group into a large room with high windows. There was no one there.

This is very strange, thought Jeanne. No one is here to meet us. Without a doubt they will come. Then, the door opened and three gentlemen entered. They certainly were not coming from inside the house because they still had their coats and hats on. Helen seemed to know these men. Jeanne listened to the conversation, but too often their voices were low and she missed many phrases, which really annoyed her. Russell was explaining in detail the architecture of the building, placing value on the richness of the decor, entertaining Jeanne, trying to captivate her attention, every so often looking at the time. When he noticed that Jeanne seemed to be wondering he said with a lovely smile, "All our friends will be here in a moment. We often meet together and you do not know how happy I am to present you to New York's elite."

Around ten o'clock, they played cards. Jeanne had let herself become somewhat intoxicated by repeated cocktails. Opportunity makes the thief!

Jeanne did not completely lose her head. Helen, who kept an imperturbable control, threw a glance towards Jeanne and said: "My little Jeanne, come with me."

The young girl got up and followed Helen. As they came near a closed door, she heard feminine voices that all seemed to be talking at the same time. Pushing her gently, Helen, whose eyes were diabolical, made her enter and added, "Do as they tell you to do." Jeanne's eyes opened wide; she sobered up and understood what was happening. Her soul revolted. They had never even considered that she might have principles of decency that had been transmitted from generation to generation, and that her soul, despite her weak moments, had been purified in royal blood. They forgot that beneath a fragile appearance, her soul was made of steel. Her will, heightened by the struggle, and still wanted to come out victorious over the immorality that once again assailed the stronghold that had been erected at such a high price for the defense of her faith and of her race. In a silent prayer, she appealed to heaven. Gathering all her thoughts, she reflected for an instant, and forcing herself to smile, said: "I understand, you can go back downstairs. I will do exactly as they tell me." Then she looked around her. There were eight young girls who were stripped of any modesty. One of them approached and whispered something in the ear of the newcomer. Raising her voice she heard; "I left everything in the passageway," and without waiting for an answer, the door opened. Running, Jeanne flung herself at a small door that led to the balcony. She went down the fire escape and in a state of panic, mingled with the crowd. Her face was livid, her lips drained of blood, and her eyes could not discern anything.

How long she walked along the streets like this she could not have told you. Was she demented? No, she was simply weakened by the strife. She became dizzy and fell.

For a long time now, a radiant sun spread its glorious rays onto a white hospital bed. A smiling face leaned toward the sick one who opened her eyes for the first time in two days. Regaining her senses, Jeanne asked what she was doing there. The nurse told her that she had been brought there one night, unable to say who she was or where she came from. She had been found on the sidewalk, bleeding, by a passerby who had her brought to the hospital. Jeanne remembered the terrible night and closed her eyes without speaking. However, a frown creased her lovely white forehead.

All day she remained that way. One night, they announced to her that Helen was there to visit. Jeanne refused to see her. Russell sent her flowers; the Baron himself came and caressed the thin figures of the young patient with his dry lips, for down deep, he had much admiration and respect for the young Franco-American. But Jeanne remained indifferent to all their attention. Her mind was kept captive, but her soul flew freely above the turmoil that shook a humanity that had fallen from grace. She would return to her father, and surrounded with his warm affection, she would regain her strength while her smile and cheerfulness would delight him in his old age.

The next day the Baron, in a joyful mood, visited Jeanne.

"My dear child," he said, "I am opening my summer home at Hampton Beach. Why don't you come to rest there. My valet will be at your disposition and in a few weeks you will regain your health thanks to the fresh air and the ocean's invigorating baths."

"You are very kind, however, I had thought of returning to Lewiston, to travel through our woods and over our lakes, all the while benefiting from the wholesome air that our numerous pine trees offer us."

"Jeanne, I have great admiration for you, and if it was possible for me to erase from your memory the too very justified opinion that you have with regards to me, I would be the happiest of men. In accepting my sincere invitation, you would prove to me that you have some faith in me."

Jeanne smiled, "Mr. Baron, I will keep the best of memories of you... that of your present and past generosity."

"Thank you, Mademoiselle." He slid his scented card under her pillow.

"Father, it is I, I have come back to you." The father smiled and through the night, in his mind, he saw his beloved daughter. A long silence reigned between the two loved ones. The father clutched his child's hand while the young girl silently let two bloody tears flow. Jeanne wanted to brighten the house with her merry laughter. Her poor father heard nothing but her voice rising in leaps and bonds, and influenced by a smile, his lips parted. The hours were pleasant, and heart to heart talks frequent.

Jeanne seemed to him more beautiful than ever, adorned with the palm of victory. With his marvelously skilled fingers, he traced his child's face. His blind eyes seized every feature. The strength of her will and her soul's energy had hollowed the young girl's temples. The father said nothing, but in a moment filled with affection and understanding, he held her young head and gave it a prolonged kiss.

It was one of those evenings when night descends warm and with its gentle shadow sets the stage for the most sincere confessions; when secrets are shared; when two souls blend into one, united by the most affectionate ties.

June arrived. The Lacombe family settled into a lovely chalet situated on a small knoll near Moosehead Lake. In the morning, the pointed roof greeted the rising sun, and in the evening, it bent its proud head over the water, so as to hear the waves chat with the half moon's reflection as it showed its pale face.

Jacques had come to spend a weekend. He found Jeanne more beautiful than before, and yet, it had been only four months ago that he had left her. Her aunt was reading the result of the election to her blind father, so the young couple strolled down the shore. In the light boat, Jacques wrapped Jeanne in his arms and together they drifted on the tranquil lake. They did not speak. Suddenly, Jacques, who incessantly looked at Jeanne said: "Jeanne, my beloved, your presence gives me strength. It seems that I could conquer the world with you by my side. Jeanne, if I were worthy of your love, I would be the happiest of humans. Together we will struggle, we will conquer, and we will love each other," Jeanne smiled. From that day on, the happy engaged couple braved storms courageously and their hearts spoke such sweet language that a strange ear could not grasp it.

Three years went by. The elderly father caressed the blond head of a young child. Happiness reigned in the house. Jacques had just been promoted and besides that, an old uncle had recently died, leaving Jacques as the only beneficiary of his large fortune.

It is too much happiness, thought Jeanne. The angel of memories unrolled before her gentle eyes the golden decree, signed with the pure blood of her race, transmitted from father to son and which had its place of honor in the heart of the young Franco-American.

BIBLIOGRAPHY

Anctil, Pierre, *A Franco-American bibliography*. New England, N. H. : National Materials Development Center, 1979.

April, Susan, Paul Brouillette, Paul Marion, and Marie Louise St. Onge. *French Class: French Canadian-American Writings on Identity, Culture and Place*. Lowell, MA: Loom Press, 1999.

Beaugrand, Honore, *Jeanne la Fileuse*. New England, N. H. : National Materials Development Center, 1980.

Beaupré, Normand. *La Souillonne, monologue sur scène*. Tamarac, FL: Llumina Press, 2006.

Beaupré, Normand. *Deux Femmes, Deux Rêves*. Tamarac. Florida, Llumina Press, 2005.

Beaupré, Normand. *Le Petit Mangeur de fleurs*. Quebec : Les éditions JCL, 1999.

Bonier, Marie Louise. *Débuts de la colonie franco-américaine de Woonsocket, Rhode Island*. Framingham. Lakeview Press, 1920. The beginnings of the Franco-American colony in Woonsocket, Rhode Island, Assumption College, French Institute Worcester, Ma, translated and edited by Claire Quintal ; with additional notes by Raymond H. Bacon and the technical assistance of Sylvia and Roger Bartholomy of the American-French Genealogical Society. 1997.

Brault, Gerard J. *The French-Canadian Heritage in New England*. Hanover, NH: University Press of New England, 1986.

Brault, Marie-Marthe T. *Mères et filles au bout de la vie : récits de femmes âgées de 55 ans et plus*. Sainte-Foy, Québec : Éditions de l'IQRC, 1998.

Breton, Raymond and Pierre Savard, eds. *The Quebec and Acadian Diaspora in North America.* Toronto: The Multicultural History Society of Ontario, 1982.

Caffee, Gabrielle Leboeuf. *La Canadienne : Memoires of a Vanishing Culture.* Lanham, MD : University Press of America, 1993.

Cather, Willa. *Shadows on the Rock.* Vintage Books USA; Vintage edition, October, 1995.

Chabot, Grégoire. *Un Jacques Cartier Errant: Jacques Cartier Discovers America.* Orono, ME: University of Maine Press, 1996.

Charron, Sylvie and Huseman, Sue : *Grapes of Despair.* Introduction and translation of *Les Raisins de la galère* (1996). Looking for publisher.

Charron, Sylvie and Huseman, Sue: "North Africans in France: A Crisis in Cultural Identity – Tahar Ben Jelloun's *Les Raisins de la galère.*" Chapter in The Francophone World. Cultural Issues and Perpectives, Ed. Michelle Beauclair (Peter Lang: 2003) 67-87.

Charron, Sylvie and Huseman, Sue: George Sand: *Pauline* and *The Marquise.* Introduction and translation. Academy Chicago Publishers, 1999.

Chartier, Armand B. ; Quintal, Claire. *The Franco-Americans of New England :a history.* Manchester, NH : ACA Assurance ; Worcester, MA : Institut français of Assumption College, 1999.

Chassé, Paul P. *Anthologie de la poésie franco-américaine de la Nouvelle-Angleterre.* Rhode Island: Rhode Island Bicentennial Commission, 1976.

Chopin, Kate, *The Awakening and Selected Stories.* New York : Penguin Classics, 1984.

-----, *Bayou Folk and A Night In Acadie.* New York : Penguin Classics, 1999.

Coté, Gertrude, M. *As I Live and Dream.* A Dirigo Edition, Manchester, Maine, 1953.

Dallemagne-Cookson, Elise. *Marie Grandin Sent By the King*, Xlibris, 2003.

DeRoche, P. Celeste, "These lines of my life: Franco-American women in Westbrook, Maine, the intersection of ethnicity and gender 1884-1984." M.S. Thesis, University of Maine, Orono, Me., 1994.

DeRoche, P. Celeste, "I Learned Things Today That I Never Knew Before:" Oral History At The Kitchen Table. *Oral History Review* 23/2 (Winter, 1996): 45-61.

DeRoche, Celeste, *How wide the circle of we : cultural pluralism and American identity 1910-1954*. Thesis (Ph.D.) in History--University of Maine, 2000.

Desjardins, Lise A., *An exploration into the health and illness beliefs of a Franco-American community : the description of a clinical reality*. Orono, Me., 1995.

Doty, C. Stewart. *Acadian Hard Times: The Farm Security Administration in Maine's St. John Valley 1940-1943*. Orono, ME: University of Maine Press, 1991.

Ducharme, Jacques. *The shadows of the trees, the story of French-Canadians in New England*. New York, London : Harper, 1943.

Dumas, Emma. *Mirbah*. National Materials Development Center, 1979.

Dumont, Micheline, et al., *The Clio Collective, Quebe Women: A History*. The Women's Press, Toronto, Canada, 1987. Translation by Roger Gannon and Rosalind Gill.

Duval-Thibault, Anna. *Les Deux Testaments*. National Materials Development Center, 1979.

Faucher, Doris, Provencher. *Le Quebecois: The Virgin Forest*. Artenay Press, September, 2000.

Faucher, Doris Provencher. *The Rapids*. Biddeford, ME.: Artenay Press, 2002.

Field, Rachel. *Calico Bush*. New York : Macmillan,1931.

Ferland, Jacques. " 'In Search of the Unbound Promethea': a study of female activism in Quebec cotton mills, 1870-1907." *Labour/Le travail,* Spring 1993.

Grant, Bridget T., Robbins. *Canuck, Françaises d'Amérique, La Jeune Franco-Américaine.* Transciber. **For info on French texts and other supportive materials::**
http://www.fawi.net/Transcriptions/Transcriptions.html

The Franco-American Women's Institute, http://www.fawi.net/

Hareven, Tamara K. and Langenbach, Randolph. *Amoskeag: Live and Work in an American Factory-City.* New York: Pantheon, 1978.

Hartig, Rachel.M. *Crossing the Divide Representations of Deafness in Biography.* Gallaudet University Press, Washington, DC., 2006.

Kennedy, Kate. *More than Petticoats: Remarkable Maine Women.* Guilford, CT: Globe Pequot Press, 2005.

King, Anette Paradis. *Growing up on Academy Hill: Remembering My French-Canadian-American Papa.* Gouldsboro, Maine, 2002.

King, Anette Paradis. *Toward Evening: Poems.* Gouldsboro, Maine, 2004.

Lambrecht, Winnie, *Sur bois: Franco-American woodcarvers of northern New England.* Manchester, N.H. : Franco-American Centre Franco-Américain, 1996.

Lane, Brigitte Marie. *American Folk Traditions and Popular Culture in a Former Milltown: Aspects of Ethnic Urban Folklore and the Dynamics of Folklore Change in Lowell, Massachusetts.* New York : Garland, 1990.

Lanctot, Gustave. *Filles de joie ou filles du Roi.* Éditions du Jour, Saint-Denis, Montréal, Canada, 1966.

Landry, Yves. *Orphelines en France pionnières au Canada: Les Filles du roi au XVIIe siècle.* Leméac Éditeur, Inc., Montréal, QC, Canada, 1992.

Langellier, Kristin M. and Peterson, Eric E. *Storytelling in Daily Life: Performing Narrative.* Philadelphia: Temple University Press, 2004.

Ledoux, Denis. *Lives in translation : an anthology of contemporary Franco-American writings.* Lisbon Falls, Me. : Soleil Press, 1991

Le Maître, Yvonne. "Littértature franco-américaine de la Nouvelle-Angeleterre." *Anthologie, Tome 5,* National Assessment and Dissemination Center for Bilingual/Bicultural Education, 1981.

Lees, Cynthia C. "Border spaces and la survivance the evolution of the Franco-American novel of New England (1875-2004)." Ph.D. Thesis. University of Florida, Gainesville, FL, 2006.

Louder, Dean and Eric Waddell, eds. *French America: Mobility, Identity, and Minority Experience Across the Continent.* Baton Rouge and London: Louisiana State UP, 1993.

Maillet, Antonine. *Pélagie.* Trans. Philip Stratford. Garden City, N.Y. : Doubleday, 1982.

Maillet, Antonine. *La Sagouine.* Trans. Luis de Cespedes, Toronto : Simone & Pierre, 1985.

Metalious, Grace. *Peyton Place.* New York : Messner, 1956.

-----. *Return to Peyton Place.* New York : Messner, 1959.

-----. *The Tight White Collar.* New York : Messner, 1960.

-----. *No Adam in Eden.* New York : Trident Press. 1963.

Michaud, Lisa Desjardins, (Ed.). *Le Forum.* Franco-American Center, University of Maine, Orono, Maine.

Nadeau-Single, Lee. *Annette : the story of a pioneer woman.* New York : Vantage Press, 1990.

Nadeau, Paula. *La Kermesse parade : a celebration of Franco-American heritage set in contemporary community life.* Thesis (M.A.)--University of Southern Maine, 1993.

Nos Histoires de l'Ile : History and Memories of French Island. Old Town, Maine. 1999.

Olivier, Julien. *D'la boucane : une introduction au folklore Franco-américain de la Nouvelle-Angleterre.* Cambridge, Mass. : National Assessment and Dissemination Center for Bilingual/Bicultural Education, 1979.

Paradis, Françoise. *Evangeline, a tale of Acadie.* Tamarac, FL: Llumina Press, 2004.

Pecoraro, Elizabeth J. *Using theatre arts skills to instruct Franco American students: a creative dramatics approach.* Thesis (M.A.) in Theatre--University of Maine, 1991.

Pelletier, Susann, *Immigrant dreams and other poems.* Lisbon Fall, Maine : Soleil Press, 1989.

Petrie, Lanette Landry, *My Mother's Walls.* Proof Positive Press, Bradley Maine, 1998.

Poteet, Maurice, ed. *Textes de l'Exode: Recueil de textes sur l'émigration des Québécois aux Etats-Unis (XIXe et Xxe siècles).* Montréal : Guérin, 1987.

Parent, Michael, Olivier, Julien. *Of kings and fools : stories of the French tradition in North America.* Little Rock : August House Publishers, c1996.

Pelletier, Cathie [K. C. McKinnon]. *Candles on Bay Street.* New York : Doubleday, 1999.

Pinette, Susan. *Alternative ethnographies : genre and cultural encounter in early modern French texts.* Dissertation: Thesis (Ph. D., French)--University of California, Irvine, 1999.

Price, Trudy Chambers. *The Cows Are Out!: Two Decades on a Maine Dairy Farm.* Frenchboro, ME.: Islandport Press, 2004.

Proulx, E. Annie. *Accordion Crimes.* New York : Scribner, 1997.

Pula, James S. *The French in America, 1488-1974 : a chronology & factbook.* Dobbs Ferry, N.Y. : Oceana Publications, 1975.

Quintal, Claire. *La femme franco-américaine : The Franco-American woman.* Worcester, MA : Institut français, 1994.

-----, ed. *Religion Catholique et Appartenance Franco-américaine: Franco-Americans and Religion: Impact and Influence.* Worcester, MA : Institute français, 1993.

-----. "Mémère Kerouac ou la revanche du berceau en Franco-Américanie." *Voix et Images: Litterature Quebecoise* (V&I), 1988, Spring; 13 (3 (39)): 397-401.

-----, ed. *Steeples and Smokestacks : A Collection of Essays on the Franco-American Experience in New England.* Worcester, MA: Institut français, 1996.

-----, ed. *Le Patrimoine folklorique des franco-américain.* Québec: Le Conseil de la vie française en Amérique, 1986.

Robbins, Rhea Côté. *Wednesday's Child.* Brunswick, Me. : Maine Writers & Publishers Alliance, 1997. 2nd Edition, Rheta Press, Brewer, 2001.

Robbins, Rhea Côté, *The River Review/La Revue rivière.* "Franco-American Women's Literary Tradition: A Central Piece in the Region's Literary Mosaic," University of Maine at Fort Kent, Fort Kent, Me. 1999.

Robbins, Rhea Côté, *L'Ouest Français et la Francophonie Nord-Américaine.* "De l'Ile à la Tortue, à la Nouvelle France, à la Nouvelle-Angleterre : lutte pour une identité vivable," Chapter 5 Something That Will Cure, Presses de L'Université d'Angers, Angers, France, 1996.

Robbins, Rhea Côté, Petrie, Lanette Landry, Langellier, Kristin , Slott, Kathryn. (Eds.). *Je suis franco-américaine et fière de l'être/I am Franco-American and proud of it : an anthology of writings of Franco-American women.* Women in the Curriculum, University of Maine, Orono, Maine, 1995.

Robichaud, Gérard. *Papa Martel : A Novel in Ten Parts.* Garden City, N.Y., Doubleday, 1961; Orono, ME, University of Maine Press, 2003.

Robichaud, Gérard. *The Apple of His Eye.* Garden City, N. Y., Doubleday, 1965.

Roby, Yves. *Les Franco-Américains de la Nouvelle-Angleterre, 1776-1930.* Sillery (Quebec) : Septentrion, 1990.

Rocheleau, Corinne. *Hors de sa prison : extraordinaire histoire de Ludivine Lachance, l'infirme des infirmes, sourde, muette et aveugle.* Montréal : Imprimerie Arbour & Dupont, 1927. (Honored by the French Academy.)

Rocheleau, Corinne and Mack, Rebecca. *Those in the Dark Silence.* Washington, D.C.: Volta Bureau, 1930.

Rocheleau, Corinne; Langford, W. F., ed. *Laurentian Heritage.* Toronto ; New York : Longmans, Green and Co.,1948.

St. Martin, Gérard Labarre, Voorhies, Jacqueline K. *Écrits louisianais du dix-neuvième siècle : nouvelles, contes et fables.* Baton Rouge : Louisiana State University Press, 1979.

Santerre, Richard Robert. *Le roman franco-américain en Nouvelle Angleterre, 1878-1943.* Thesis (Ph.D.), Boston College, 1974.

Shideler, Janet L., *Camille Lessard-Bissonnette: The Quiet Evolution of French-Canadian Immigrants in New England.* Peter Lang Publishing Group, New York, 1998.

Stewart, Sharon. *Banished from Our Home The Acadian Diary of Angélique Richard Grand-Pré, Acadia, 1755.* Markham, ON: Scholastic Canada, 2004.

Theriault, Jeri. *Catholic.* Columbus, Ohio: Pudding House Publications, 2002.

Theriault, Jeri. *Corn Dance.* Troy, ME: Nightshade Press, 1994.

Therriault, Mary Carmel, Sister. *La littérature française de Nouvelle-Angleterre.* "L'Hermine" Université Laval, Montréal, Fides, 1946.

Thiébaux, Tamara. *When Heaven Smiled on Our World.* Written by Corinne Rocheleau Rouleau, text adapted and illustrated by Tamara Thiébaux-Heïkalo. Fitzhenry & Whiteside, 1992.

Toth, Emily. *Inside Peyton Place : the life of Grace Metalious.* Jackson : University Press of Mississippi, 2000, 1981.

-----.. *Unveiling Kate Chopin.* Jackson : University Press of Mississippi, 1999.

Touchette, Charleen. *IT STOPS WITH ME MEMOIR OF A CANUCK GIRL.* Santa Fe, NM.: Touch Art Books, 2004.

Tremblay, Remi. *Un Revenant, One Came Back: A Franco-American Civil War Novel.* Trans. Margaret S. Langford with Claire Quintal. Bennington, VT: Images from the Past, 2001.

Trottier, Maxine. *Death of My Country The Plains of Abraham Diary of Geneviève Aubuchon Québec, New France, 1759.* Markham, ON: Scholastic Canada, 2005.

Trottier, Maxine. *Alone in an Untamed Land The Filles du Roi Diary of Hélène St. Onge Montréal, Upper Canada, 1666.* Markham, ON: Scholastic Canada, 2003.

Vachon, Josée. *Déracinée / Uprooted.* CéVon Musique, 2001.

Weil, François. *Les Franco-Américains : 1860-1980.* Paris : Belin, 1989.

676894

Made in the USA